Praise for Raffaella Barker:

'A writer of talent' *Times Literary Supplement*

'One of the cleverest, and freshest, British young novelists'
Daily Mail

'Raffaella Barker is so good at drawing her characters and
making them likeable that within about ten pages you feel
you know them intimately . . . Very, very well done'
Daily Express

'Charming . . . engrossing' *The Sunday Times*

'A gripping read' *Heat*

'A beautifully written novel' *Bella*

'Not only does Barker's prose often ooze delicious sexual
tension, but her lush descriptions of a summer garden or a
walk in a bluebell wood were enough to make me grab my
Barbour' *Spectator*

'A gripping family drama' *Independent on Sunday*

'Pure therapy: Barker's books are good for you' *Country Life*

'Enjoy it – I certainly did' *Literary Review*

'An engaging work, sewn up with a dry line in wit and illu-
minated with a strongly felt devotion' *Scotland on Sunday*

A Perfect Life

Raffaella Barker

headline
review

First published in 2006 by HEADLINE REVIEW
An imprint of HEADLINE PUBLISHING GROUP

First published in paperback in 2007 by HEADLINE REVIEW
An imprint of HEADLINE PUBLISHING GROUP

1

978 0 7553 2410 1

Typeset in Fairfield Light by Palimpsest Book Production Limited,
Polmont, Stirlingshire

Printed and bound in Great Britain by Clays Ltd, St Ives plc

Headline's policy is to use papers that are natural, renewable and
recyclable products and made from wood grown in sustainable forests.
The logging and manufacturing processes are expected to conform to the
environmental regulations of the country of origin.

HEADLINE PUBLISHING GROUP
A division of Hachette Livre UK Ltd
338 Euston Road
London NW1 3BH

www.reviewbooks.co.uk
www.hodderheadline.com

This book is for Sarah Lutyens whose grace and patience I have tested and found limitless.

Nel mezzo del cammin di nostra vita
Mi ritrouvai per una selva oscura
Che la diritta via era smarrita.

In the middle of our life's path
I found myself in a dark wood
And the way forward was overgrown.

Dante, *Divina Commedia* 'Inferno' canto 1

Angel

The air is gentle but the heat is flexing, and summer is at its most perfect blooming point. In the heart of the flowering day, a woman lies, as if thrown, on the black mesh centre of a trampoline. Nothing moves. High hedges and soft red-brick walls have caught the flaring July sun, and the world swims like the view through warped glass in the mid-afternoon. The sky is limitless blue, no clouds, no birds, but one thin pink scar appearing in silence from a high-flying jet. The trampoline sways and resettles beneath the woman; she raises her arms above her head, scissoring her legs, slithering naked oiled skin against the springing latex. She is restless. The whole experience would be improved if she could be bothered to go and get something to lie on but she can't move just now. Maybe in a minute. No one is in the house; none of them will be back for hours. The sweat and oil on her back soak down into the trampoline and she sighs, shifting her hips so every notch of her spine eases and her body pulses with sensation, with being alive and alone in the heat.

Usually she would fill this spiral of time. In fact, time has not existed like this for her since she was seventeen. Lying around doing nothing is for losers, for people whose lives are not full enough. Lying around is an absurdity for a mother, a wife, a woman with a career, a clockwork model spinning and spinning on adrenalin and guilt. No one would ever equate the flung defenceless form, gleaming now and turning pinky golden all over, with freckles appearing on her cheekbones and her shoulders, eyes sleepy, mouth soft, hair a hot coil, with the sharp-edged creature who clacks around the house, an apron tied over her sundress, a telephone wedged on her shoulder like a modern-day parrot and a sense of form-less panic rising in her chest. Like dough – and there is some even now proving in three bread tins, as well as a plait made by Ruby before she went to the beach – panic can only rise so far and then it will overflow, pouring sticky elastic chaos over everything, coating all feelings and thoughts with impenetrable glue.

Angel turns over on to her front and stares down through the black, porous, undulating trampoline skin at long vibrant shoots of grass. All around, the turf is cropped yellow and dry, but beneath the trampoline it has continued to grow. It looks cool and inviting. The sensa-tion of lying under the trampoline in the damp, soft grass might be soothing if only she could get there. But moving is impossible. It is as if she has been hit. Violently hit so that everything in her brain has shifted a little, and when she breathes in, the warm air comes into her lungs in a jagged rush; when she breathes out, it whooshes away and it won't slow down, the momentum is fast and shocked. And the space between her breaths isn't space at all, it is a drum filled with juddering emotion.

Crying was the last thing on her mind when she came out into the garden with a pair of scissors to cut a bunch of sweet peas. She had been meaning to get round to it for days; in a blue jug on the hall table the flowers from the weekend were dried up and smelled of mouldy hay. To actually come out here with the scissors and a basket to pick a bunch of flowers seemed to have become something she needed to book into her diary if she wanted to get it done. And then, as she stood in front of the delicate hazel skeleton on which the sweet peas had woven themselves into a soft cascade, Angel could suddenly see herself with her shoulders hunched and her jaw set as she poised the open scissors over a perfect bloom. She cut the first stem and then the second and laid the two flowers in the basket. She looked at the long, tangled stems, and behind them saw herself so clearly it was like a mirage. There she was, a woman who could not enjoy cutting flowers in a glorious summer garden surrounding a beautiful comfortable house, because even flowers can become yet another thing that needs to be done. She searched around inside her mind for some scrap of enjoyment, a shred of belief that this life, this perfect garden, this beautiful never-ending yet never-returning summer day could bring joy, but her head felt sleepy and distant. The effort of caring was too much. She snipped another wiry sweet-pea stalk, and then two more, which were twined together, and held them under her nostrils, inhaling, eyes shut.

Smell is the most primitive of the five senses. It can evoke memory and feeling; with overwhelming urgency, it hooks in and tweaks at a part of the heart under which layers of life have been buried. Smell can overwhelm anyone, anywhere. As long as we breathe, we are susceptible to its power. The combination of the warm essence of flowers, the harsh dry whiff of grass, and the always present hint of the sea pierced Angel with ferocious sorrow. A blade plunged deep into her and tears she has not shed for many years began feebly seeping, small and tight from the corner of her eyes. They would dry up and stop in a moment, she was sure. Crying was something she couldn't imagine doing any more. Like dancing in the rain and putting her hair in bunches, it belonged to the past. But the tears swam in her eyes and welled bigger, splashing on to her cheeks, warm and so wet. Her nose was running now too, and when she wiped it on the back of her hand a huge sob leapt from her ribcage into her throat and out, the first one rusty like a machine coughing into life, but the second and third gaining momentum as if lubricated by tears. Stunned and absorbed by her own anguish, Angel had hurled herself on to the trampoline and surrendered to misery. Abandoned sobbing is something she has not done for years, and if she had ever thought about it she would have laughed at the notion that she might ever again need to be so melodramatic. For her, life is on an even keel, and there is no time or energy to spare for it pitching or tossing. Over the years, her passion has somehow atrophied, shrivelled and transformed without her noticing, and her tears of sorrow and of joy have desiccated and together they have become her determined belief that if you just keep putting one foot in front of the other you will get there in the end. But where? Now, in the grief she cannot control, she is suddenly afraid, afraid of wanting highs and lows again in her life, afraid of losing control, and afraid of her own unstoppable tears. The sun moves slowly on through the relentless blue of the summer sky. Angel watches it through hot swollen eyes, humbled by her own insignificance in the face of the voltage of light and energy pouring yellow through dust motes down on to her, beating heat on to the yielding earth. And the strength around her is calming, the unconquerable force that is nature harnessed within the structure of the minutes and hours of a day reassure her. Nothing is happening, the world is ordinary, and gradually she surrenders, becomes still and loses her fear.

Afterwards she lies spent, blinking, focusing a clean gaze upon the pear tree and the garden wall. The tidal weeping is over. Angel can only match her flat-out feeling, her veins electric and delicious, as if nectar is being injected into them, with the sensation of lying close to someone, skin touching skin, sated after sex. She is aware of the layers of flesh, blood and bone in her body, alive and potent, vital and relaxed. She shuts her eyes and the sun pulses red against her lids. And now it is gentler, like a caress, a hand tracing the planes of her face. Her breathing is calm and soft, well-being wrapped around her like a man's embrace. She wants to have this after-sex feeling for real. After having sex. It is as surprising as the crying had been to realise this.

Nick

In the car on the way back from the office in Cambridge, Nick Stone is in his shirtsleeves, his suit jacket bundled on the seat next to him. He has attended a lunchtime Alcoholics Anonymous meeting, he has put forward an unassailable argument to the powers that be at Fourply Elastics, where he works, for his trip to New York, and has spent an hour watching his son Jem play cricket for the under-sixteens at school in Ely. A good day. Well, that's how it looks from the outside. Nick hits the accelerator on the giddyingly straight road from Waterbeach and the tarmac rushes loud beneath his tyres, drowning the whisper of the engine. Just to irritate himself, Nick deliberately sets his thoughts to wishing his car was a motorbike, and he has a gorgeous babe on the back. She would have long blonde hair, like the waitress in the Neil Young song. The motorbike would have to be a Harley Davidson, but that's fine. Who would complain about that? The babe would wear shorts, sawn-off pale blue denim jeans, and her legs would be smooth and brown.

He would, of course, have a leather jacket. The one he owned years ago in California. They would be on the road somewhere in America – where ever they were in the Neil Young song would do fine. Nick doesn't want to waste too much time on those sorts of details; the bits he is interested in are, in reverse order: the girl, the speed and the freedom. Actually, maybe speed is number one. He is almost hitting a hundred now, and the featureless green of the fenland fields keeps moving past him, the only landmark a distant black row of pylons, ink cartoons scrawled on the landscape. The back end of a lorry, a real blot on the horizon, dawdles into his path from a turning up ahead. Within seconds he is close up behind it, his eyes level with a balloon of yellow writing. The lorry has Netherlands plates, the writing is incomprehensible, and is presumably in Dutch. Probably something to do with windmills. Or sex. Nick suddenly thinks of Amsterdam, a place he has never been to. He has always thought he would rather not go there, as the pleasure of imagining it, bursting with sex and drugs, could never be bettered by a reality.

A moment later he is pinging past the lorry, flying like an arrow towards home, hearth and, of course, heart. He unwraps a piece of chewing gum and flicks the paper out of the window, a small act of lawlessness, but nonetheless enjoyable. His phone rings, he turns it on.

'Hello?'

'Nick? It's me.'

Angel sounds ghastly.

'What's the matter?'

'Oh, nothing. I just wondered what time you would be back. I've got to pick up the children and I was wondering if I should cook something before I leave.'

'I won't be long.'

His automatic response to a question is to hedge. Even an indirect one, and Angel has learned over the many years of their marriage to phrase her questions obliquely, but still Nick hates to be tied down. Freedom, a girl on a motorbike and speed. None of them fits very well with picking up the children and a wife cooking supper.

He makes a small effort to sound helpful, knowing what the response will be.

'Do you want me to get anything?'

'Don't worry, it's fine. I'll see you in a bit.'

'Bye, Angel.'

The phone beeps a final full stop on the conversation. The whistle blows on Nick's little afternoon fantasy and everything that seemed lit with possibility is dull now, as if a cloud has passed in front of the sun. Nick turns on his phone again and calls the office. He gets Janet, his secretary.

'I need the US documents faxed home, I've got calls to make tonight. I did ask you to get the stuff to me earlier.' He doesn't say please, and Janet's hurt is like a bell clanging persistently in his conscience. He has enough awareness to know that he does this often when he is irritated by Angel, and in the pause when Janet doesn't speak, he wonders if it comes out of a smarting and unresolved frustration that he works for his wife's family's business, and although he is good at his job, it feels to him and looks to the world that he got where he is by marrying the boss's daughter. Uncomfortable with this thought, he coughs into Janet's silence.

'Oh, sorry. Yes, I'll do that, Nick. Did you want me to post it to you as well?'

'No, I don't need a hard copy at home, I just need to get on top of it before I come in tomorrow. I keep forgetting Angel's on sabbatical.'

Nick is not sure why this is relevant, it just popped out, but it seems that it was the right thing to say.

Janet is being won round; he can hear the motherly smile in her voice when she says, 'Well, it has only been a week so no one would expect you to remember.'

Nick cannot allow himself to be let off the hook so easily. 'Very kind of you, Janet, to be so loyal.'

Janet sighs, papers rustling as if she is folding them while talking.

'You don't have to worry, Nick. Have a nice evening, and we'll finish everything off before your meeting tomorrow afternoon. Bye, Nick.'

'Bye, Janet. Thanks.' Before he has spoken, the line is dead – she did not hear his thanks. Honestly. Why be nasty to poor Janet? It's not her fault. Nick castigates himself, flicking off the cruise control as he turns out of the Fens and into the plush arable farmland of Norfolk. Neat high hedges run along both sides of the road, punctuated by gates painted robin's-egg blue. Getting back here, sliding under the rural canopy, always has one of two effects on Nick – he either feels safe or he feels trapped. Today's feeling is trapped. There are so many parts of life that are full of possibility; it's just that sometimes the possibility comes with a dead end.

The driveway to his house is a dead end. It was actually one of the things that made Nick want to buy it, odd though it seems this evening. The wall in the yard where cars turn, looms large and solid in Nick's mind and from long ago the plummy tone of the estate agent rolls into his thoughts. They first saw the Mill House eighteen years ago, and the Locksley & Parks representative deserved full marks for digging himself into a hole and then climbing out again with only a small whiff of mortification about his person. 'The original carriage drive was obliterated by the erection of the conservatory, but that is in itself a massive bonus, and of course you are saved from the danger of drive-through burglars,' Martin Chistleton had droned. His habitual cravat-smoothing with one hand and hair-rumpling with the other speeded up when Angel climbed out of Nick's car wearing a pink fluffy jumper she insisted was a dress but which Nick knew was just too short. Angel didn't care. She told him so on the way, when he looked across at her, ran his hands up from her knees and said, 'You can't go around like that, you look much too provocative. Where's your coat?'

Angel smiled and bit her lip, parting her legs a little so his hand could move between her thighs.

'I forgot it,' she said, wriggling in her seat, looking sideways at him, adorable and adoring. Nick had a rush of excitement and joy so mood-altering he could have sworn it was medicated. She was lovely, she was sexy, and she wanted him, too. It was extraordinary, but it appeared to be true. There was no need for him to find reasons or excuses; he could just enjoy the pleasure of being with Angel.

But that was then. Now he is almost home. He skirts the village centre, noticing with a small part of his mind that the scaffolding is off the church and the bench has been dragged out of its usual position overlooking the duck pond. And although thinking about that time plunges Nick back into nostalgia for the heady feelings of love and lust and lost youth, he only affords himself a moment to rub a hand up over his forehead and into his hair. That phase of limerance, so intoxicating and consuming, is the beginning, the foundations: it is not meant to last. Or is it? Ever since then he and Angel have been getting on with building the rest. Or so Nick believes. Of course, he loves her, she knows that. They have a life together.

The crumbling of tyres on the gravel, echoing hollow as the car passes in through the gates, is one of the sounds

Nick knows best, and it brings texture to his memories of first seeing the house, Actually it is a miracle he can remember anything about that time. His life ten years ago is mostly lost in a fog of confused fragments, memories torn apart by being drunk, or rows over drink, or attempts to stop drinking, or lies about having stopped drinking. Most of his sober moments were spent juggling two questions: would Angel have married him if she hadn't been pregnant, and where will the next drink be coming from?

There is no possibility that they would ever have bought a house like this if it hadn't been for Angel's family. There is no way he, Nick, ever thought a rambling idyll in a picture-book village was an achievable dream.

Frankly, it often looks to him more like a nightmare. A giant money-guzzling monster parked in the middle of his life, demanding everything he can ever muster and more. If they hadn't bought this house, things might have turned out differently. He might have been able to do something other than work for Fourply, rival to Angel for her father Lionel Mayden's affections, as Angel used to joke, but the joke was thin because Angel knew the business had won long ago.

The Mill Stone House, as Nick secretly called it to himself, was their wedding present from Lionel. Nick's pay-off, or rather Nick's high-interest loan. Lionel has been dead for ten years now, but still Nick feels he is paying with his life.

And it is true; every day Nick goes to work in Cambridge

at the head office, as sales director of the company, doing a job that is vital in a small British manufacturing business, but which he still believes no one needs him to do. It's enough to turn anyone to drink. If they haven't already been turned off it.

Nick has stopped the car at the front door and the engine cooler buzzes in the silence.

In the house, music throbs in the kitchen, and Coral, teetering in high-heeled shoes with a cigarette in her mouth, eyes narrowed to the smoke, is breaking ice in the blender.

'Hi,' says Nick, pointlessly he feels, as there is no way she can hear him.

Coral turns round from the dresser and moves towards the sink. Her eyes widen seeing him. 'God! Nick. I didn't know you were back,' she says.

'Evidently,' Nick replies, grinding his teeth to curb anger he has no reason to feel. Coral brushes her hands down her thighs, automatically smoothing her clothes, even though they are not crumpled. She twists her hair into a loose plait and smiles, flashing on and off automatically, calculating the effect on Nick of a strange youth in his kitchen.

'This is Matt. Matt, this is Nick. Nick is my, my –' Coral laughs angrily. 'Oh well, you've met my mum, this is the other half.'

Matt doesn't stand up, though he smiles and nods his head at Nick and carries on rolling his cigarette. Nick wants to make a cup of tea, to sit down at the table and read his post and catch up with the cricket score on the radio. He stands in the doorway for a moment. Coral and Matt ignore him. Coral shovels the crushed ice into two glasses then throws the blender into the sink. There is no suggestion that she might pour a third glass. The music is impenetrable, loud and feverish. Matt says something Nick cannot even hear. Coral runs her fingers through her long hair and laughs. Smarting slightly, and at the same time knowing it is absurd to be hurt by any teenage behaviour, Nick leaves the room. Coral lowers the music to shout after him.

'Oh, by the way, could you tell Mum I won't be home for supper? We're going to the cinema.'

On the sofa in the snug, Nick flicks on the television, and thanks God for the invention of cricket.

Angel

The children have gone into a trance of tiredness now that Angel has got them back in the car after a day playing with school friends. Ruby and Foss are bundled on the back seat in an array of play implements which should have been stashed in the boot. Angel is regretting her own feebleness in not insisting on this with every corner, as plastic spades clatter and fall on the floor, or a rush of beach pebbles spills from a bucket down between the seats. Driving with dark glasses on through the lustrous pink and gold evening cornfields, Angel wonders how many conversations and thoughts it is possible for one person to have at one moment and not implode. Radio Two is playing a song from her past, getting lost in rock and roll, drifting away.

Part of her mind is transported back to a summer when she was seventeen, and had too much time to lie around feeling sorry for herself. It was hot, like today, and every day Angel lay naked on the flat roof of the woodshed at home in the suburbs of Cambridge, soaking up the sun. She breathed in the sticky earth smell of bitumen tar, inhaled one cigarette after another and deliberately closed her mind to revision. Her mind hummed and buzzed through all of that summer, with the rush of nicotine from the stolen cigarettes she sneaked from her father's pocket.

Angel turns the car off the main road and slows down for a tractor dragging a trailer piled high with a gold glacier of corn. She shivers involuntarily. The first field is harvested, the path cut to make way for the end of summer; this moment always makes her sad, even though it is still only July.

Her thoughts return again to the wilful destructiveness in her teenage self that took her tiptoeing into the bedroom where her father lay gasping for breath, only half conscious. His prone state, incapacitated from smoking, drowning in his own lungs from emphysema, enabled her, unnoticed, to slide her hand into the cool silk of the inside pocket of his jacket for his always-present packet of cigarettes. The hot, ironed smell of his shirts, the whiff of lemon aftershave and tobacco curled like smoke through her memory. She could take the cigarettes and no one knew. No one cared what she was doing or wondered where she was. Her father was dying, a process which would take ten years. Her mother Dawn was distant. Fourply, the family business set up by Lionel and his brother Terry, was run by the board. In its heyday the company had flourished, supplying school uniform manufacturers and swimming-costume makers with stretch nylon, but at the time Lionel became ill it slumped, and

Angel remembered Terry's glee when Fourply won a shell-suit contract with a removals firm.

'I don't think this is what Lionel built the company for,' her mother had sighed. 'Anyway, I'm going upstairs to see him. You'll find some lunch for yourself later, won't you?'

It was late morning. Dawn was in her dressing gown and had just put the telephone down. She went through to the kitchen, opened the fridge and took a glass from the cupboard next to it. As she poured vermouth, then tipped her head back to drink it in a gulp, Angel realised with vague unease that she had seen her mother do this every day for as long as she could remember. And until she left home, she measured time by this small deliberate routine of her mother's, though she never told a single person. Now, more than twenty years have passed, and Angel still remembers the ache of feeling unwanted that opened like a chasm when she heard her mother telling her father, 'And we don't have to worry about getting her up for school for a while. She's revising and she can get the bus. And then she'll be gone. She'll look after herself, Lionel.'

The present intrudes sharply, a voice in Angel's ear commanding her attention, bringing a focus.

'Mummy, how much pocket money would it cost for me to buy hair straighteners? Will it be more than twenty-one?'

Angel is never sure what currency or denomination seven-year-old Ruby works in.

'Um, I think that will be plenty. I reckon about seventeen would be enough.'

Ruby leans forward from the back seat, much further than she would have been able to if she was wearing her seat belt, and waves a magazine picture. 'I want to get this one. Can we go to Marshall's on the way home?'

'It's shut now. Please will you put your seat belt on? And Foss, you put yours on too, please.'

Coral, Jem, Ruby, Foss. Girl, boy, girl, boy. Eighteen, sixteen, seven and four. It is so neat it belongs in a nursery rhyme. Angel can never quite get used to adding them all together and finding that she is a mother of four. Sometimes she is convinced that Ruby and Foss, separated from the other two by almost ten years and brought up by her with a different awareness, are her second chance. She is supposed to get it right this time. Even so, it has taken her until now to break the mould and leave her job at Fourply. And of course it isn't really *leaving* to take a sabbatical, but maybe it will give her time to work out why her life has become overwhelming. She cranes to look in the rear-view mirror at Foss, but he is invisible behind her seat. He doesn't often speak, so when he is with Ruby who is never silent, it is easy to forget about him.

His voice rises from the back. 'I've done my seat belt up already. I want some water.'

'Well, there's some in that bottle.'

'No, not for drinking, it's to wash the snails. They're muddy and hot.'

'Oh. Good. I mean bad.' Angel has no idea what the right response is.

'What exactly do you mean?' comes Foss's voice politely from behind her.

'Err. I don't know,' replies Angel, feeling mad.

Ruby whacks something with her magazine. 'Oooh, Mummy! He's got insects too. I really hate woodlice. Why do we have to have them in the car?'

Foss's small voice is utterly reasonable. 'I like them. I found them in the flower bed. Mummy, why is it called a flower bed not a flower table or a flower carpet?'

'I wonder?' Angel muses. 'Beds are nicer, I expect that's why.'

Bed. Yes. Bed. Lovely. Feeling slightly demented, and sure her brain is being burnt out by overexposure to children, Angel allows herself to go into a trance, abdicating responsibility for herself as she keys in her replacement Jake's number on her phone, her heart slamming. It is so absurd; she bites her lip, smiling, thinking about Jake Driver. His copious aftershave, nice green eyes, engaging smile and short-sleeved yellow shirts are superficial guides to Jake. Thank God. Angel scratched the surface almost by mistake at first and found more in his lively voice, his enthusiasm and, most importantly, his toned athletic body. His promotion from first sales rep to head of marketing, even though it is only in Angel's absence, has caused a rash of irritation through Fourply. Nick, who supported Angel in choosing Jake and worked with him to make the transition smooth, says he is riding it out well.

'Actually, I don't think he's noticed, which is thick-skinned of him, but good for his morale,' he said to her last night. Angel has no excuse for ringing, so feeling like a naughty teenager with a crush, she has convinced herself to believe her own internal whisper that she is just checking he is OK and letting him know she is available if he needs her. Oops, no. Not available, but accessible. Yes, that sounds professional. Jake's answerphone cuts in immediately. Relieved, Angel turns off her phone.

'Mummy, my verruca has grown and Jamie Matthews said I wouldn't be able to do swimming because it's infectious like the plague. I think I caught it from someone sneezing on my foot.'

'Mmm. That sounds lovely,' says Angel, aware that she is expected to respond, but not listening because her mind is miles away wondering if her number will show on Jake's missed call list, or if she has hung up quickly enough for it not to register.

Ruby waves her hand in front of Angel's face. 'Mummy. I KNOW you aren't listening. I need you to hear to what I am saying.'

Reluctantly, Angel yanks herself back again to here and now. Goose pimples rise on her bare arms as she drives up to the house and sees that Nick is home.

* * *

'Mummy, come on! Daddy says we can have a bonfire and cook supper on it and he's lighting it and Foss is crying because a snail just popped in the fire and it's dead.'

Ruby's excitement is like quicksilver, flowing over and around lead-heavy Angel, standing in the kitchen in the dusk's mauve-shadowed evening half-light, tears dripping, unbidden. She presses her fingers into her eyes and turns, her smile tight.

'Let's have marshmallows,' she says, searching for a paper bag in the cupboard under the sink.

'What are you doing?' Ruby likes to be part of every-thing, so she gets a bag too.

'I'm expelling panic,' says Angel. 'Do you remember the book Jem gave me for my birthday? It's called *The Outlaw's SAS Handbook* or something. Anyway, this is one of the things we do.'

'I'm going to expel some too,' says Ruby.

'Good,' says Angel. 'Here goes.' Breaking off, she blows a huge breath into the bag, so does Ruby. They look at one another and start laughing.

'We could do some more,' Angel suggests, grinning, 'or we could bite a knotted handkerchief or emit a series of "Oooms".'

'Oooms!' says Ruby, almost bursting with the silliness of this game with her mother. They attempt a couple of limp 'Oooms', and collapse giggling and coughing.

'Panic over!' says Ruby and darts into the larder. In a

23

second she is climbing up the shelves like a monkey, expertly on target for the hidden packets of sweets. She turns and smiles at her mother, and Angel sees her dimple, her busy innocence and is suffused with the delicious adoring love that runs largely unnoticed and unacknowledged through family life.

Ruby waves the packet. 'Yes, here they are! You guessed exactly what I came back in the house to get. Yummy, come on, Mum, hurry up!' Nothing is ever fast enough for Ruby.

Angel opens the fridge and looks inside, wondering as she does so if the fall-out of Ruby's speeded-up character, her impulsive problem-solving energy, is Foss's pensive dawdling, and perhaps even his love of snails.

'OK, do you want sausages too?' Angel gets out a packet of chipolatas and a bottle of ketchup; finds some buns in the bread bin and half a bar of chocolate. On a tray she piles plates, glasses, ginger ale, a box of straws and a bottle of wine. Ruby dances ahead, a huge yellow-and-green-checked rug swagged around her. Angel grabs a couple of cushions on her way to the garden and another sigh slides through her. Out into the garden for a sunset supper with the children and Nick. Could it be idyllic? It certainly should be, and it looked it from the outside. But no amount of props and flowers, scattered cushions and cheerful activities can swamp the tension that occupies the space between Angel and Nick. Or assuage the guilt Angel feels for being unhappy. Still, she kicks a small purple-faced nylon vampire off the doorstep, walks into the garden, determined to find the best she can in the evening and to enjoy it. Music might be the key. Ruby would play the harmonica, Nick would play guitar and they could probably muster a couple of songs; it would be better than silence. And better than talking to Nick.

Roses and the raspberry canes she was inspired to plant among them, thinking the thorns would keep the birds away, scratch at Angel's legs as she passes along a narrow path and through on to the lawn. The peonies have died now, and recent rain has left their heads like filthy tissue paper flung by careless children. Angel wants to put down the tray and pull off the dead heads, but changes her mind as she is about to do it. It is not the right moment for gardening. The trouble is, in the summer there is no right time for anything, and with no working week, and the children beginning their school holiday, structure vanishes. Life plumes away in July and August with no timetables for children's swimming lessons or work. Everything normal stops and everyone disappears. Jem says it is because of exams and people passing their driving tests, but that is just the typical view of a solipsistic teenager. The only chance of holding on to a shred of real life is to get into the garden and observe the change there as summer reaches its zenith and then begins to falter.

Deadheading flowers is the best way Angel can mark time. But not now. Now she must stop procrastinating and go and find Nick and the children for supper. Talking to herself, chastising and chivvying herself along like a mother hen, Angel seeks in her mind for more distraction to bring to the evening. Where is Coral? An eighteen-year-old daughter is a useful decoy and Coral can always be counted on to fill most silences, as long as Nick doesn't start digging at her.

There is Nick, crouched over the fire, Foss leaning on his back. The angle of his head, the peach-pink evening light and the crack of the bonfire shoot together like an arrow into Angel's heart and she remembers a moment long ago when she knew she had fallen in love with Nick. It could be yesterday it is so clear; but actually it was winter, and the peach-pink light was not the sunset, but was cast by a lamp wearing a pink silk camisole, flung off in Angel's student bedroom. Nick was standing smoking by the open fire, the only heating in the room. The fire cracked and Nick turned to look at her. Angel was in the bed and she looked back at him in silence and in that moment a lingering knot of fear or doubt gave way between them and some unspoken but mutual willingness unfurled in its place. Or so Angel felt, and she loved Nick for showing her that.

Nick and Foss are still at the bonfire. Angel approaches, every inch of her purposeful and cheery.

'Hi there. Any sign of Coral? I thought she might like to have supper with us.'

Nick doesn't get up or look at his wife, who is leaning

over the table to put the tray down. He chucks another small log on to the fire.

'Coral's gone out on the tiles with a youth. I think his name was Matt. I'd never seen him before, but he seemed nice enough.'

'Oh yes?' Angel's heart sinks. No Coral. And she would be angry that Nick has seen the new love interest so early on.

'They were going to the cinema and Coral was dressed to draw blood from the bloke.' Nick shakes his head. 'You should talk to her about what she wears, Angel. She's going to get into all sorts of trouble, you know.'

Angel's spine contracts, her shoulders slump, she does not want to have this conversation.

'The fire looks good,' she says. 'I've got some sausages, and ginger beer.' It is easier to talk about nothing. It is always easier to talk about nothing now, and she wishes it were not the case. She wishes she could walk up to her husband, put a hand on his shoulder and kiss him hello. On the mouth. That is what anyone who values their marriage would do, anyone who wants to keep their life safe. That is what someone who can see trouble coming would do to avert it. Angel thinks about it. Nick pokes the fire with a green stick. His hair flops over the collar of his shirt at the back, but at his temples it is receding. Stubble across his chin of salt-and-pepper grey, brown and black, and his strongly arched eyebrows give him a piratical look. A little frayed around the edges, and certainly in need of a haircut, but he is still attractive. Angel knows this, though she cannot for the life of her feel it. The thought of kissing Nick when he hasn't shaved is about as appealing as eating sawdust.

'I watched a bit of Jem's match this afternoon.' Nick still doesn't get up, nor does he look at her; he speaks into the fire. Irritation rises like vomit in her throat.

'Oh really?'

'Yes. He got a few runs. You didn't tell me it was the end of term next week.'

'Oh. Didn't I? Well, it is.' How can she, a grown-up woman, a sophisticated person, bring herself this low? Feeling despicable, Angel wants to make it worse. 'I don't suppose you've remembered about the Fathers and Sons Cricket match, have you?' Bingo.

Nick stands up, hands on hips, and looks at her, his expression a mixture of unease and anger. 'I'm going to New York on Friday, you know that.'

'Well, YOU know that the school has this match on the last day of term every year.' Is there any need to sound so venomous? No, there is never such a need. It achieves nothing except pain.

'Why do you care, Angel?' Nick glances at her then crouches to pierce holes through the sausages with the barbecue fork, before chucking them in a string into the old black pan Ruby brought out. Angel feels as though she is built from ice with a single living vein of aggravation coursing through her. The only way to prevent herself from freezing over completely is to keep on needling Nick.

'I don't. But I would have thought you would care. I would have thought you would have liked to play.' Her voice is rising and tightening, her jaw is tense. She hasn't noticed that she has folded her arms tight across her chest.

Foss is between them now, holding up a ball. Nick takes the ball and tosses it from one hand to the other. 'I'll delay the trip. I can miss the conference, it's no big deal, and I'll just go to the Trade Fair.'

Glancing uneasily at Angel, Foss says, 'Daddy always wants to play,' and the wheedling in his voice is another flail to Angel's conscience.

Jem

It's my school holidays at last and I have been home for two days. Mum is weird. She's not normal and she made Ruby cry today. She's got this new habit of talking mad psycho stuff. So this morning – well, I suppose it was after lunchtime really, but just now, when Ruby wants to make bread and it is really hot and I have just got up and am getting my breakfast, she comes into the kitchen talking on the phone as per usual, and she stands and glares. It's the beginning of the holidays for all of us. She has given up work because she says it's too stressful with all of us to look after, but I think she would rather have given us up and kept on going into the office. She should chill out, but she is fired up and anxious. I don't like it. She isn't concentrating on what she is saying to whoever it is on the phone, because her eyes are darting about in a really stressy way at me and Ruby and all the flour and cereal and spilt stuff that just comes if you leave a seven year old to do their own thing. It's Mum's job to look after Ruby, in fact, it's Mum's job to look after all of us, and if she's on the phone or in her office then she can't expect us to do everything her way. And just because she's decided not to go to work any more doesn't mean we all have to be perfect hologram people.

'Listen, Janet, you'll have to wait for Nick to get back. Or call him in New York later. The children are all making bread and there's a kind of *In the Night Kitchen* insanity in my house and I must focus on that now. Let's talk later on. Actually, you should call Jake. He'll have a good take on it, and he's responsible with me out of the picture and Nick away. Look, I must go, we're about to be engulfed by dough!'

God. I so know this one. Mum is so good at making it sound as though whatever we are doing here is wonderful and creative and she is enabling it. Other people are always saying, 'Angel, you give your children a perfect life.'

Well, if this is perfect I may as well shoot myself and save Mum and Dad a whole load of money and grief. And by the way, if this is perfect, please never show me flawed. Mum presses the off button on the phone, slams it on the dresser and stomps over to the kitchen sink.

'Can't any of you even pick up a teaspoon?' she demands, standing like a wooden martyr at the sink. 'I do feel, Jem, that you could take responsibility for yourself now and get yourself up and dressed before lunch. How can you have a sense of fulfilment if you're asleep all day?'

'I don't want a sense of fulfilment, I just want some

sodding breakfast,' I snarl back at her. Mum raises one eyebrow – a really irritating thing she can do which I have tried to copy.

'It's lunchtime,' she says, trying to be withering and not succeeding.

'Mummy, when you do that you get wrinkles on one side of your face,' says Ruby, pulling Mum towards her with a floury hand, commanding her attention. 'Mummy, help me make this plait. I need you to do it and put sprinkles on it.' Ruby is kneeling on a corner of the kitchen table. Actually, she looks as if she is rising out of a big flap of greaseproof paper, a bit like the *Venus de Milo* in that seashell which we have just been doing in art. The reason that it springs to my mind is that Ruby is wearing a bikini decorated with felt cut-out conch shells and she's got ice cream on her nose and a streak of green in her hair where Coral sprayed it with a can of coloured dry ice. She looks quite neglected, but also very like my art project. I need a photograph of her. I think there's a camera in the dog bed – most things seem to end up in the dog bed. Except the dog – she is behind me eating an egg that has rolled off the table and smashed on the floor.

'Mummeeeee. Help me!!!!!' bellows Ruby, more like Goebbels than the *Venus de Milo*, but that's another whole project for History and I am not going there today.

'Just a minute, darling, let me finish talking to Jem, he needs – Oh look, Jem, where did you find my camera? I'm sure you could take a better picture of Ruby if she wiped her face and we got all that mess off the table, and what about some flowers – oh look, there's that jug of hollyhocks over there –'

Racing about, Mum starts trying to ruin everything by poncing it up, but I've got the picture already so it doesn't matter.

'Mum, what are we doing today?' I interrupt her because I don't want to hear her half-baked rubbish about what she thinks I need, what she thinks I should photograph and how cute she can make it. I am so bored of life with my family I could lie down and go into a trance and never stand up again.

The phone rings again, and Mum shrieks, 'God, I can't stand it!' and starts scrabbling around on the dresser because she can't remember where she put the handset down. She's got no bra on and her boobs are drooping like pancakes and more or less showing at the sides of her strappy dress. The phone is in the dog basket. There is so much stuff in there it's like an office and there is actually no room for Vespa. That's my excuse for why she sleeps in my bed. I fish the phone out and hand it to Mum, clicking the on switch. She is so lucky to have me instead of a total crack-head teenage son. I wonder if she realises. A clue that she does is that Mum smiles at me – the fastest smile I have ever seen. It's gone almost before I register it existed. It's not much, but it will do for now. It'll have to.

'Hello? – Yes, this is Angel – oh, Jake. Yes. No, not at

all. Of course I can talk, I've been thinking about you and wondering how you are getting on.' Suddenly everything is different about Mum. Her shoulders drop about three inches, she lounges over to the sofa in the corner of the kitchen and she sits down, flopping back, not sitting perched with her hand clamped tight on the phone as she usually does. Now she is swinging her legs. She runs her fingers through her hair and giggles into the phone. You would not think it was the same harridan of one second ago.

'Yes, well, the figures suggest that we can pull it off, but what do you think?'

'Mum, can we go to the beach? I need to dig a hole to do a poo.' My mini-brother Foss comes in with his bucket and spade, shouting because he always does and Mum says he needs an operation – grommets. I think permanent head-phones for all the rest of us would do the job fine. He looks even more neglected than Ruby. He is chewing a piece of gum I remember him having yesterday when he went to bed, he has a snail of snot running from his nose, and he is only wearing a T-shirt. He stands in front of Mum and starts hitting her on the knee with his spade. He is more or less totally charm free. That's what I like about him. Mum makes a horrible face and shoos him away with one hand. I heard her telling her friend Jenny last summer that she never meant to have him. I can remember every word and she was pretty emphatic. 'The thing is,' she said, 'because Nick and I more or less never have sex, I completely forgot about contraception, so I was astonished when I found I was pregnant, and by the time I realised it was actually true, it was far too late to do anything.' Mum never talks loudly, but her voice carries when she is sitting in the kitchen with a friend and I am on the computer in the playroom and all the doors between are open. I don't actually know what acid dropping on stomach tissue feels like for sure, but I wouldn't be surprised if it is a similar feeling to hearing your mother talking about having sex, and worst of all with your father. Anyway, I felt sick for a while and then I forgot about it, though I do feel sorry for Foss every now and again. It isn't great that he wasn't wanted, but he's here and everyone loves him in their own way. I wonder if they wanted me, come to think of it? They already had Coral; they might have wanted another girl, or an only child. I'll ask them sometime.

'Mum, come on, let's go and dig a loo,' Foss bellows. I can't stop laughing because Mum is glaring and waving her arms as if she is being attacked by a wasp, but from her voice on the phone you would think she was in a totally peaceful empty room.

'I'm so glad you're enjoying the work, and thanks for getting in touch, it's really thoughtful . . . I do feel a bit spare without my job at the moment, but family life is pretty fulfilling.'

There is a shriek from Ruby. 'Mummmmmeeeeeee,' she yells on a crescendo of frustration, 'you've got to help me, I need to put this in the oven now. Come ON!'

Mum climbs backwards off the sofa, speaking in staccato snatches into the phone. 'That is so perceptive of you. Well, Nick is often away and –' she breaks off and I wish she was on a photo phone so Jake could see her scowl, wipe Foss's nose with a tea towel and lift him out of her path.

'Yes. You're right, I try to –' She lifts Ruby off the table and pushes her towards the sink, miming hand washing. Mum grabs the dough plait. A bit of it flops off in her hand. Ruby turns on her – more like Medusa now than the *Venus de Milo*, and whacks her with a wooden spoon. Mum grabs the wooden spoon and chucks it in the dog basket before turning her face to the wall, literally, and carrying on her conversation looking into the corner of the room.

She giggles at something Jake has said and fluffs up her hair again.

Ruby has not finished with her. 'Mummy, you've ruined it. I am glad you are in the corner. You ruin everything of mine. I was going to sell it at the fête and now it's too small and I will have to make another one or else it will have to be thirty-five instead of seventy pounds. Or pence. I haven't even decided which yet.'

I pat Ruby on the head. 'Good maths, Roobs.' I smile at her but she is working up for a big scene, and won't be distracted.

'It's half,' she snarls at me. A familiar tension is building like clouds before a storm in the kitchen. And in fact, weirdly, I glance out of the window and the sky is mental – grey and purple, too, and a couple of birds are frantically trying to fly to a tree for shelter but they don't seem to be making headway. Anyway, it's probably a mistake as the tree could get struck by lightning. Ruby starts to howl and on the phone this guy Jake is obviously still yakking on.

'Oh, I would love to do that. What a nice thought,' Mum burbles.

I wave at her, Mum scowls at me, and tucks the phone under her chin. Standing on one leg she puts her hands together as if she is ready for prayers. She always does yoga when she's stressed. Her concentration is ragged, though, thanks to the mayhem in the kitchen, and she wobbles and drops the phone and it falls in Vespa's water bowl.

'Shit,' says Mum, bending over to fish it out, but Jake has gone. 'Oh well,' she says, and putting her hands on her hips, she tries to get organised in a cheerful Boy Scout way that doesn't suit her. 'OK, everyone, what would you like to do now? It's your holidays and you can choose.'

'Good,' sobs Ruby. 'I choose you. I want you to talk to me, me, ME. You have hurt my feelings.' She yanks at Mum's skirt, making her wobble and topple on to a chair.

Mum looks sad and young. 'I didn't mean to upset you, Ruby,' she says quietly. It seems to me there is a good chance she will start crying, but luckily she pulls herself together and winks at me.

'Put the kettle on, gorgeous,' she says to me. She isn't

making me feel safe or happy to be home. She is not acting like a mum. I feel like she is talking to a parrot, and I am not getting that cosy family feeling there sometimes is in our kitchen. Or used to be. I don't blink but I stare and stare at her. She must be deranged. Her mood swings are worse than Foss and he's four. She is forty, for Christ's sake. Maybe she's getting the old lady thing where they don't get the curse any more and their bones go brittle. Apparently it drives them mad – well, that's what Coral says. Thunder whacks through the sky and a hiss of rain starts instantly like a sprinkler being turned on. Mum is wiping the table and putting cups for tea on it, and trying to chat to the little ones.

'We could play Hide and Seek?'

'Nope,' says Foss.

'Or Snakes and Ladders?'

'It's lost,' snaps Ruby.

'Mum, this is crap,' I say, and I didn't mean it to be as forceful as it sounds in the room. Mum's face crumples; she pulls it together and tries to smile. If she didn't make everything so difficult I would feel sorry for her right now.

'Oh,' she says quietly, rocking Ruby in her arms. Foss climbs behind her and his arms are locked around Mum's neck under her hair. She has a way of looking very primitive when she is surrounded by my little brother and sister. She kind of huddles with them, and she wears a lot of ethnic jewelry and big, buckled belts which intensify the cavewoman thing.

'You get in too many stress situations and you shout a lot. If I didn't know you, I wonder if I would like you?' I feel mean because, cavewoman or not, she suddenly looks like I have thrown a bucket of snot over her. She has almost no wrinkles and a small face with a lot of big hair. She is quite pretty for a mum as old as forty, I think; I can only go by what my friends tell me, and they say she's quite cool.

'That's what you think,' I always tell them, even though of course I am secretly pleased. 'She keeps another personality at home – it's the one with a haggard old face, bad breath and the nastiest temper outside the Mafia.' My favourite film is *The Godfather*. And it's true – Mum does have a split personality. I try to concentrate on the part of Mum I like, and I relent a bit.

'Oh, I probably would like you,' I offer, 'but I doubt I would ever meet you if we weren't mother and son.' I get myself out of the room before she or one of the mini-brethren begins to cry. What a stupid conversation to have begun with my mum. I sound like one of Coral's stoned friends.

Angel

Angel's alarm clock prods her awake, and her sweat is another skin in the hot night, sheet tangled around her legs. Three o'clock in the morning. She must have miss-set the alarm. Turning over, Nick's back faces her, she turns again on to her front. Her nightdress and the sheet catch her, and she sits up, wide awake now, mind racing out of the room and away. A comforting yeasty smell, warm in the air, brings her back and she remembers why she is awake now. She has to turn on the breadmaker. Ruby needs bread hedgehogs to take to Brownie Camp tomorrow – today, in fact. It is not even term-time any more, but there are still non-stop child events, opportunities to fail in optimum mothering skills, scattered through the holidays. It was the obvious answer last night to bring the breadmaker into her bedroom. It would work if she turned it on in the night, and the hedgehogs would be ready at breakfast time.

Angel presses the switch and the machine begins to churn. She lies down again on her side, her back and

Nick's curved away from one another, a channel of cold linen between them. He does not stir, but his breath rasps on the verge of snoring. She feels resentful. He can sleep. He can hop on a plane to New York and call it business, but Angel knows it will be fun. She would like to be going and it is shaming after only one week away from work, to acknowledge this. The company could really benefit from some good strong orders in the US and Angel knows Nick will be very good at generating them; while she is not working and not managing to do the hedgehogs on time.

Angel wriggles to get comfortable in the bed, insomniac fear beating like a muffled drum in her head. What if the sabbatical does not make her life work better? So far it isn't showing any signs of improving anything. Angel has set a lot of store by it, unable to look past it at anything else. A mother needs to take stock of life sometimes, and to do that she must be able to give things up. But what will be next? How much of what is important to her must she lose to find herself?

The rattling of the breadmaker and Nick's snoring are joined by the first birdsong of the morning as dawn breathes grey light into the room. Angel is chilly now, and wide awake, her resentment increasing with every noise Nick utters in sleep. At least he is going away, so she can have some peace at bedtime. Angel is glad not to have a witness to this thought.

She gets up, unplugs the breadmaker, and takes it out

and down to the kitchen. The table is already laid for breakfast. Another day. Angel puts the kettle on and sits down at the table. Ruby will be pleased about the hedgehogs. She stands up and opens a cupboard, taking out a tin lunch box and putting it on the floor in front of the door. Now she will remember the hedgehogs when she and Ruby leave in a rush. Nick's jacket is on the back of a chair. On the table in front of it lies his passport, the ticket tucked into it, and next to it his car keys. Familiar parts of her husband. There used to always be a packet of cigarettes with his most closely guarded items, but Nick gave up smoking a year after going into Alcoholics Anonymous. Then there were worry beads and nicotine chewing gum for a while, but all that has gone now. Remembering how he struggled, and how she appreciated him for doing it because her father never had, Angel shivers, remorse creeping like cold water through her. She wishes she wasn't glad he was going to be away.

The kitchen chair digs into her spine. Angel moves with her cup of tea over to the sofa and lies down, kicking aside a large cuddly bear, a pair of headphones and a ball of red wool with knitting needles trailing a scarf small enough to spiral round a worm. A pink glow is creeping round the corner in the yard and filtering through the kitchen window. The timer pings on the breadmaker, and as she decants the dough, Angel thinks how often she has seen the dawn in. Kneading hedgehogs, sewing on name tapes, sitting up with an ill child, breastfeeding a new baby, so many nights with Nick asleep or away. So much time inhabited alone.

The twelve hedgehogs are ready now, each with a pair of raisin eyes and quiffed spines, achieved by the use of a wide-toothed comb – not entirely clean, but Angel hopes the heat of the oven will kill anything living that might have lurked on the comb. She slides the tray into the oven and resigns herself to being up for another hour. It is five now, so it isn't worth going back to bed. She turns on the radio and out swim fluid notes, liquid sound, flowing into the kitchen, soothing and invigorating. Angel does not know the piece, but its effect, of removing her from her circular guilt and inspiring civilised thought and emotions from a different, deeper part of her, is lovely. The moment of surrender to the inevitable, in this instance a night of wakefulness, is a moment of joy. Angel decides to perform a small act of love for Nick. She gets out the ironing board.

Jem

I am getting used to the boredom of the summer holidays now. Every day comes and goes and could be any old day. It's nice not knowing when a week has passed, and it's a different kind of boredom from being at school; it's a kind of free boredom, whereas at school it is enforced. They make you bored when you are there and at home I can choose to be bored. So it's not bad.

The last few days have been thundery then hot, and today is similarly bad-tempered feeling. Coral is lying on the lawn with Matt, her new boyfriend, and Melons her best friend from school. They have finished their A levels and they are free to live the rest of their lives. Lucky bastards. No surprises for guessing the big thing about Melons. Matt has glasses and is comic-book handsome with a square jaw and he blinks a lot. Could be the glasses, I suppose. I reckon he is a bit like Clark Kent with a hidden Superman lurking inside him. He is a rower and he is in a team at university. And he smokes. Him being Clark Kent would make Coral into Lois Lane which is about right as she is skinny with dark hair and a face full of sharp edges and flat planes and the biggest brown eyes imaginable. Matt passed his driving test last year, so Coral has done well to get him as her boyfriend and now she has wheels for this summer.

Coral swipes her arm towards me and catches my ankle as I try to walk past. 'What are we doing today?' Coral has perfected an almost effortless way of speaking that means she hardly opens her mouth. It's quite hard to understand her, but she never says anything very interesting anyway, so it doesn't matter. I like her a lot even though she is my sister. One of the best things about her is that she is eighteen, which means her friends are, and one day I will get somewhere with one of them. Hope it's Melons. Coral is still looking at me, in fact they all are. Like I know the answer to anything.

'Dunno. Let's go somewhere.'

'You're insane. Mum will never let us go in Matt's car with him. She is utterly against teenagers driving other teenagers. Haven't you heard her banging on about it?'

'Does she need to know?'

Coral raises her eyebrows and shades her eyes with her hand to look at me in the glaring sunlight. 'You are so devious,' she breathes. 'I like it.'

'Where shall we go?' Melons stands up. Actually, she's called Mel, but I really like referring to her as Melons even though I know I can't do it to her face. I can't think of anywhere we could go. There is nowhere remotely cool or even bearable for miles. It is better not to even think about going somewhere because the options are so limited it's lowering to the spirits.

Suddenly Mum and the tiny twosome appear round the back of Matt's car. Ruby and Foss are dressed up like American tourists with shorts, sunglasses and backpacks. Both of them have sun cream on their noses and base-ball caps on. They look purposeful. So does Mum. She is waving money around, a sure sign she wants to get rid of us.

'Jem, Coral. Here, let me give you some money. Foss and Ruby are desperate to go to the sea – could you big ones take them, please? And I'll come and meet you later.'

'How are we getting there?' Coral has the money pock-eted before I can even see how much there is. Today is our day for making Mum look freaked. She presses both hands under her hair and lifts it off her neck. 'Oh God,' she murmurs under her breath. 'I hadn't thought of that – I forgot Delilah is on holiday. How could I forget that when it has made my life such hell?'

Delilah is our au pair and I don't think she's on holiday, I think she's left. I went into her room to see if she'd left any fags behind and there was nothing of hers in there at all – not one photograph, not one hair clip or pair of knickers. I know because I looked in all her drawers, and not one fag, which was a pain. Mum hasn't even been up there yet and I can't face telling her, neither can Coral.

'She'll go psycho, let's not do anything. She'll find out

soon enough,' was Coral's decision when I took her to look yesterday evening. She gave me one of her cigarettes and we climbed out of my bedroom window on to the flat roof to smoke, silent together when we peered over the edge and saw Mum strutting along the path through the long grass with Foss whining behind her.

'I'm never having children,' said Coral.

'Me neither,' I agreed. 'They're far too much hassle and it takes years to grow them – piglets are better.'

'Yeah, piglets on leather leads,' said Coral dreamily, and we both started snorting with laughter – no reason except maybe nicotine.

'I could take them,' offers Matt, waving his car keys in a provocative gesture from the keyring he has hooked around his middle finger. I don't think he really means to be cheesy, but he has a bit of a crush on Mum and she is twisting her hair around and letting it fall down her back again, and smiling at him, and she is not tall, and has such an air of being rescued. She looks up and widens her eyes. I've noticed she can't help coming on to any male – she almost does it to me sometimes which is gross – anyway, whatever her motives are, she has made Matt feel massive, cool and important, like he makes a difference to someone.

'That would be great,' she says. Just like that. As if she has never gone on about teenage drivers, or over her dead body, or any of her so-called abiding principles. I open my mouth to point some of this out, but Coral pinches my arm and whispers, 'We've got thirty quid.' So I keep quiet and we pile into Matt's very small hot car. He starts the engine and Hendrix comes on loud all around us and the car howls as we rev and lurch out of first gear and down the drive. I look back, anxious that Mum might have seen this evidence of bad driving, but she is already back in the house, not so much as waiting to see us out of the gate. Coral lights a cigarette.

'Phew, we've escaped,' she sighs.

'I feel sick,' says Ruby.

'Are we nearly there?' Foss asks, wriggling back so his head is cushioned by Mel's enormous shelf of – well, by Mel.

Nick

Nick feels slightly retarded for admitting this, even to himself, but being away these days without Angel or the kids is like taking drugs. He can do anything. Really. He can do whatever he wants with whomever he fancies – and there are so many girls to fancy it's unbelievable. No one need ever know. It's a mid-life crisis for sure, but it's fun.

And this is how he can revisit the free-fall sense of irresponsibility, the light-headed whim-led state that took him in the mid-seventies to Sausalito, California to live on a houseboat with a girl called Tree. He didn't ever pretend to love her, but they smoked a lot of opium together, then they took cocaine, and somewhere along the way Nick got a job as a chef.

Even though he has not picked up his knives for years, Nick's fingers still sometimes ache with the memory of the cuts and wounds that never really healed through his early twenties. There is nothing else left of that part of his life now. The restaurants he worked in were gone, and

Tree has changed her name back to Theresa and lives in ecological splendour with a green banker husband and IVF twins in Marin County. He remembers her as ethereal, but it could just have been the drugs, as he also recalls she gave the best blow jobs of any woman he has known. That surely takes some practical application, but maybe that, too, is just a fantasy of Nick's from his own internal twenty-four-hour soft porn channel.

The dreamlike propulsion which was his youthful impetus is now taking him out of the fashion buyers' fair on West Broadway, Manhattan and along three blocks to a former municipal building where he will meet a real estate agent with a view to purchasing an as yet unbuilt apartment. He is feeling good, he has charmed Susie Streid, a big blonde buyer from a national supermarket chain, and has convinced her that the chain needs to revamp its image and invest in a new uniform of stretchy trousers for all its employees. From there it is a tiny step to getting them to stock the trousers to sell as well, and the deal will be worth a shed load of money. Sexy money. Not sexy trousers unfortunately, but that would be a miracle.

He should have taken Susie Streid out to dinner, but he has a bit of property to speculate over today. Susie can wait. The 'unbuiltness' of the property is what makes him able to contemplate spending several hundred thousand dollars of as yet un-borrowed money on a bachelor's loft he has no intention of telling his wife about. Compartmentalising is what Nick's life is all about. He kicks a Starbucks paper cup off the sidewalk and crosses in front of a heaving row of taxis, motorbikes and delivery vans at the traffic lights.

New York, even though he only arrived yesterday, and is still treacle-legged with jet lag, is full of promise, and Nick intends to extract every ounce – or do they deal in grams now? – from it. The triggers are all here, and unconsciously he scratches the palms of his hands with his clenched middle finger, an echo of a past but never-to-be-forgotten sensation, as he walks past a metal double-height door where he dimly recalls he may once have scored a bag of useless smack. The heat is sticky already, although the sun has not yet beamed down between the tall blocks on to the narrow SoHo street. It is a good thing in Nick's opinion that he put on a black T-shirt when he got up today, and not the white linen shirt Angel had packed in his case with a post-it note saying, 'Thursday for Trade Fair. Make sure you hang it up in the bathroom as creases will drop out that way.'

The shirt is still in the bottom of his case, and Nick has no plans for removing it. He has never entirely shed the remnants of his youthful musical aspirations, although now all that is really left, apart from a collection of guitars and twenty-three pairs of cowboy boots, is a tendency to wear over-tailored jackets with jeans and to leave his hair a bit too long. Angel's determination to style the whole of her life even extends to her husband, and his packing for a business trip. Unbelievable. But, as Nick likes to remind himself, she can't help it. It's a disease, and boy does he know about disease. And Angel, governed as she is by guilt, is a great wife. Nothing is too much for her, and there are times when Nick is overawed by her determination and her strength. For example, when she decides to clean the back of the cooker and inside the kettle after a day of meetings and business administration, she honestly seems to believe that if she scrubs hard enough, she will get rid of her own demons. Pour out a bottle of bleach on the world and let there be light. And the more Angel purifies her surroundings, the more Nick obscures his, covering his tracks, keeping every bit of his life separate so no one can see the whole of him. Least of all himself. He crosses the road, and because he has time to spare, and the brick wall of jet lag has just hit him on the head, he enters a coffee shop, orders an espresso and drinks it on the sidewalk. The hot bitterness jolts him into the present, and he winces at the honking of car horns and the pulse of a pneumatic drill a few blocks away. A girl with black, belligerent sunglasses and a snake of plaited hair gets up from the round table outside the café door and glides away on roller blades. Nick sits down in her place, and the sun glances off his wedding ring.

Angel's sense of guilt has given Nick a lot of slack rope, and her desire to assuage it keeps him in luxury. He's not complaining, or not on the surface, but those whom Nick shares with in his twice-weekly AA meetings know a different truth. The real truth. Nick doesn't really accept it at all. He is fed up with doing life Angel's way, and he's fed up with his own guilt for the things he does in defiance. He may be powerless over her actions, but he is accountable for his own, and the marriage is suffering.

In his quietest moments he wonders if he and Angel were ever really suited. He was drinking, he rescued her, and she was grateful. When he stopped drinking he saw the confusion that had brought them together, or as much of it as he could deal with, but there were the children by then, and life just kept on going. And like he always says, Angel is a great wife, and he loves her. He has to believe this truth, and that she loves him too. Without this, Nick knows the whole of his life would have to be rewritten.

He finishes the coffee and, leaving three dollar-bills under the sugar shaker, he crosses the road and turns the corner. He walks half a block then pauses, looking for a number on the building he has reached. It makes no sense to think about Angel now anyway. She's miles away and right now she is not his problem.

'Hey, Mr Stone, good morning.' A glossy girl with peach-pink lips and huge pale purple sunglasses turns to walk up the steps to the building alongside Nick. Joy of joys, she is wearing a miniskirt and her legs are not especially long, but are the right shape, bare, honey-brown and smooth as a caffé latte.

'I'm Carrie from Holder and Casey, pleased to meet you.' She smiles, her eyes sweeping up and down over him with practised bold flirtation.

God. Oh, God. I love American girls, thinks Nick, following her in through the rusted black door, his eyes glued to the hem of her skirt, his mind entirely occupied now with how many steps behind her he must walk in order to see up this skirt and win his mental bet with himself that she is wearing red knickers.

'Of course, all you can see today is the space, and it's fifteen hundred square feet of prime Manhattan loft, so it's quite something, or it will be.' Carrie's shiny hair swings across the white crisp back of her shirt, and she smoothes her skirt across her hips and steps back to allow Nick to press the elevator button

'Seventh floor,' she says. Her breasts are high, and although it would be fantasy to say that the buttons of her white shirt are straining, Nick can see the faint suggestion of the pattern of her bra, and when he looks away from her he notices the bump of a nipple is reflected in the shiny brass panel of the lift door.

'How many floors of the building have you sold?' Nick wants to say her name, he wants to put his hand under her shirt and kiss her then press his leg between hers and lean down to lick her collarbone. He wants to put his hand on her neck, under her hair, and bring his mouth to hers, kissing her, pressing against her. He wants to push her back so her shoulder hits the 'Doors closed' button and he can reach under her skirt and let his fingers explore her hot, wet cunt. Or do they call it 'snatch' in New York? He might ask her that in a minute. His cock is hard in his jeans, and the pressure of the zip against his foreskin is further arousal.

The elevator doors open. Carrie has been talking all the time. Or so Nick believes, though he has not heard a word of what she has said.

He listens now. 'You are lucky this became available, you know, Mr Stone –'

Nick puts up a hand, snatching it down again to stop himself touching her cheek.

'Oh, it's Nick, call me Nick.'

Carrie smiles; her eyes are blue and grey-flecked, with thick lashes like a smudge around them. 'Oh, OK, Nick. A film studio wanted to buy the whole lot and make it into apartments for actors like a kind of condo for Hollywood types, but they have decided to go for the two penthouse floors only now, so this is up for grabs, and it is just a great space.'

Carrie flashes her even white teeth, bites her bottom lip and swishes her skirt as she walks beside him along a corridor, pushing open big dark wooden doors to a concrete and plaster space. Nick is confused – he is meant to be talking about price per square foot and asking about air-conditioning and service charges and timing – and all he can think of is shagging Carrie.

'This building is incredibly light, and that is what has sold it to Hollywood types who want to come and live in New York. I think they get seasonal affective disorder there more than we do, and I notice that all the calls we get are more to do with light than space. Oh –'

Carrie stumbles on a cable snaking down a black square cut out of the floor.

'Watch out, the place is such a construction site I guess we should be wearing hard hats.'

She gurgles with laughter at the idea, Nick laughs too, but in triumph – her knickers *are* red, so he owes himself now. What's it to be?

There is nothing to see in the space that will be an apartment, but Carrie marches him around, valiantly conjuring up pictures of bathroom, kitchen and living space.

The sun glances on her hair and her freckles, then like an arrow races down her body, over her breasts, down the gentle contours of her stomach before it fades out on the hem of her skirt. She catches his eye and he knows that she knows he has been looking at her more than he has looked at the loft space.

He clears his throat. 'So, this is the bedroom, is it?'

Carrie is leaning against a column, her back to the window. Close to her, Nick breathes in her scent, and her scent is sex. He thrusts his hands into his pockets. She wants him, he is sure. Or as sure as he ever is in anticipation.

'Yes, there is the option to build a platform, too, for a second sleeping area here.'

Nick swivels towards her, Carrie puts her hands into the small of her back and arches her spine, and she looks up at him from under her lashes. He is pretty sure she will be sensational in bed, he's got four nights here and there are a lot of apartments he can look at with her. Why waste any more time?

'Shall we go for a drink?' he says.

'It's lunchtime.'

'I know.'

Nick pulls open the door of the brasserie and Carrie walks through in front of him. Inside, a marble-topped bar is crowded with people sitting at it. The espresso machine hisses, waiters carrying plates of oysters weave between the mass of bodies, bending and yielding to find the line of least resistance. Nick puts his hand on Carrie's waist to guide her, and he could swear that she softens and moves closer. She is separated from him for a moment by a waiter spinning with a tray of empty coffee cups, and in that instant Nick steps closer to the bar to get out of the way. A girl on a stool reaches out and touches his arm.

'Hey,' she says. She has slanting dark eyes and a diamond stud in her tongue. Her lips are dark, like good red wine, and her teeth are small and even. Nick is bewildered. The girl smells of spice and incense, expensive and complicated.

She must have mistaken him for someone, or maybe the person she wants is behind him. He looks round, but there is no one. The girl is smiling at him, so she must be someone he knows, but who and from where? He searches as fast as he can through his mind to find out who she is.

'Would you like to come and buy me a drink, or are you with her?' She shoots a sly glance towards Carrie, who is further down the bar now, perched up on a stool, running her fingers through her hair and looking back to see where Nick is.

Nick realises that he doesn't know this woman after all – she is picking him up. This is thrilling. And so unexpected. What a waste that it has happened now when he is hot on the trail of Carrie. Two sensational chicks – the obvious thought flashes across his mind for a luxury moment – 'Two!' but he dismisses it right away – it is just too difficult to pull off. Undoubtedly he would be left with none, or worse, two very cross women. He looks at Carrie. She has taken off her sunglasses, and leans her elbow on the bar playing with her hair, shifting in her chair. She glances down the bar again to Nick and the stranger and tosses her hair back before reaching into her handbag. Any minute now she will leave. Nick needs to act fast. Decision time.

'Yes, I am with her.' Blinking regretfully – this girl has great tits under a soft, tight, brown velvet top – he steps away. Making a mock-sad face, she reaches for her drink, sipping from the straw. She looks up at him with a sideways smile.

Christ, she's even got dimples – that is cute, Nick sighs.

'Lucky for her, pity for me,' she murmurs. Nick laughs, moving away, his testosterone flying now as he slides on to the stool next to Carrie.

The barman is there immediately. 'What can I get you, sir?'

Nick raises his eyebrow at Carrie.

'I'd like a Diet Coke,' she says.

'And I'll have an espresso and a soda water. No ice, no lemon.' Nick has to press both feet firmly on to the floor and shove his hands into his pockets to stop himself seizing Carrie and kissing her. Some small talk. That's what they need right now, it's a great libido controller.

'So, tell me where you come from and what you like about New York.' He reaches a hand out and pinches the hem of her skirt on her thigh.

Carrie laughs. 'I thought we were here to talk about the loft,' she says.

'I'd rather talk about you.' Nick gazes intently at her.

Carrie looks at him, but cannot hold his gaze. She crosses her legs, swivelling nearer to him, and runs her tongue around her lips. Nick has not had this much fun for years. Adrenalin is pumping though him and he experiences the heady joy he knows is so temporary, of feeling immortal. He reaches out and pushes a strand of her hair back behind her ear. The jolt he feels is as good as a needle full of heroin.

Angel

The sound of Matt's car, idling at the bottom of the drive, engine speeding up as he changes through the gears, hangs in the still afternoon and Angel leans against the closed front door, her eyes shut, listening to the sound shrinking, becoming engulfed by other sounds, a black-bird chirruping, the summer coo of pigeons and, further away, the drone of a small plane. Once she has nothing to listen for, she opens her eyes and summer leaps on her, dancing green in the freckled beauty of the beech tree. The peaceful stillness is shocking in contrast to the holiday invasion of children's clamour, their voices echoing in every waking thought, and often every dream, too. Inescapable until they go out somewhere, and the silence of their absence is more penetrating still. Angel steps away from the house and almost sways, dizzy with a sense of being lonely, her mind travelling as if she is able to see all the way around herself with a video camera. If she was standing on a tall plinth in the middle of a waste-land a million miles away she could not feel more alone.

She needs to do something, or see someone, to fill the space somehow. Dithering, she begins to kick gravel off the lawn using her bare feet, flicking with her toes, enjoying the concentration it requires to pick up one small stone between two toes and flick it back on to the drive. There is a lot to be said for low-grade labouring at times of emotional stress, and in Angel's mind, peace begins to flower as she remembers Levin in *Anna Karenina* and his simple pleasure in scything the hay on his estate. She moves slowly down the side of the lawn, becoming more methodical, right foot up, curl big toe, stretch and point over the stone, gather, twist and fling. So satisfying. And probably very toning, too. The telephone rings and Angel runs back to the house, only marginally distracted from her labours, and trying to remember the name of Levin's brother.

'It's Jake. I'm on the road not far from you and I thought I'd drop by and fill you in on how it's going so far.'

Angel swallows but her throat is dry. 'OK,' she says. There is no reason for her to be filled in. She is not working. She is out of the loop. He does not need to come. 'Yes,' she says. 'That would be great. I'm here. Do you want to come with me to the beach to pick up—'

'I'll be about two minutes.'

The floor tiles in the hall are cool, calming the pulse in her bare feet. She stands for a moment holding the telephone, excitement spreading through her veins. Suddenly, for no particular reason, she remembers Levin's brother was called Nikolai. She catches sight of herself in the cloudy mirror by the door into the kitchen and rushes for the stairs, unknotting the ties of her blue dress as she goes. And into the fluttering quiet, a car speeds up to the house crunching gravel like gunshot. The door clunks open, and the music floating from the car stops. In the silence Angel freezes, suddenly alarmed that she is quite alone in the house. A moment passes. Angel yanks open her wardrobe and pulls out a pair of shorts and a purple T-shirt. Oh God, no knickers and she has already put on the shorts. No time to change. Shit. Now she looks deliberately provocative. Mind you – how can he know that she has no underwear on?

The car door slams and she hears Jake coming through the open front door. Suddenly it seems suggestive to be running downstairs from her bedroom. Too embarrassing. Thinking quickly, Angel darts through to the back of the house and hurries down the dairy stairs into the laundry room. The door from this room through to the front part of the house is shut, and she opens it, arming herself with yet more sweet peas, today's crop from the relentless harvest, left until now, gasping for water on a chair by the washing machine.

Jake is sitting on the front doorstep reading a news-paper.

'Hi there.' Angel crouches next to him then wishes she hadn't and stands up again. He looks up her bare legs and slowly brings his gaze up to her face. He stands up too, and kisses her cheek. Angel blushes, and excitement courses through her. They look at one another and Angel smiles and half turns and he takes her hand and kisses the other cheek. Oh God. Angel bites her bottom lip and looks away, then back at Jake. He lets go of her hand slowly, still looking at her. His eyes are green and changing like a moving kaleidoscope, pulling her in. What else could he have done to greet her in the heat, the closeness, with Angel barefoot in skimpy, hippy clothes he has never seen a colleague wearing before? Shaking hands would have been absurd, doing nothing too suggestive.

'Good T-shirt,' he says, still not moving away. Angel flushes again – the T-shirt has 'Bitch 1' written in white flowing script over the right tit. Angel can hardly breathe or move; she is melting with heat, Jake's focused interest, the beating of her pulse and the heady scent of the flowers in her hands.

'It's not mine, it's my daughter's – not the little one, obviously,' she gabbles. 'Anyway – do you like sweet peas?'

Jake laughs, snapping the tension. 'I love them. Did you pick them especially for me?'

Angel steps back, and pulls herself together. 'Of course.' She unclips the clasp from her pinned-up hair and looks straight at him. 'Come on. Let's put them in some water. Then we can go to the beach to collect the children.'

'OK. I'll brief you on work on the way, shall I?' Jake walks back to his car and reaches in through the open window for his sunglasses, still talking. 'The beach sounds great – can we swim?'

'Yes, I think the tide will be coming in by now,' says Angel. 'I'll just get some paper for these to go in.'

Angel retreats to the kitchen and leans against the closed door for a moment, glad to have breathing space. She walks back outside, blinking in the bright light and heat. Jake goes round to the other side of the car and opens the door for her.

'Ready?' he says, grinning.

Angel imagines a parallel scene where he pulls her towards him by the belt loops on her shorts until they are touching all the way up their bodies, and their eyes meet and then their mouths.

'Almost.' She suddenly realises she hasn't got a towel or her handbag or anything.

'I've just got to get my stuff,' she calls, retreating into the house again, needing to escape the intensity coursing between them.

Nineteen years ago Angel was escaping something else the day she met Nick Stone. A wrong love affair that lasted three weeks, so never had real wings on which to fly. Angel didn't know she was pregnant when she got on the train to return home to her parents, having said goodbye to Ranim. He was returning to India, he was never coming back, he lived in an ashram there and his expansive views on free love got Angel into bed the first night she met him. There she stayed, consumed, falling, and allowing no safety net in herself, cut off from her friends and family, drunk on headlong sex and passion, pretending to herself it was safe because he was going away. 'Three weeks won't hurt,' was her promise to herself, 'and then I'll get on with my life.'

The man opposite her on the train that day was the antithesis of sleek, small-boned delicate Ranim whose liquid dark eyes promised everything, whose sensitive hands and smooth body gave her pleasure she had not known before. She mistook pleasure for love, and was yearning to see him again even as he kissed her goodbye and boarded his plane. She never did. The shock of his going numbed her, and she could only measure the extent of her pain some years later, when she noticed it had gone. Life was too big and full for her to dwell on a memory, no matter how lovely, and the affair with Ranim was more a memory than anything else.

Out of the fantasy of what she wanted to believe at the time was the biggest love affair of her life, she allowed Nick to rescue her, a damsel in distress. He seemed strong and sure and he wanted her in his life. The distress became self-disgust when she found that she was pregnant, and Nick asking her to marry him was affirmation that she was lovable. She found it hard to believe he could still want to have anything to do with her, but Nick was drawn to complexity, and the more Angel revealed of the mess she believed herself to be, the more he loved her for being herself. And without noticing it happening, over the first year of knowing him, Angel fell in love with Nick's courage, his willingness and his determination.

Nick stopped the raging voices in her head, and in the silence she heard her own heart and was amazed it was still in one piece. And relieved to have a father for her baby. She would never stop being grateful to Nick for that.

Searching in the kitchen for her sunglasses, Angel cannot get the grin off her face. She feels reckless and young. Desired. Just the way Jake looks at her is waking up her body, and sparkling energy runs through her, making her want to sing and dance and kiss and touch. In this moment she cannot connect with the notion that she has four children and a husband, and she runs out of the door and into Jake's car, more or less not touching the ground but floating in a pink-tinted fantasy.

Jem

If she wasn't my mother and therefore beyond sex, I would swear that Mum has been shagging when she arrives at the beach. She's got Jake the Spaz with her and she's wearing one of Coral's T-shirts which says 'Bitch 1' on it and is tiny so a lot of Mum's suntan is showing and more of her tits than I ever want to see. Ruby sees Mum first and she runs back past the beach huts and up the steps to where Mum is at the top of the dunes, her back to the pine trees, shading her eyes to look for us. She knows where she is looking though, because we always go to the same place on this beach. Ever since we saw the poo floating by, we have made our encampments well away from the popular stretch where the sand is soft, and instead we have gone for the Neolithic option with giant pebbles and sand like a mosaic with broken razor shells.

Quality of life on the beach is not about texture, it's about waste levels and pollution. Or escaping them. I like to tell Mum that we are eco-warriors. I tell her because it's true, but also because it puts her in a really good mood to think of us having any sort of conscience or cause. Sorry to be cynical, but it's true. We have given up buying one make of cereal completely because the company exploits African babies, and even Foss knows to look at the brand before he chooses an ice cream and he boycotts the bad one.

Ruby has adopted an African child to make up for the wrongs of this cereal company. So far she has written her child ten letters and sent biros, pencil cases and three pairs of my old trainers. She hasn't had anything back yet but Mum says life is all about giving, so it's supposed to be fine. Mum's given two hundred quid for this baby. I wish she'd dish it out to me – I could do with some new speakers.

Anyway, Ruby makes Mum and Jake swing her, so they come across to us like some perfect family threesome. Mum's eyes are sparkling and her cheeks are flushed; she looks amazing, and completely different from how she looked when we left the house earlier. It is a bit like a facelift. I have to say, I am not the one who notices this; it is Melons who whispers to me, 'Hey, look at your mum, she's cheered up,' and Coral adds, 'She could do with growing up a bit. I don't know why Nick puts up with it.'

Coral always calls Dad 'Nick'. I think it makes her feel grown-up, like swearing at him, which she does as well. He never shouts back like he does at me, but I guess that's to do with her being a girl. Mum always says so anyway.

'Oh my God,' says Mel, 'but she's your mum, she wouldn't. Would she?'

Coral turns her back on Mum. She looks furious. 'She's wearing my T-shirt as well. She should just get on with being grown-up and leave the teenage behaviour to us lot.'

Mel is anxious now, it was supposed to be funny and it's getting ugly. 'Let's go and swim,' she says, handing Coral a cigarette. They both light up from the same match cocooned in Matt's hand.

Foss trudges up with his bucket slopping with seaweed and water. He is doing his heavy breathing thing, but it's just concentration, not a special need. Mel and Coral scoop him up on to Coral's back and make sure they are off before Mum reaches us. Matt follows them more slowly, after having a good look at Jake. I don't know what I want to do right now. The problem with going down to the sea with Mel is that when she swims her bikini is see-through and everything – like EVERYTHING shows. I don't know how girls can cope with being so full on. Maybe she doesn't know, but Mel is better than any poster from a magazine. It's just as well she isn't my sister.

Luckily, and maybe because it is what I am related to, I don't go for the slight dark type at all. Coral is like a tube. All her limbs and her body are round but narrow. She looks like she weighs nothing, and she is quite short, like Mum, and very exotic-looking, like no one in our family. Her hair is so black it often looks green. She could come from Mars. Or Tibet. But actually I suppose she was born in King's Lynn hospital with Dad standing around looking anxious like when Ruby was born, which I can remember because Coral and I had to go too. Luckily there was a Nintendo machine in the waiting room. It took the length of time needed to complete Golden Eye for Mum to give birth to Ruby. Then we went home.

Ruby is yakking away as usual. 'So, Mummy, we made this castle and the fairy stables are at the back but a bit smaller than I wanted because Matt and Jem got bored, but there is still enough room for three Brat ponies – did you bring them?'

'Err no, was I supposed to?' Mum isn't even looking at the castle; she's playing with her hair and glancing at Jake sneakily from behind her shades.

'Ooooh, Mummmmyyyyy!' Ruby's voice can rise on a crescendo like a dentist's drill. 'I sent a text from Coral's phone to you TELLING you to bring my Brat ponies. So why didn't you look at your messages?'

A lot of the sparkle leaves Mum's eyes now as she tries to talk Ruby down from her flight of fancy.

It is never easy, and particularly when Ruby is hot and thirsty, and Mum feels guilty. 'My phone is off. Actually, I haven't seen it since you had it in the tree house yesterday, Ruby, when you were texting Daddy.'

Ruby's mouth is screwed up so tight and red and witchy it looks like a sea anemone in the middle of her cross little face. She whacks Mum right in the stomach.

'Ooff!' Poor Mum reels back and looks like she wants

to kill Ruby. 'Don't. Hit. Me,' she says through clenched teeth, and walks away towards the sea.

Ruby starts howling, 'Mummmmmyyyyy' and runs off after her. Before she can catch up, Mum starts jogging and then she is in full flight escaping from Ruby. No one is having a good time. I lie down on the sand and put my hat over my face – the bloody sun is still shining, even though it must be four or five by now. There is a sigh and someone else stretches out beside me, and without taking my hat off my eyes, I work out it must be Jake. It's the smell of his aftershave that tells me. Quite weird. I hope he doesn't speak.

He does. 'How old is your little sister?'

'Err, dunno . . . maybe seven or something,' I mutter and feign sleep, but he is not going to be shaken off.

'Where's the other one?'

'The other what?'

'You know, the other small kid – you've got two, haven't you?'

'Well, I haven't – Mum and Dad have got two as well as me and Coral. I dunno where he is. I think Coral took him somewhere with her friends – I was only supposed to be in charge of Ruby.' I tell him all this in an energy-saving monotone and I hope it is enough to shut him up. I don't dislike him, it's just that I want to chill out now I am finally horizontal on the beach with no small children dangling off me, and I can't chill if I have to talk to some bloke I don't know.

'It looks like fun being part of a big family,' he says, and I realise that there is nothing I can do to shut him up, unless I actually get up and move further away. I am flat out, with warm sand shored up around me. I suddenly remember this book Mum used to read about five children and some little creature with eyes on stalks. 'Can you remember that psycho little thing that lived in sand in a gravel pit in some old children's book?' I even prop myself up on one arm to squint over at Jake. He puts his sunglasses on his forehead and squints back, looking confused.

'The first book I ever read was the *Highway Code* when I took my driving test.' He laughs. It doesn't sound to me much like there was a follow-up, so I don't ask what the second was.

Anyway, I have remembered by myself now. 'I think the swivel-eyed creature was called It. I dunno why I just thought of it.' I pull my hat over my face more and try to burrow down a bit because I can hear Mum and Ruby on their way back and on to a smooth bit of the emotional ride.

'Here we are,' Mum puffs, staggering up to us with Ruby clinging with all arms and legs around the middle of Mum, which seems very small. 'I think you could walk now, couldn't you?'

'Or fly or dance or do anything like holding hands with you,' agrees Ruby, schizophrenically altered from ten minutes ago.

Jake leans up on his hand and mutters to me, 'Blimey, is this normal?'

'Yeah – don't you know anyone this age?'

'I suppose I don't – but I like them, they're crazy.'

'Stir her up and watch her spin,' I say, and Jake and I snigger for no reason. Mum, kneeling by the castle, looks over at us; her hands are on her hips and her sunglasses are on her head and she is doing her sixties impression which would be quite good if it wasn't so dated. She nearly speaks then changes her mind. I wish Dad was here to play a game of beach cricket. I don't really want to ask Jake – it would please Mum too much.

Nick

The hotel has walls like suede or fudge but they are not soft. Nick's back is against the wall – literally more than metaphorically. He is lounging in the lobby waiting for Carrie to come out of the Ladies' lavatory. She could have used the one in his room, but she didn't even glance through the door at it – quite unusual for a girl.

Is it unusual for a girl to come and have sex in the afternoon with someone she has just met? Maybe not in America, which just shows how excellently his instincts were functioning when he conceived the plan of buying the apartment. Nick has never experienced this version of adultery before. It seems a lot more practical and sensible than dating, and it's exciting, too. Three hours in his hotel room with shadows from the tops of trees outside moving on Carrie's back when she lay on her elbows on the bed, looking at him, not talking, but playing with her hair and propping her feet one on top of the other. She had a bikini mark slicing high across her arse and a tiny scar like a hidden pocket zipped shut on her hip bone and her skin was golden, soft and taut, everything skin should be. She smelled of fruit and daisies, not exotic and sultry, but clean and preppy. And what she could do with her mouth, her tongue, her lips, her hands. Mmmmm. This is what Nick is in New York for, affirmation that he is alive and successful. He may not have cracked the deal with the US elastic manufacturers, but he can fuck and ejaculate as well as the next man.

Probably better, he thinks, remembering Carrie's second orgasm, when he had her up against the hard-backed yet soft-surfaced suede wall. Oh yes. That was what it was all about. And she was so yielding, so open. Mmm, lust is a great feeling. With a flourish he turns his phone on and it beeps with a message. He listens to it, turning towards the window as Carrie comes out of the Ladies and stands next to him, fresh lip-gloss shining on her smile. He blinks at her and steps away a little, instinctively wanting his own space now he is focusing on the rest of the world again.

'Daddy, it's Ruby and Foss. Please can you ring us? We want to know when you will be back and how do you make the car work when Mummy left the lights on? Also Jem isn't letting us watch the big TV and Mummy says we have to sort it out ourselves. Love you.'

It is only by taking a deep breath and shutting his eyes that Nick can keep from crying out in pain and rage. His head contracts as darts of guilt pierce him. He would like to double up and fold over but all his instincts and his whole life of male conditioning make him stand up taller, inflate his chest and take the blows. He only knows how to walk on, walk away, keep going and never let it show, never let it hurt. Never stop and hold pain because it could kill him. It's just too big. A waitress from the hotel bar walks out of the Ladies door Carrie has just come through. She is blonde, tired but raunchy looking. Her bracelets rattle as she goes. Nick closes his eyes and inhales the air she moves through. There is a smell of musk and cigarettes and a metallic whiff of pharmaceuticals that sets his pulse racing through time. It fishes him out of his guilt and brings him back to here and now in a New York hotel lobby with his fingers smelling of sex. It's time to get out and go to work, but there's Carrie. What will she want to do now? Where is Carrie, anyway? He had forgotten her as he dealt with the message, and now she seems to have vanished. He looks around. In the same moment Carrie coughs a small, ironic cough from behind him and fishes into her bag for her phone. Glancing up sideways at him she smiles, and having got his attention, touches his arm and tiptoes to kiss him.

'I gotta go now, it was nice spending time with you,' she says, and turns and walks out of the door, her phone clasped to one ear.

No exchange of numbers, no 'Will you call me?' Just out of the door and into a cab. Nick looks after her and for a bittersweet moment regrets that he will never know her better. The yellow cab pulls away from the building and with one, smooth, easy movement Carrie is gone from his life. It's so simple it should be patented. Nick sighs and presses the recall button on his phone; five hours and several thousand miles away the telephone rings in his house.

Angel

A homecoming is always fraught; glancing at her watch, Angel has yet another burst of creative energy. She has been busy since early this morning, rewriting a mental list and adding to it constantly in a fevered and successful mission to have no free time to think. The truth is actually unthinkable anyway; today Nick is on his way back from New York and Angel doesn't want him to come home. Pulling the heads from three amber-scented roses she sprinkles the petals over the table outside. Nick will be here in half an hour; his plane should have landed at breakfast time and he will be on the train. Coral and Mel have laid the table. The only way Angel can get any teenagers to do anything is to make sure there is one with no relationship to her in their midst. The presence of the outsider always shames the other progeny into most chores.

Angel straightens one or two place settings, and begins to gather up the glasses, polishing them on her skirt, not even conscious that she is doing it. Conditioned for years now by her own pointlessly high standards, she notices

cloudy dishwasher residue on the glasses and automatically begins to clean them. The shade of the pear tree and
its low-embracing branches creates a domed chamber
filled with dappled green light. The cloth on the table is
a cool green backdrop for the mainly murky glasses, the
cutlery and the soft peachiness of rose petals. Eighteen
place settings stretch away. Angel cleans three glasses and
stops as tears begin to drip off her nose. She digs her
hands into her apron pocket and her fingers claw the
seam, tearing at the fabric, scratching until the tip of her
finger burns with friction and her nail goes through. Then
she presses into the flesh of her leg, sniffing and blinking,
trying to focus on the irritation of physical pain but preoccupied with organising. Why has she decided to ask so
many people to lunch on the day of Nick's return from a
week away in New York?

She knows the answer: it is simple, it is quicker to form
than the question. She lives with the answer all the time
– it never changes; she cannot bear to be alone with him.
It is as if she has run out of petrol. She feels empty and
worn out. And frustrated. Actually, she cannot see how
she or Nick could have done more, and yet, today, the
reality of daily domestic life with her husband is unbearable. It was not always like this. Other parties, other family
occasions were different, and Angel is reminded of one,
Coral's birthday when she was twelve or thirteen. She
leans on the wall looking over into the water meadows
beyond. Nick built a huge bonfire, planning to roast a

whole sheep on it. But the heat was so extreme that to get near it he had to wear protective clothing, and a passer by, seeing him stamping out sparks with a spade, called the Fire Brigade. This was the best thing that could have happened. The firemen helped Nick get the sheep roasted and a lot of the children thought it was meant to happen. Angel sighs. The gulf between where they were then and now is best filled by castles in the air and peopled with guests. In the ever-moving merry-go-round of family life with friends there is no time to be still, and no time to examine how far removed the reality of their life together is, from the picture they present to the world.

A saucepan clattering from within the kitchen window reminds her that there is food to be got out of the oven, an opulent pudding to decorate and wine to open. Angel stalks back to the kitchen yelling for the children to come and help her.

'Come on. Granny will be here soon, and everyone else, and Daddy will be back in a moment and I need some help if we are ever going to get lunch on the table.'

Foss and Ruby are already in the kitchen stirring a bowl of lime-green liquid, both standing on the table and as usual wearing more or less no clothes. Why can no one else dress the children? Angel wonders with a stab of irritation, peering into their cauldron.

'Christ, what's that?'

Foss drops his spoon, Ruby raises her eyebrows and huffs, offended.

'It's jelly and we're going to put flowers in it and turn it upside down in the mould.'

'That's lovely,' Angel says guiltily, turning to crouch by the oven. She pulls the chickens on the roasting tin out and backs towards the table. The door from the hall swings open, Angel's hand slips through a hole in the tea towel and her skin sticks to the hot metal of the tray. 'Oh buggering bastard!' she screams.

Ruby glares at her, hugging Nick, who appears through the swinging door at this moment. 'Daddeeeeee!!!!' she coos, frowning at Angel and hissing, 'Mummy. Don't call Daddy that. You should be pleased to see him. I am.'

Fierce defiance radiates from Ruby, stinging Angel like a small slap. Chastened and caught out, Angel wonders if leaving work is the catalyst for her to behave like a five year old, or if the osmosis has happened through exposure to the children. Nick moves round to hug Foss, and with both Foss and Ruby in his arms, clinging like small monkeys, he reaches across to kiss Angel's cheek. All she can see are the whites of his eyes. His mouth on her cheek is cold and her heart flares for a moment then contracts with a hiss as though it is hot metal and has been immersed in cold water.

'Hi, Nick, how was your trip?'

'Mummy, why do you never talk to Daddy in your nice voice?' Oh God, they miss nothing. Angel spins lettuce savagely, pulling the string of the salad spinner so hard that the lid flies off and the lettuce twirls across the room.

'Bollocks,' says Angel. Ruby giggles, 'Stressy', and bats a bit back to her. Angel gathers up the salad and plonks it in a huge bowl. She would like to put the bowl on her head, to have some space between herself and the children, to redress the balance a bit. Maybe Nick being home will help. Ruby has her small palms flat across Nick's face, pressing his skin, wrinkling his cheeks and fluffing his hair. With jet lag and coffee-stained teeth, Nick looks rough. Angel cannot find any part of herself that is pleased to see him, and an anaesthetic of cold fear begins to seep through her. Nick, in front of the kitchen window with Foss and Ruby loving him, is not what she wants any more. It has never occurred to her not to want it, or to even think about it before. Until now, this was life.

Nick puts the children down and opens the fridge door, a reflex reaction he makes every time he comes into the kitchen. Angel cannot speak or look at him as a flame of irrational rage leaps through her.

Nick drinks a can of Coke in greedy gulps, flips his sunglasses down on to his nose and says, 'So, what's the big lunch in aid of, or is it to welcome me home?' Angel hears the defensive clip in her voice and despises herself as she rises to his challenge.

'My mother hasn't seen the children for weeks and Nat Rosstein was in Cambridge for some accounting meetings so I thought I'd ask a few people to lunch. I invited Peter and Jeannie Gildoff. Oh, and Jake Driver.'

Nick groans, 'Oh, for Christ's sake, Angel, I've just got off a plane. I don't want to do all this. Nat Rosstein. I mean I like him, but I do not want to track the accounts today, or even think about the business.'

He stalks to the fridge and takes another can of Coke.

'Anyway, it's a fucking charade,' he adds. Tears spring in Angel's eyes; she turns the tap on at the sink and blinks them away, distracted by her new capacity to cry and not wanting Nick to see.

'I don't know why you have to be so negative about everything,' she mutters, not really wanting him to hear and start a row, but unable to keep the bitterness within her. She slams salad, spoons and a salt cellar on to a tray and marches out into the garden. Nick gazes after her, then takes himself into the playroom, shuts the door and flips through the TV channels to Extreme Sports. Surfing in Australia. Excellent. He stretches himself on the sofa and turns the volume up.

The breeze catches the corner of the tablecloth and shivers through it, moving the leaves of the catkin tree, rattling them like sequins on an Indian shawl. Goose pimples rise on Angel's arms as she kneels behind the courgettes in the vegetable patch, picking a bowl of strawberries from Foss's tiny edible garden. Foss is meant to be doing this with her, as he was meant to plant the sunflower seeds and pumpkins and the row of radishes, but he cannot be persuaded to leave his snail emporium, well established and flourishing in the stone sink in the yard. She stops picking them mid-bowl and goes back to try again with Foss.

'Come on, darling. You and Mummy can do it by ourselves – we can pick the strawberries with no one else,' Angel urges him. It is absurd that he spends all his life in the same dank spot, though, she reminds herself cheeringly, he did come out to make jelly this morning. Now, though, he is back with his bucket, some stones and his signature snotty nose. She wipes it on her apron and he roars, 'Get off, Mum – that's my nose you're picking. Leave it alone.'

'I am not picking it,' retorts Angel, trying to hold his hand and lead him through the gate in the wall to the vegetable patch. Foss shakes her off and crouches to pull a slug off the bottom of his bucket.

'Come on, let's go and pick strawberries.'

'No.'

Angel takes a deep breath and counts to five. Children are so insane. Half their lives they are moaning and crying that she doesn't see them enough, that she isn't there to pick them up from school or watch them on the climbing frame, and the other half of the time they are refusing to interact and want to keep her at bay.

'Look, we're running out of time and we need strawberries for Granny to have for lunch,' she wheedles, looking at her watch and calculating that she needs ten minutes to change and pick another bunch of bloody sweet peas. Why do they die so fast? She must try and find some endurance flowers; in fact why not just go for plastic ones and forget the sodding garden?

'Well, you get them then, I don't want to.'

Jem, bouncing a basketball, pauses with a grin. 'Mum, you can't make people do what you want just because you've suddenly got time. He's been working on that slug centre for days now and he thinks picking strawberries is for girls. I bet Ruby will help you.'

Angel looks anxious for a moment then bursts out laughing.

'OK. You win. I think you're right. How did you get so sane, anyway?'

Jem grins again. 'I learn from your mistakes,' he says, and chucks the ball in through what appears to be an open upstairs window. A sound of smashing glass follows.

'Oh fuck,' says Jem.

Angel's eyes follow his gaze.

'I can't stand it,' she sighs, not sounding as though she minds at all. And in fact she doesn't. She has no will for anger and it is such a relief not to care.

Nick

Dawn Mayden had been a very good advertisement for mothers-in-law when Nick met her. Just the way she poured a drink, oily gin beneath slow bubbles of tonic as she added an inch of it to the warm glass until it brimmed over and slopped on her fingers grasping it, her nails painted powder-puff pink, a little chipped but charmingly so. The unspoken, almost unconscious recognition of another drinker was, for Nick, like a Masonic handshake. Or like he imagined one to be. Lionel was overpowering, confident, a king among men, his chest a puffed-up pillow in front of the rest of him, his chin imperious, his nose an angle to look down. He was already ill with the first stages of emphysema when Nick met him, but it did not show then in anything save the gusts of command that were his conversation.

'So you're a chef, are you? Well, that will have to stop. No call for that here.'

'Nick wants to open a restaurant, Daddy.'

Nick had never seen Angel so meek as she was in the

presence of her father. He rather liked it, though he didn't like Lionel. But his breathless bullying made Nick all the more grateful for Dawn's acceptance when he met Angel. That was a long time ago, a million light years from now and jet lag and Angel's bloody lunch party. Nick has drunk four cans of Coke and feels that his eyes may pop out of his head at any moment. Too bad, Dawn needs his attention. She walks across the lawn to the shade of the lunch table and the nearby arrangement of deck chairs and rugs, moving slowly, reminding Nick that she is widowed and arthritic. Her face is still beautiful, but her eyes are opaque with gin and bitterness. Nick hasn't seen her smile for ten years.

Angel says she is sure her mother must have smiled since Lionel died. 'But now you come to mention it, I haven't any proof,' she said last time Dawn came to lunch, adding after a moment's thought, 'I have begun to notice that the only events Mum likes to go to now are funerals and she'll travel a long way for one.'

This thought, along with a determined effort not to grind his teeth, is uppermost in Nick's mind when he rises to greet Dawn in the garden this hot summer afternoon. He takes her to a chair in the shade and pours her a glass of Pimms. Angel hasn't even noticed that her mother has arrived, her bottom in a red skirt visible behind a low rose hedge, her head out of sight.

'I suppose she's picking flowers or weeding or something,' says Dawn, looking for a second towards her daughter before turning back to her drink.

Ruby appears at her side, waving a silver fan. 'Hello, Granny, shall I cool you? Mummy's making nasturtium salad. It's disgusting, you have to eat flowers.'

Dawn lifts her face, presenting her cheek for Ruby to kiss, but gives no other sign that she has seen her.

She continues to address Nick. 'It's almost August. I wonder what will happen this year? Through the years I have noticed that August is full of endings.'

'Really?' Nick wishes he had placed a bet on how long it would take her to start talking about death, and scans the gate eagerly. He never thought he would be glad to see Peter Gildoff because he is giddyingly boring, but the sight of him and Jeannie, she in a bright yellow dress with a pink hat as if she is attending a garden party, is very cheering.

'Nick, hello.' Jeannie kisses him, and he shoots her a glance to see if she is in the mood for any suggestive gesture. There has been the odd occasion over the past five years when they have slept together. Nothing serious, though the emptiness Nick felt afterwards did not stop him doing it again. Jeannie is not available today. She switches on and off a smile of greeting, but she is more interested in who is coming to lunch and what Angel has cooked. Close up her skin is browned by a thousand freckles joining up to create a colour, and she reminds Nick of a lizard – a beautiful, cold creature, narrow-limbed and white-bellied. He has to stop an enjoyable scaly fantasy about her to greet Nat Rosstein, the company accountant. This ends when Jake arrives in his open-top car wearing shorts, and lopes across the lawn to where Angel is emerging from the kitchen with a tray laden with different blooms, a glass full of Pimms and borage, a bowl full of nasturtiums, a vase of mint and tiny wild strawberries. Jeannie is the first to exclaim at Angel's cleverness.

'Oh do look, the vase has got the things we might eat in it and the bowl has got the decoration – that's a charming trick, Angel.'

Angel smiles. She is hot and disarrayed and at her most sexy. Or so Nick can see Jake thinks. Nat Rosstein, sitting between Angel and her mother, has only to lose concentration for a second when he pulls a red spotted handkerchief out of his pocket to wipe his forehead, and Jake is away, both elbows on the table, leaning towards Angel, making her laugh and throw her napkin at him. Dawn could do with a handkerchief herself. On her other side, Nick passes his napkin to her, hoping she will take the hint. She wipes the condensation of her glass with it and takes a swig of white wine. Nick feels drunk from inhaling the alcohol seeping out of her pores and into the ether. He would love to sneak away and watch the cricket, but there is no chance. It is not worth pissing Angel off; he would never encourage Jem to do that so he shouldn't either, and anyway, it will be over soon. Come to think of it, where is Jem? Nick can guess. Bugger it. How can he leave? Pudding arrives, a few strawberries, and the jelly made by Foss and Ruby is greeted with applause. Foss has left the table and returned to the dank corner by the waterbutt. He waves but does not move when Angel calls him. Ruby, standing on Angel's chair, is happy to have all the limelight. She grins and curtseys.

'We made it with Mummy this morning. Actually, we did it ourselves because Mummy was busy.'

'Marvellous,' mutters Nat Rosstein, as Ruby sits down next to him.

'Do you like cooking?' he asks her.

'Yes, if I can sell it,' says Ruby, her eyes dreamy as she spoons heaped green dollops of jelly into her mouth.

Nat sits up, properly interested. 'You like selling things, do you? Good. They need you at Fourply, or they will. As your family accountant I am very pleased and rather relieved to meet you.'

'I love sums,' adds Ruby, batting her eyelashes at him and enjoying being taken seriously.

Good for you, Ruby, thinks Nick, overhearing his daughter, and he turns to his mother-in-law with renewed optimism and energy. If Ruby can do it, he can. Surely?

'Have you caught any of the cricket?' Nick says hopefully to Dawn. After all, you never know people's hidden passions, and he might get lucky and have a racy interchange with her about the scorching West Indies innings yesterday. Dawn's mouth purses slowly, and she shakes her head.

'I loathe cricket,' she says, and then, breathing her

mouth big again on an exhalation of cigarette smoke, she continues with her own train of thought.

'When Angel has time, I'd like you to come and bring the children to Great Dunham. I'd like to show them the church again. It's important they know Lionel's grave.'

'Yes,' agrees Nick, and feeling that it is important, too, that he knows the cricket score, he shakes his empty Coke glass, mutters, 'There is more in the fridge, I think,' and leaves the table.

Angel

How does it reach this stage? Is there a moment for every woman in her situation when she is turned on by her husband that is followed by the next moment in which she no longer wants him, never again desires him? Or are there a thousand moments in between these two states? Moments when the eroticism between two people can be reclaimed, when attraction has not burnt out but requires just the fan of focused attention to bring a spark, to ignite a flame. If there are a thousand of these moments, does Angel have to find the enthusiasm tonight? Can she leave it for a day when she might feel less exhausted, less distracted, or will even the possibility of passion go cold if it is left unattended?

Angel sits down on the edge of her bed. Nick is in the bathroom. He has been up here for most of the evening, watching cricket on the bedroom television. Flicking it off with the remote control, Angel remembers her friend Jenny insisting that a television in the bedroom is the kiss of death to passion. Angel doesn't like to add up the many times she has been grateful to it for buffering her from intimacy with Nick.

Getting into bed, the sheets are cool, and she lolls, limbs naked, stretching so she is right in the middle, arms and legs spread. It is such an effort to find all that erotic feeling, and bring it to bed when it has been buried deep beneath years of familiarity and resentment, unmet needs and frustrated expectation. The only reason she is thinking about sex at all right now is that, while Nick was up here with the cricket, she and Coral watched a French film downstairs about a libidinous sixteenth-century queen. It was quite arousing and reminded her that somewhere, locked up inside her, was a small flame of desire, and though she had not even noticed it for months, it lived.

A sudden thought of Jake, his flat stomach visible when he stretched to reach Foss's balloon from the apple tree earlier at the lunch party, shoots through her and lands, quivering, in her. Angel almost gasps, shocked by the volt of sexual feeling surging in her body. She remembers feeling like this years ago, but not since she had children. It is exciting. She wriggles in the bed, her nipples hard against the ironed linen. She pushes her forefinger into her mouth and rolls her tongue around it. She shuts her eyes, and slides her wet finger in between her legs, now scissored together tight and hot. The thump of desire in her slows as she opens her legs again, and quickens when she slides her fingers deep inside herself. Nick comes out of the bathroom, pulling off his T-shirt over his head. His chest is broad, barrel-like, thrust forward, his stomach round but not fat. He is not in bad shape, and in the semi-darkness Angel stares at him, bites her lip hard and holds the pulse between her legs. With her other hand, also hidden by the sheet, she rubs her thumbnail across her nipple. Her hips begin to move and the sheets are smooth and sensuous against her thighs, her arse. She closes her eyes and lets her breath come faster. Nick has his back to her; he pulls off his underwear then sits down on the bed, turning the light off as he lies down. In the dark Angel does not move away from the middle of the bed, so Nick's body meets hers all the way down one side. Angel stretches her foot down as far as she can, and gasps, taut excitement in every nerve. She rubs her leg against Nick's thigh and hears him catch his breath as she moves on top of him. She shuts her eyes and leans forward to kiss his mouth. In her mind, Jake's mouth opens to hers and she thrusts her tongue deep inside, her lips soft, her jaw relaxed. His mouth tastes of peppermint and sex, giving and also wanting. She still has her fingers inside herself, pressing hard between her body and Nick's. She rolls her pelvis and gasps with the bolt of a fingered orgasm, lying along him now, so all the front of her body is soft, yielding to his hardness as he turns her over and lies on top of her, his breath in gasps, his hands around her hips, on her breasts. And he doesn't stop moving, stroking her along the curve of her back, thrusting hard against her, running his hand around and under her, caressing her, holding her close and never still.

'This is hot, this is good,' breathes Angel, arching against his thigh between hers, her hands on his back, her nails tracing a path to the hollow in his back from where he begins to thrust, wanting his cock inside her. She opens her eyes and the room is velvet-dark, the man on top of her is whoever she wants him to be. She begins to breathe faster, pulling him in, guiding his cock and pressing splayed hands across him.

'I want to feel you hard inside me, I want you hot and holding me, fucking me gently, fucking me slowly,' she whispers, and her tongue touches his ear between each word, her mind full of words whispered to someone else, her mind full, her body flexing, wanting. Angel's hips begin to move in a rhythm like a slow drum beat, all of her throbbing towards him, sweat on her breasts, her neck, licked off his shoulder when she presses her lips to suck the taste of him from his skin. Nick's cock is hard inside her but in her mind it is not Nick, it is Jake, and the hands moving on to the flat of her back, strong and sure, pushing her towards him, the fingers moving down over her arse belong to a man she hardly knows.

She moans. Jake in her head whispers, 'Tell me what you want,' and she whispers back, 'I want you to bite me, on my neck, and on my breasts, I want you to lick me.' And she pushes her finger into his mouth then rubs herself and him together, faster. Nick gasps, Angel groans and comes, shudders rolling over her. Nick thrusts harder and the hot centre of them together is wet with both of them spent and gasping. Angel's eyes are open in the blackness of the room, and she sees Jake's green-speckled gaze looking back at her in the dark.

Nick

O n goes the summer. Party time for all the family. Nick's jet lag from New York lingered for a few days but has now been submerged by a sense of walking through quicksand. The game of tennis this afternoon with Jem was the moment he felt he broke through to the real world, for the first time in weeks, and since then Nick has noticed smells and sounds as though he has had his senses peeled. Coral came home this afternoon with love bites all over her neck. Lucky her, was Nick's first thought, but Angel went mad.

'You are not valuing yourself. And if you don't, how can you expect anyone else to?' she screamed.

Nick, safely hidden behind the Sunday papers, swallowed and rubbed his hand through his hair when Coral yelled back, 'Well, Mum, you are a fine one to talk about valuing yourself. How happy are you these days? Or any of us, with this crap atmosphere in the house? You should sort your life out before you get at me.'

'That will do.' Angel's dignity was palpable. Nick lowered

the paper and Angel was radiating strength in a way she didn't normally. Her clenched hands were the only sign of tension as she walked right up close to Coral and said, 'In the end, Coral, we all choose the lives we lead. That's all I want to say.' Angel walked out of the room.

Coral raised her eyebrows and opened her mouth. Then she shut it again and flicked on the television, watched it for a moment then, flinging the remote control on the sofa, she said, 'I'm going to have a bath,' and departed upstairs.

Rather to Nick's surprise, she appears in the hall as Angel, Jem and he are leaving to go to the Gildoffs' for supper.

'Are you coming, Coral?' Nick knows it is a foolish question before he has finished asking it. She throws a withering glance towards him and sweeps out of the door, her arm hooked into Jem's.

'Am I under arrest?' Jem teases, and he and Coral start scuffling and play-fighting in the back of the car as they did when they were small.

It is a rare experience, Nick muses, to be going out with his wife and family – not counting the little ones who are at home with a new human monosyllable, apparently named Gosha, who comes from Poland.

'This is a treat,' he says to Angel as they accelerate away from home. She smiles back at him. 'Yes, it's nice.' They both face the road and the windscreen again, and Nick wants to hit out at the emptiness between them, the nothing that this small exchange evokes.

A Perfect Life

The Gildoffs' house is mostly a backdrop for their pool, and the curved concrete walls and suburban tidiness as well as Peter Gildoff's big iced tumblers of whisky always remind Nick of *The Graduate*. Arriving with Jem and Coral heightens this sense and Nick leans against the mosaic wall, looking across the humming blue of the pool at Peter, a little red-faced with pink oven gloves on at the barbecue. Jeannie bustles up with a jug of elderflower cordial.

'Here, Nick darling, I know you won't touch alcohol, so we made this for you,' she says, licking her lips and flashing her eyes at him.

Raspberry lips in her tanned face, a white linen shirt loosely buttoned so there is a glimpse of coffee-coloured lace underneath. Mmm. Mistress clothes. The linen outfit, which includes shorts, reminds him of an animal nurse in *Daktari*, a TV programme he used to watch as a child. Even better, a mistress in a nurse's uniform. Very sexy.

There is a splash, and Coral and Joanna, the Gildoffs' daughter, dive like synchronised swimmers into the pool, followed by Heath, the son, who does a flashy somersault and lands flat on his back.

'Christ, that must have hurt.' Nick holds out his glass to Jeannie for a refill and looks round to see if Jem is next in. Jem, though, is lurking behind Angel, staring at the ground, hands pushed deep into the pockets of his shorts. Angel whispers something to him and he shakes his head. She rolls her eyes. Nick feels a stab of disappointment for himself as well as for Jem.

'Coral is so pretty these days, isn't she? She's a most exotic-looking creature.' Jeannie waves her sunglasses towards the girls, now chatting and dripping on the edge of the pool. Coral's bikini is silver and green, her black hair drips iridescent, drops of water cling to her black eyelashes and she looks like a dragonfly or a paradisiacal bird, her limbs so long and slim, her hands fluttering as she explains something to Joanna. Nick wonders if the comment is barbed. He wonders how many of the people they know speculate over Coral's paternity, and why it has gone so far without him and Angel deciding something about it. Even Jem doesn't know, unless Coral has told him. Exhaustion washes over Nick, a grey sensation, and he can't see the point of anyone knowing, or the point of anyone not knowing. This is the kind of thing that erodes the joy in life, and right now he could do with a lot more joy. In fact, it was probably their unconscious desire to keep their family joyful that stopped him and Angel ever deciding on a moment, or a day to come out about Coral. Life has a way of smudging and blurring the need for confession, confusing memory and myth until there is no truth, just a story it is easier not to tell. Nick finds it better by far to think about Jeannie's flesh, a little reptilian, perhaps, because she has spent too much time in the sun, but eager. Jeannie has always been available for urgent, secret sex; it turns her on to do it standing up and somewhere where she could be caught. Nick has cautiously enjoyed this over the years, though he has no desire to be caught with her. He remembers her bush, red like her hair. Were they both natural or dyed?

'I like your underwear, Jeannie,' he says. That is a safe bet, as she is practically flaunting it now. She has put down the jug and is standing close to him, one leg forward, hands on hips and her elbows well back so her tits thrust forward. She is up for something, most definitely.

'Good,' she says and walks away, smiling. Nick follows her, his curiosity roused.

Nick knows it is the first of August from the moment he wakes up the next morning. The day his father died. Thirty years ago, and it is maddening to Nick that it is the first thing he thinks of on the morning of this day, every year. It always has been. He gets up and leaves the room without waking Angel. It's a thrill to walk downstairs and outside naked. He and Angel have had sex twice recently. He knew he was pushing it last night, but he got his own way, more focused in his determination than he might usually have been because of the great shag they had last week. This time was nothing like as good, but at least it happened. Angel doesn't often give him blow jobs and he is never sure if she likes oral sex either. Funny not to know that about your own wife. Anyway, fuck it; he got laid, even though it was as a direct result of being turned on by Jeannie. Sex with an uninterested spouse might be a hollow victory, but at least it is an affirmation that he is alive. As is sobriety. Nick is standing outside the kitchen, feeling a little foolish now with nothing on. There is a rumble of thunder coming from the coast, and lightning licks across the sky. A pair of shorts belonging to Jem is in a crumpled heap beside a huge super soaker gun in the yard. Nick puts them on. It is a shame Jem didn't join in the water fight at the Gildoffs' last night. OK, so he and Coral, Peter and Joanna were in the two teams, but Joanna was doing it to impress Jem. There was no doubt about it, from the lingering looks she cast his way when they were sitting on the edge of the pool eating the kebabs Peter had made. Nick felt he might have looked foolish joining in the children's game, but fuck it, Peter did too. Angel was always complaining that he didn't get involved enough, and frankly, he felt so randy he needed to get in the water to cool down. Angel was subdued all evening. She said she had a headache, but it must have gone or he never would have got her to have sex with him. God, Peter Gildoff must have a headache this morning; he must have put away half a bottle of whisky last night. Nick shudders, standing in the kitchen doorway in the gently malevolent pre-storm morning. Whisky would never be his weapon against himself.

'A man can say he is truly successful when the Scotch he drinks is older than the woman he is sleeping with.' This was Nick's father's dictum. A difficult one for his teenage son to respect, and bewildering too, as the years passed and Nick's father's hairline receded, his stature diminished and his girlfriends got steadily more nubile.

A man can say he is truly a loser when his son is older than the woman he is sleeping with – Nick was waiting for it to get to that stage, looking forward to toasting his dad with a superbly barbed speech on some God-awful family celebration, but he never got the chance. Silas Stone died with much less of a flourish than he lived, in pain, alone in hospital, visited regularly by his ex-wife Naomi and less often by his only child, his sixteen-year-old son Nick. Nick was appalled when his mother first began visiting Silas.

'Why are you doing that? He doesn't deserve to be visited by you. He's nothing to do with you, Mum.' Naomi smiled her sepulchral smile, and Nick realised that to her Silas had stopped being the focus of her heartbreak and become her favourite thing – a duty.

Nick's anger was directed at his mother. He saw her feeding Silas's insatiable need for women; he did not recognise that she was feeding her own yearning to be needed. Nick was isolated and confused; his mother had cared only for him since Silas left ten years before, and now she was returning to the man whose absence Nick had experienced in her crying into her pillow night after night. Nick could not understand how she could forgive him. He didn't realise that forgiveness becomes a compulsion, no longer a choice, in the face of death. Or it can. Nick's resentment of his father was something he kept locked in himself. He felt he had no choice but to be Naomi's companion; he was a reluctant Mummy's boy, he was afraid of her need of him, but if he did not stay close to her, she would be alone. He could not imagine his mother alone.

It was ironic then, that once Silas died, Nick's fury redoubled and the heat of it took him across the Atlantic and on to west coast America. Three years in San Francisco were enough to cool him right down to the chilled-out dope smoker he became, and enough time for Naomi to become fully involved in piety. Nick found it too irritating to deal with. Or that was how he presented it. In fact, he was too smashed to deal with anything at that time, and the months, then the years rolled by and in no time at all he was twenty-one, Silas had been dead five years, and, no surprise here, Nick had a big problem with drink just like his dad. But not whisky. Anything but whisky.

Angel

A week has passed since the Gildoffs' barbecue, and the thunderstorms and humidity have intensified, creating lassitude. Worn out by infantile bickering and lack of domestic routine as the holidays spool on and on, Angel is glad to be in London, even though it is mainly to sign some papers at the bank. Not even the dullness of her appointment can diminish her gratitude for a day and a night off. A romantic treat was how Coral saw it.

'You and Nick can go out to dinner and have some fun,' she said, wandering into Angel's bedroom as she packed.

'Oh yes,' said Angel, and guiltily put in some nice underwear. Coral sat on the bed, flipping through the clothes spread next to her.

'If I get married I am keeping my own bedroom,' she said dreamily, then focused again on her mother. 'You know, I was thinking we should all go on holiday again like we did when we were younger. I found these. I wanted to show you them.'

They were photographs of a family holiday in Spain, taken with a child's blurry camera. Most of the pictures showed Nick and Angel laughing, holding hands, leaning together smiling to pose. Angel glanced at Coral, now lying flat on the bed looking at the ceiling.

'This seems like a long time ago,' she said lightly.

Coral glared at her. 'Yes, but it should be every year,' she said and marched out of the room.

The night is restless and suffocating, so walking in the streets is an effort for the body, and thinking or speaking an effort for the mind. It is frustrating. Angel's hair flops hot like a scarf against her neck and she takes off her jacket and swings it on her finger. Coming to London to be with Nick is a stolen moment, a touching affirmation of the importance of their marriage. Well, that is how the children see it, and Angel's friend Jenny, when she mentioned the trip on the telephone yesterday.

'Good,' said Jenny. 'You need to do that from time to time to remember why you like one another.'

Angel is uncomfortably aware of finding it an ordeal already. Nick has a room he uses in his friend James's house, and although James is never there, the smell of the house, musty, not quite masculine but like unclean hair, is alienating.

Angel is unrelaxed when she is there; she feels out of place and unsure, and she wishes she had wanted to suggest a hotel. But when the idea flashed into her head, she dismissed it urgently; unable to face the expectation of sex, and feeling a hotel would throw a lot of unwanted pressure on to what was actually just a quick business trip to London.

Nick takes her out to dinner along the road from the house. It might have been nice to go somewhere special, but impetus drains away while Angel has a bath, scrubbing neurotically with a scourer at the stilton-crackled enamel surface, and Nick is on the phone calling Los Angeles. The success of the New York trade fair has galvanised the whole of Fourply towards the American market, and Nick is the figurehead. Listening to him setting up meetings with buyers from Tuscon, Huston and San Diego, Angel feels very homespun as she takes her mobile phone into the bath and calls home. Trying to luxuriate in the oily and lukewarm depths she gets through to Gosha whom she always avoids talking to as far as possible in person.

'How are the children?'

'Oh yes.'

'Are they in bed?'

'Oh yes.'

Angel thanks God she is not standing in front of Gosha, as she might have to strangle her.

'Is Jem there?'

'Oh yes.'

'Well, can I speak to him then?'

'Oh yes.'

* * *

113

The pleasant myth that has run through their marriage was that Nick was the main wage earner and Angel a fluffy housewife. Now it is true, and it works as a stereotype, particularly in London, where Angel has nothing to do except focus on Nick. He has been in town all week, mainly in Great Titchfield Street seeing suppliers, as well as talking to accountants and generally making himself busy. And unreachable. His phone was off every time Angel rang it, and she planned to bring this up over dinner. When they finally sit down, the need to confront him drains out of her. Is it worth it? She hadn't had anything important to say to him anyway. They order and begin trying to talk, but the conversation is desultory.

'I saw that article about Elastex in the paper today,' offers Nick with the main course, scratching a patch of dry skin on his arm. 'Their shares are up.'

'Great.' Angel stabs a cherry tomato and forks it into her mouth, hoping it will block the stream of frustration rising in her throat and beginning to course through her. How can he be so – so NOTHING? How can he not have a life? How can he still have eczema?

How can he not have anything to say to her that a man should say to a woman, not even, 'Your hair looks nice'? Angel tries to feed him that line by telling him she had it cut that afternoon. For her this is a sensual experience, and her fingers return every few moments to comb through the silky coolness of its length.

Nick looks past her at the waitress standing by the bar and his eyes dart up and down her body. Angel follows his gaze with her own eyes and sees a ballet dancer's poise in the slender back and waist, high buttocks and long legs of the waitress. Her hair is tied in a long ponytail, and her shoulders are brown beneath a scoop-necked top. She is about nineteen, Coral's age. Angel looks back at Nick and the pupils of his eyes are deep black wells of desire, a tiny ring of blue around them. He is still watching the waitress. Angel eats another tomato and examines in herself the feeling of lonely realisation. Nick would like to sleep with this girl. Right now he is lost in the fantasy of having sèx with her and Angel's presence is forgotten. It surprises Angel that this hurts her so much. After all, she stopped wanting to sleep with him long ago, and now only does it to fuel her own occasional fantasy or because she knows she ought to. But human feelings are not always rational, or containable. Angel feels sick and drinks some water, and imagines Coral who is afraid of nothing, making a joke out of it.

'She's sexy,' she says, finally deciding that to ignore Nick's behaviour is cowardly.

'Mmm, I guess so, if you like the Eastern European model,' says Nick, reverting his gaze to Angel with a blinking, wide-open-eyed stare that she mistrusts far more than any amount of refusing to meet her eyes.

Walking home, Angel crosses the road before Nick to

look over into the canal at the water beneath the lacy grace of a summer-green weeping willow on the bank just south of the bridge. Nick is behind her, fiddling with his phone; he pauses beneath a street lamp sending a text, not glancing in Angel's direction.

'Hey there, dude, what the fuck are you doing?' A teenager, not looking where he is going, walks into Nick, and recoils exclaiming. Angel is walking ahead now, and several of them surround her, passing her, jostling, hitching up their jeans to maximise their loafing gait. Nick catches up; he leans towards her and his breath is on her neck.

'Do you find this lot intimidating?' he whispers. He has tucked his phone into his inside pocket and he pats it now, reminding Angel of someone middle-aged. With a feeling of something solid crumbling for ever, she realises he is old, and he is scared.

She smiles at him. 'No, they're just trying to be cool. They're just like Jem, I'm not afraid of them,' she whispers back. Nick is reassured and saunters away from her a little to read a billsticker on the bridge. The boys are still around them; Angel is conscious suddenly that one is talking deliberately loudly.

'Hey, yeah – there's that white guy we saw the other night. I guess this must be his woman.'

Curiously, Angel glances behind her. A tall youth with a black and yellow baseball cap turned sideways on his cropped hair is looking directly at her. There are no other white people on the street. Angel's heart pounces in her throat: they are talking about her. And Nick.

The boy looks hard at her and goes on talking to his friend.

'Yeah, that white guy. He's the one we saw kissing that redhead the other night.'

'Yeah, man, he had his hands all over her.'

'And this is his woman, lookin' at us right now.' They grin a challenge at Angel. She can hardly breathe. Nick is just within her vision, walking beyond the two boys, his expression closed, his eyes on the ground in front of him. Angel realises he is not listening. Nick crosses the road towards the house, fumbling in his jeans pocket for keys; the boys slow down for a second, pivoting on their rubber-soled trainers to watch as Angel crosses too. One of them wolf whistles. Nick looks back, flashing a proprietorial grin that Angel wants to slice off his face with a blade. The boys carry on walking, still talking, their voices a singsong ballad.

'I saw that guy right outside that house the other night. He was kissing that redhead so hard.'

Nick unlocks the door.

'Come on, Angel, let's have a cup of tea in the garden.'

Angel sees Nick's face, tired, exposed and preoccupied in the streetlight.

'You didn't hear what they were saying, did you?'

'What, those boys? No, but I imagine it was about drugs.'

'No, it was about you.'

'Me?' The whites of Nick's eyes shine green with the reflection of the digital clock on the cooker then vanish as Angel turns on the overhead light in the kitchen.

'Yes, they said they saw you kissing a redhead in the street the other night.' Angel's voice, strong and pure inside her, comes out small, dull and level. She is shocked to find that she cares, and cares a lot. It isn't so much that he might be kissing redheads, it is more that he has lied, and that he lied in the restaurant, maybe not in actual words, but Angel knew he wanted to sleep with the waitress, and it feels like betrayal. All the more because she has betrayed Nick in her fantasies. She knows what it means. And everything that seemed dreary yet safe in the grind of their marriage suddenly seems at risk. Angel has a sense of stepping off the edge of her life when she says, 'I don't want you to lie to me.'

Nick slams his fist on the table.

'For fuck's sake, Angel, they are a bunch of trouble-making crackheads. Of course they didn't see me kissing a redhead, but it's a very clever way of making trouble for a middle-class white guy.'

'I don't believe you.'

'Oh, fantastic! So you believe a load of fucked-up teenagers you have never met, who would rape you as soon as look at you. You believe them and not me. How can you live with me and not trust me to that degree?'

'I don't know if I can live with you any more.' This is said so softly Angel realises Nick cannot even hear it, but it doesn't matter. She has said it now.

Jem

I really quite like it when Mum and Dad are both away. It doesn't happen so much now Mum isn't working, but she's gone to London and I don't know when she'll be back. I wish she had said, as we have to tidy up before she gets here or she stresses out. Maybe she did. I'll ask Coral later. Right now I am just enjoying the laid-back atmosphere of no parents. For example, there is no point in opening the curtains in the TV room like Gosha wants me to. Even though her English is not great, I know that's what she wants because she kind of mimes it at me, then she sits down, looking like a puppet whose puppeteer has just got bored and chucked the strings down – so she is sitting with her hands flopped out beside her and her head kind of wobbling with disgruntlement, looking at me and then at the curtains. I carry on watching Extreme Sports – today it is whitewater rafting and some of them are wearing gorilla suits, I'm not sure why. Coral comes in, and I can't quite believe it but she starts on at me too.

'Jem, you are such a slob. Get off your fat arse and

pick up your shoes and open the curtains. It stinks in here.' Honestly, you'd think she was Mum or something.

'Piss off, Coral. You can't tell me what to do. You are not in charge.'

'Well, you don't seem to be doing what Gosha asks you, do you?'

She waves ostentatiously to include the whole room in the things I am not doing. Gosha just stands there, blocking the TV, holding a duster and a bottle of spray cleaner.

'You are a major pain in the backside, Coral.' It is definitely one of those situations where it is much easier to look as though I am doing what Coral wants.

I take the spray stuff from Gosha and squirt the TV screen. Coral kicks the bottle out of my hand.

'What the fuck are you doing?' I hiss. She is nuts. Her eyes are all popping and swivelling around and she is biting her lip so hard I reckon she will draw blood. Gosha backs towards the door and slips out, closing it behind her, leaving me with the psycho.

'You know that is just so annoying, don't you?' Coral pounces on my duster and tears it in half. I watch her and I just can't help it, I start laughing. She is making such an idiot of herself. She hasn't noticed me laughing because she is stamping on the ripped-apart duster. I reach for her wrist. My hand fits around it so easily it is like holding Ruby's wrist, and she suddenly notices I am laughing. There is a moment when I am almost scared. She is like a snake. She kind of rears back on her spine, and her hair runs like scales down her back and her eyelids go down like hoods, and when she lifts them again her eyes are black and they gleam for a flashing moment with anger so deep I could never get to it. Her face is a jarring collision of angles. I find I am running out of laughter, and then, just as I remember happening in every argument we ever had when we were little, at the moment I think, Actually, this isn't a joke, it's not at all funny, and I am trying to stop myself, Coral starts laughing too.

'God, you're a bloody bastard, Jem,' she says. 'Look, I want to clear up this dump so Gosha doesn't grass me up. I'm going to have some people back this evening for a party after the pub. Gosha will be in bed and I don't think she'll hear them, but you never know. At least if I've tidied up I've got more chance of her doing what I ask. You can ask some of your friends, if you like.'

The trouble is, my friends can't drive yet. And none of them lives near enough to bicycle to my house. It makes me feel such a retard that we all have to ask our mums to drive us still, and then they pick us up from someone's house and get in a real psyche if we're drunk. It's a lose-lose situation and it just isn't worth trying to get anyone over.

I tell Coral, 'No, I'll be all right, thanks,' and then just to please her, I pick up three sweet wrappers, a yoghurt pot and an egg cup full of dog-ends and take them through to the kitchen. She is slamming plates in the dishwasher. It is a miracle they don't break.

'When are Mum and Dad back?' I don't care what the answer is, I just want to distract Coral. It works. She shuts the dishwasher and leans against it to light a fag. She offers me one and I take it. It is weird to be smoking in the kitchen.

'Too soon. Well, Mum is. I don't know what Nick's doing. He's never here at the moment.'

'Yeah. It's crap. It's better when they're both away. Mum notices too much on her own.' I flick ash into the sink and zap the radio into life with the remote control. Coral turns on the tap and puts her cigarette out under it.

'Mum is a real pain in the neck on her own,' she says.

Foss has left some snail shells on the kitchen table, and some twigs. I remember there is a wren's nest in the greenhouse I want to show him, and I go out to find him. I know he will be in the dank green corner by the water butt, and sure enough I find him there.

'Sssh, Jem. This is toad school,' he whispers, pointing to where Ruby is crouched with a small stick pointing at three inattentive-looking toads. I must say, Ruby looks as though she might have crawled out from under a stone herself; her legs are pale green in the shade, and when she turns to look at me the bags under her eyes are almost bruises.

'Hey, sis, you need an early night,' I say. This is definitely my day for getting it wrong with sisters.

She hurls a scornful glance in my direction and hisses, 'Just be quiet. This is charm school and anyone who is rude becomes a toad and any toad who misbehaves becomes a Prince, but did you know that the way toads misbehave is by being polite and charming?'

The pressure becomes too much for one toad and it flings itself into a patch of hogweed. Foss dives in to retrieve it, oblivious to the nettles among the foliage he is groping in. Foss never feels a thing. I always think it's because he's the youngest and he has evolved into this part-subterranean being because his life experience is that it just isn't worth making a fuss. I feel like that most of the time myself, actually, but the girls never do.

My job when Mum is away is to feed the sheep. It's a miracle they are still alive, as I only remember about once every couple of days. Actually, it isn't that bad; I usually feed them when I go to the shop and that's almost every day because the only excitement around here is heading down to the village for a bit of commerce. Mum doesn't like the shop selling us fags, but it's tough luck. There are not many good things about being sixteen but buying cigarettes is one of them. The only reason I can afford the fags is that Mum and Dad have gone mad with dishing out cash at the moment. It usually means something is wrong, and if the wrong is proportional to the amount of money, then we are in for a major car crash in our lives. Mum has given me about forty quid in the last week or so and Dad has given me seventy. He actually gave me a fifty-pound note the other night on the way back from the stinking Gildoffs'.

He said, 'Here, Jem, this is some summer pocket money.' Coral went mental, huffing in the car next to me, but she was glaring at Mum, not Dad, when she said, 'Well, Mum. How about it? What happened to your promise that I will always get the same treatment as the others?'

My fifty-pound note was too big to fit in my wallet. I rolled it up and tried to imagine what sniffing cocaine through it might feel like, but I could only imagine it to be like sniffing sherbet by mistake which makes you cry, or inhaling cigarette smoke up your nose, which also makes you cry, so I didn't feel very authentic. I tried folding it in a concertina instead. Mum was having a go at Coral, leaning her elbow on the seat, twisted to more or less face us in the back of the car, her face looking pretty evil and not unlike the swivelling child in *The Exorcist*. Anyway, she had her teeth gritted when she said, 'Don't try and get clever with me, young lady. Emotional blackmail is not on. Do you understand me?'

And she flounced herself round and put on her dark glasses in the front, even though it was late at night and dark outside. And blow me, then Dad got another fifty out and passed it to Coral.

'I had one for you all along,' he said.

But Coral pushed his hand away and said, 'I don't need

paying off, Nick,' which was so rude I was gobsmacked. And stupid, I mean, if she didn't want it, I would have had it.

Mum and Coral have more rows than I have with anyone, but they also really like one another. Just as well.

Mum gets back from London far too early in the morning. Around twelve. I hear her because I seem to have slept in the playroom on the sofa, so her voice, shouting from the kitchen, 'Hi, everyone, I'm back,' is much closer than I want it to be. Luckily Coral is in there, so I don't have to get up, but they don't bother keeping quiet.

'Hi, Mum, did you have a good time?'

'Well, some of it. Boring at the bank, good at the hair-dresser and I did some shopping. Look, I bought these.'

There is a lot of rustling while Mum gets stuff out of a shopping bag. Coral chirps and gasps, the way girls do over clothes, then she starts laughing.

'Mum, you've got a lot of stuff.'

Mum laughs too. 'Some of it is definitely coming your way. I mean, how can I have thought I would look OK in this? It's like a horse's hay net.'

'No. It's great, it's a halter-neck. Look!'

'Yes, I had a feeling that would be better on you. I wish you had been with me.'

'Didn't Nick come?'

Mum laughs again. 'No, he went to Birmingham yesterday.'

'So why didn't you go too?'

'To Birmingham? No thanks. I'm on sabbatical exactly so I don't have to go to Birmingham. Now tell me, what's been happening here? Should I be suspicious that it's so tidy?'

She suddenly opens the door into the playroom and shouts, 'Good morning, Jem.' I groan and pull a cushion over my head, but not before I hear Coral giggling.

'Yes, be very suspicious, but don't worry, it's fine and everyone has gone home.' I am always impressed that they get on when they do. And relieved.

Nick

How many condoms is it reasonable to buy? One packet seems a bit un-macho; there are only five in a packet and five is somehow weedy and sissy. Two packets might be all right, but two the same or different kinds? Maybe the pack of twelve boxes is the best idea. Twelve boxes of five. Sixty condoms. Sixty shags. Chance would be a fine thing and he'd probably be dead halfway through, but there are worse ways to go. Nick picks up the pack and moves on to the painkiller section. He stares at the rows of coloured boxes, and when his arm reaches out to take one, he sees his hand, separate, brown and leathery-looking. His hand picks up the box and he almost drops it again – he cannot feel the cardboard in his hand, he cannot feel anything. Is a night once in a while with Jeannie Gildoff an affair? Is this guilt? A breakdown? Is this a heart attack? He can feel nothing, but feeling nothing hurts like a cauterised vein – a pulse denied and aching with molten blindness. He heads for the counter and pays, hardly pausing for the checkout girl to wrap his purchases and then he is in the main body of the station and walking towards the train.

He is on the way home and he is numb. Angel doesn't want to live with him any more. That's what she said. Of course he heard her, but it was easy to pretend not to, easy to crank up a temper tantrum to eclipse her voice, her feeling, her truth.

Nick has done this so many times he can feel the pattern before it happens – Angel tries to say something, having built up to it over some time, weeks, maybe, of sighing and reproachful looks, through which he is expert at maintaining a smooth exterior of denial. Of course he knows that she has something she wants to say, but he isn't going to say it for her. How can he? Angel is always dissatisfied about something. And he is so tired of being sorry, of being in the wrong. Actually, he stopped saying he was sorry long ago, but he can't remember when he stopped feeling it. That's what happens with sex in marriage too; at some unnoticeable point it changes and just doesn't seem worth doing again. It's like getting a magazine on subscription – it's always available, and desire doesn't get a look in. Nick can't remember when fantasy and his interior sex life became so much more than escapism. It must have been around the time he realised that Angel didn't really fancy him.

He walks down the platform, glancing in the carriage windows, idly wondering what or whom he might find on this train. Does the 4.15 to Waterbeach contain his destiny? Why not? Anything is possible. Nick realised that Angel didn't want to sleep with him a couple of years after he got sober. She had presumably never wanted to, it was just that he hadn't noticed before. He did his best not to give himself a hard time about it. He was having a hard enough time staying clean. Of course the whole process was a big deal. He knew from his Alcoholics Anonymous meetings that many relationships foundered and collapsed when the drinker stopped drinking, but he was determined that he would be different. He had rescued Angel, and having rescued her, they had built a life together. Now he was rescuing himself. Nick gave up drinking the year Ruby was born. He and Angel then entered a second honeymoon phase – almost more honeymoon than the first, and they began to experience life together with no rows over drink, and fell into the trap of believing that alcohol had been what was wrong. They wanted to be happy together, and so they did not notice that the chemistry just didn't work for them.

He peers in the window of one carriage, but sees a young family settling at a table, the father removing a rucksack from his back and pulling a baby from a kind of holster on the topside of it. One, two, three tiny children. A mother with a halo of black curly hair and a huge pouting mouth. The father long-haired, craggy-faced, and fit. He looks to Nick like a climber, though maybe it's all the heavy-duty nylon baby kit. Nick decides not to go into this carriage. Why would he want to spend a train journey with a load of small children when he can spend it in peace flirting with a pretty girl? He just needs to find one. He moves on to the next carriage.

The one thing Nick has always been pretty sure of is that he is appealing to women. Maybe it's the direct way he looks at them, maybe it's something in his pheromones, but Nick has never had any trouble attracting women. Keeping them used to be another matter, but then he found Angel. His view on himself was always that he was in tune with women, but he didn't see the large boulder in the midst of the ebb and flow of every relationship he had ever had. He did not recognise that the chase was the bit he liked, and once he got her, whomever she might be, the sexual charge began to diminish like a worn-out battery. He was too busy believing his own press release – that he was an understanding new man in shining armour, who had taken the road to recovery and was on course for the Holy Grail of successful intimacy.

If Jem, on a male-bonding exercise such as gathering wood or rolling the lawn into perfect stripes, says, 'Mum's in a real psyche,' Nick is the first to say, 'Yes, we must ask her what the matter is. She won't come out of it unless we talk to her you know. That's what girls are like.'

There are no girls luring him into any of the carriages. He finally boards the train and walks down inside. The scent of coffee lingering, the trace of musky bodies and synthetic perfume in the carriage mingled with the oily heavy smell of the tracks and the engines oozing through the open windows, catches in Nick's throat. He passes a pair of boys Jem's age, heads bent together over a mobile phone.

'Send her a text.'

'No, fuck you. You send her a text, you fancy her. You got her number.'

'Yeah, but what shall I say?'

Nick feels it is very important that Jem understands what women like. Above all, possibly even above oral sex – though sixteen is not the time for Jem and he to talk about that, and indeed when would be? – what women value most highly is communication. It is odd, given his belief that all women love oral sex, that he does not know if it is true of Angel. He wonders briefly if finding this out could be the key to their problems. But it seems more likely that the key to their problems is lost for ever. Anyway. Having given this understanding to Jem, and even knowing it himself to be one of the great truths in the world, has not helped Nick to feel it or act on it.

'And one thing is certain, you can't do oral sex and talk both at once.' He grins to himself, stuffing the paper bag from the chemist into his briefcase as he sits down in the restaurant car. It is four o'clock, so he can have tea. Nick has a rare moment of feeling good about himself and spreads out his newspaper on a table laid for four. The napkins are shaped like swallows in flight. Nick is still smiling to himself when he looks up straight into the blue gaze of a waitress. At last, a pretty girl. Mid-twenties, small tits like cupcakes, small arse, small body. Delicious hair, blonde but with dark roots. She brushes a strand behind her ear and another bit falls on the other side. He imagines it sweeping across her naked shoulders, though she is in fact dressed. That doesn't matter, he can see all of her, as if the green-leaf print uniform is transparent. She blushes, looking directly at him; her eyebrows are dark, straight and very fine, her skin glows with luminous health.

He wants her. He wants her to fill the hole that Angel not loving him leaves; he wants her to test drive the condoms – oh, what the hell – he wants her because trains are horny and she is sweet and young with soft pink lips and hair tied back waiting to be let loose. Slowly, without taking his eyes from her sweet open face, Nick lifts the swallow-shaped napkin off the table and slides his fingers into the folds. With almost no resistance, it falls open, snowy white and soft.

Angel

Angel deliberately brings a wicker basket into town today for her shopping. Releasing Foss and Ruby with Gosha at the toy shop, she heads for the WI market. The basket is a part of the uniform here, or rather the armoury, as the Friday rush requires invincible purpose and forward planning just like a battle, Angel always thinks. Angel loves the WI market and there is no part of it that she leaves untouched in her shopping, from the brightly coloured hand-knitted doll's clothes she buys for Ruby to the glistening cakes and jars of perfect jam. Superficially, the market suggests timeless nostalgia and an otherwise lost decorum, but really it is ruthlessly organised, financially successful and almost, cutting edge – Angel's finest moment was her purchase of a knitted iPod cover for Jem last term.

The church hall doors are open, some bunting flaps halfheartedly, and a queue of shuffling elderly ladies inches its way in towards tables covered with gingham cloths. Smiling in response to the nods and smiles all the ladies greet one another with, Angel allows herself to be carried along into the room. She struggles out of the queue at the sausage roll section, extracting herself with difficulty to reach the edge of the table, slowed by the deliberate obstacles created by carefully wielded baskets, umbrellas and elbows.

The wicker basket is heavy, but full of the spoils of war, and Angel lugs it along cheerfully. The best find today is a caramel-coloured jersey for Foss, so stiffly acrylic that it stands up by itself, but adorable, and he will look like Jeremy Fisher in it. Walking down the high street Angel feels happy. The café is noisy and hot, she threads her way through to the courtyard at the back, and sees Jenny at a table in the shade. Jenny and Angel have been friends ever since Coral and Jenny's daughter Ally were at primary school together and Coral joined the pottery club that Jenny had at her house after school on Tuesdays. Jenny's bracelets jangle when she and Angel hug, and Angel breathes in deeply, loving the smoky tea familiarity of her scent and her gentle voice.

'Angel, I've been thinking about you so much, and look at you, you've got so thin.' Jenny pats Angel's shoulder as they sit down.

Angel presses her hand. 'Oh God, it's so nice to see you, I feel as though I've been locked up. You look lovely, Jenny, I like your earrings. How is everything? Coral said to say "Hi" to Ally.'

'Thank you, thanks to Coral.' Jenny radiates calm and

peace. Angel suddenly feels that sitting with her is like sitting in the sun. A waiter hovers, they order coffee and look at one another.

Angel grins. 'God, the school holidays are mad, aren't they? I just hadn't realised quite how consuming they are before, I suppose I've always been working for part of the time.'

Jenny nods. 'I know. When Ally was small I used to get up at five every morning to have some time to myself. I think everyone finds some sanctuary somewhere. Yours was probably work.'

'And yours. How is the Art School?'

'Well, it was demented at the end of term, but now I am free until October and the new term, the new intake and the beginning of another year.'

Their coffee arrives. Angel looks around and sighs. 'This is so nice,' she says.

Jenny smiles too, and says, 'So, tell me about what's happening. Steve's been finishing the barn, driving me crazy because he is so perfectionist, but it's done, so we have just got to sweep up the rubble and you can come and have supper.'

Angel nods. 'Oh yes. That sounds lovely. I can't wait to see it.'

'How's Nick?' Jenny's tone is the same, but Angel feels as if she is about to step off a cliff.

'Oh Jenny,' she says.

'Oh Angel,' says Jenny quietly.

Angel looks at her friend; kindness glows around her almost visibly. Angel blows her nose. 'Well, you know how it is. There were probably a thousand signs before, but it is not until you choose to recognise them, or are ready to, that they reveal themselves to you.' Angel's heartbeat seems to come from her throat. Jenny says nothing.

'I haven't told anyone this, Jenny,' she says, 'but I have begun to realise that even though Nick and I have been married for eighteen years, I don't know him. I don't think I ever knew him. And I don't love him.'

There. It is out in the real world. The truth Angel had known without wanting to know, and which had been corroding within her, is out. She wants to be sick, but instead she takes one of Jenny's cigarettes and continues.

'It was the carelessness that was so hurtful.' Angel lights the cigarette and inhales deeply. 'I was unpacking Nick's bag last week – I should have learned by now to let him do it himself, but Jem wanted the bag for his art trip. Anyway –'

'Oh, I think I know what's coming.' Jenny's face, open and unjudgemental, is so loving, Angel begins to cry.

'I don't know why I looked in the zipped-up inside pocket, but I did and I found a box of condoms – actually, it was an empty box which used to have condoms in it. Sixty. They were called Durex Featherlite Easy Glide and there weren't any left in the box. And we don't ever have sex with condoms – in fact, we very rarely have sex at all, but when we do, the contraception is my business and I've got a coil.'

Angel stubs out the cigarette and lights another one. 'I know there could have been a reasonable explanation, but the thing that I found intolerable was that he didn't care enough to make sure I didn't find this. He did it in my car as well.'

Angel reaches over to the plate in front of Jenny and breaks a corner off the remaining half-croissant, feverishly hovering, finding things to put in her mouth, wanting to fill the gap within her.

'What do you mean, he did it in your car? He had sex with someone?'

Angel laughs. 'No, he was using my car for a few days and then he went away. I was clearing out the rubbish – once again, I guess it's my fault because I am so stupidly tidy and anal. Anyway, I was picking up crap and I found three condoms.'

'Used?' Jenny's pale eyes flicker, but no disgust crosses her face. Angel laughs again, wondering how many versions of this conversation are going on all over the world right now.

'No, not used. In their foil packets. I think they must have fallen out of his washbag; he's always got a few in there along with all the other rubbish. He always has had.'

'But why does he have condoms in his washbag?'

'Do you know, I have never asked him. I have no idea. The thing I want to know is why the hell do I keep clearing up after him? Or anyone. It doesn't do me any good. I would be better off spending the time reading or learning to knit.'

Jenny laughs. 'Do you mean to say that with all that domestic accomplishment you can't knit? I don't believe you. You can cook, you can grow stuff in your garden, you can make your home a place everyone wants to be, even your own teenage children like being there, and you're telling me you never learned knit one purl one. What was your mother thinking of?'

'Appearances,' replies Angel promptly. And as if a machine is working inside her head she feels a shift and she has a sense of an egg breaking in her head, its contents flowing slowly through her consciousness. 'Oh God. That's what I've inherited from her, I think. Look at what I'm good at – folding and tidying and giving everything a right place.'

'It's not a bad thing to be good at.' Jenny stretches across and puts her hand over Angel's. Her hand is cool and steady. Suddenly Angel senses that she is missing something, and it is something in life she would really love and respond to.

'What, Jen? What are you thinking?' Angel's throat is tight with tears and her voice comes out small.

'Just wondering why you feel you need to try so hard.'

There is nothing Angel cannot fold or iron. She could give seminars on the perfect ratio of clothing to shoes to books in the perfectly packed suitcase. Her clothes drawers are the same, and her wardrobe. To leave things untidy makes Angel feel mad and out of control. It is impossible, at times of unhappiness, it becomes a compulsion overriding everything, including exhaustion.

There was a row with Nick just after Foss was born. Angel had left the baby crying, while in a trance she folded sixty-four muslin squares and a stack of cot sheets in the airing cupboard.

'You have no love in your heart,' Nick had yelled at her, carrying tiny Foss on one arm. 'Didn't you hear him?'

'No.' Angel had a twitch of exhaustion at the corner of her eye, and panic rising in her chest. She looked at the blotched face of her small son and waited to feel something. But nothing came. Nick was right, she was incapable of love. The panic became clear, cold fear.

'Well, how the fuck could you not hear him? The sound of a baby crying is meant to pierce a mother's heart – it's a primal instinct.'

'Well, I didn't hear him, and you did, so what's the problem? It doesn't always have to be me, you know. Today you had the primal instinct and I was too goddam tired.' Angel was only aware of her shouted responses on the lowest level. She was barely ticking over in terms of living, and just now a slumped survival was the best she could hope for. The gloom that engulfed her after Foss was born had never happened with any of the others; its force had taken her by surprise – she did not know how to come to terms with it. She was afraid that coming to terms with it meant coming to terms with not loving the baby. Better to keep everything tidy and hope it would pass.

'Well, what the hell are you doing in the airing cupboard, then? Leave the sodding laundry. There are people here in this life, you know. Your kids need YOU, not a tidy cupboard. And let me tell you something, Angel, no one ever died wishing they'd folded more sheets.'

Nick's raging hardly penetrated Angel's fog, but the thought of a life of uninterrupted sheet folding, and the vision of the baby propped on Nick's forearm, calm now, looking around like a parrot while Nick gesticulated and swore at her, made her laugh. But by then it was too late for laughter to turn a quarrel into love. Nick passed her the baby and stalked out to the garden where he vented his frustration on the molehills. Angel stopped folding sheets and went and lay on her bed with Foss. She didn't know what to do, so she did nothing, but she did it with her baby right next to her.

Ruby, Foss and the silent Gosha, bubblegum a vast pink distortion swelling from the side of her mouth, are suddenly at the café table, standing too close. 'Mummy, Foss wants to buy more buckets and spades and we've got about ten at home and I told him so and he hit me with a balloon sword and the display fell down and I got stuck with my foot in the basket-ball net and quite a few people laughed.' Ruby blinks and pouts, steaming with indignation at the injustice of life. Angel rubs her daughter's bare arm, and the skin is thin beneath her touch; smooth, cool and fragile like porcelain.

'Mummy, I've still got seventy-five so can I buy an ice cream? Is it enough to buy Foss one too? He lost the change when I asked him to hold it when my foot was stuck. I think I had fourteen then. It's so annoying.' Ruby is revving up.

Hastily, Angel waves to get the attention of a waiter.

Jenny smiles. 'Hello, all of you. How nice, can I kiss any of you?' Jenny reaches out and swings Foss on to her knee where his solid summer-brown boyishness engulfs her, so only her eyes are visible to Angel, peering through the gold frizz of Foss's curls.

'Let's all have some ice cream and not worry about a bit of lost change,' says Angel, summoning her brightest head girl voice, a useful feature she only discovered many years after leaving school. Gosha pops her bubblegum and the pink crumpled remains fall on the floor, flaccid and small at Angel's feet. Jenny and Angel look at one another and their grinning splits into laughter.

Angel

Waking up hurts. Struggling back to consciousness Angel moves from a warm deep dream in which she was driving a camper van across a river with Foss and Ruby in the back eating sausages. In the dream Angel's camper van was purple and had a skull as the knob on the gear stick and it was blessed with surround sound and a stereo system. Her dream mind swelled then overflowed and tears rolled down her dream face as the Led Zeppelin track 'Babe, I'm gonna leave you' flooded into the vehicle. Outside, water flooded around the camper van as it floated into midstream like Chitty Chitty Bang Bang.

Angel, followed by her biddable and non-whingeing dream children, opened the door and dived out into the smooth silky green of the river. Coming up for air, she found the camper van had floated to a mooring among some hazy sapling trees. She swam to it and tied it to a hitching post. A family who looked as though they had stepped from another seventies rock album, maybe by

Fleetwood Mac, stretched out their hands to pull her in. Foss and Ruby ran out on to the bank, shook themselves dry, and disappeared into a teepee with some tall children whose brown skin and slanted cheekbones and tangled mops of hair reminded Angel of Mowgli in the Disney film of *The Jungle Book*. A fire crackled in a clearing and the people who had helped her out of the water returned to it now. A man threw a log into its peachy pink heart. The heat wrapped around Angel, and she turned to smile at the adults who gestured to her to sit down among them.

The music got louder, changed tempo, becoming strident and invasive: '*It's getting hot in here, so take off all your clothes.*'

The shreds of the dream seep away and Angel shifts, groaning and burying her face in her pillow, trying to reach back into her subconscious and find more of the intoxicating golden feeling. There is nothing left; it is as if the dream was liquid in a vessel, and it had tipped on its side and every drop had spilled out. '*If you take your clothes off I will kiss you all over.*'

Ruby is perched on the side of Angel's bed with headphones on, her eyes closed as she sings along to something on her Walkman. It is unspeakable.

'Oh go away.' Angel pulls the sheets over her head but it is too late, she is raw and awake, reality throbbing between her eyes. Reality is looking like a bad film this morning. Angel wishes she didn't have a part in it. Or if she has to have a part, she could be a maid cleaning in the background or someone driving a car past the action. Feeling ludicrous, she flings back the sheets, gets out of bed, and thinks better of it. Not yet. She lies down again. Ruby continues to sing. '*Yoooouuu can take your clothes off,*' she warbles.

Last night Angel asked Nick for a divorce. He didn't even put up the pretence of a fight. He stood up from the kitchen table, and walked around the room, his eyes fixed on the floor as he navigated the chairs and the strewn water pistol and squirting camera left by Foss before he went to bed. Reaching the sink, where Angel stood, both hands behind her gripping the edge of the worktop, he stopped and ran his hands through his hair.

'If that's what you want,' he said, looking through her, not at her. Angel shuddered and nodded; her head felt as though it was full of marbles rolling across her brain, pulling her down into something black. Nick picked up a postcard his mother had sent the children that morning.

'It isn't what I want. I mean, it is what I want. Oh! It's just that there is no other way now.' Angel rubbed her palms across her face.

Nick turned the postcard towards the light and scrutinised the postmark. 'She's in Greece now,' he said, his voice incredulous. 'I wonder if she's gone to another retreat?'

Angel crossed her arms and gazed coldly at her husband. 'How can you?' she muttered, jaw clenched, fists forming involuntarily.

He smiled at her, a big flashing grin that didn't reach his eyes and he replied, 'How can I not, when it has such an effect?'

After that the conversation disintegrated. Anger flared in Angel's ribcage and flooded up, crashing through the marbles in her head, driving splinters through her nerves so she thought her whole body might burst through her skin. She slammed three plates into the sink with such force that she broke a glass, cutting herself on its jagged rim. Sucking her finger, she searched through the drawers of the dresser for a plaster, dripping scarlet drops of rage across a pile of photographs of Jem playing cricket.

'Shit! This is crazy. How come you don't have anything to say?' On the dresser Angel found a wide piece of blue ribbon; it was the nearest approximation to a plaster available and blood was seeping down the back of her hand and slipping along her wrist.

'Why don't you want to defend yourself or change my mind?' She caught the end of the ribbon between her teeth and began winding its length around her finger.

'What am I supposed to say? What do you need from me, Angel? For whatever reasons, I make you angry. I have disappointed you, and that's how it is.' Nick swatted a fly with a rolled-up newspaper, then sat down on the sofa and began reading Jem's music magazine. Angel reached the other end of the ribbon and tucked it under itself, pulling with her teeth to make a knot.

She looked at him sideways. 'You could bloody well help put something on my finger for a start.'

Nick's glance up at her was so swiftly retrieved that Angel wasn't sure it had happened. He spoke through gritted teeth, holding the magazine close to his face and angling it in exaggerated interest. 'Why can't you ever do anything normal? Use a bloody plaster like other people.'

Angel ignored him. 'I don't know what I want you to say, but you are not supposed to say nothing and do nothing. I feel like I've got to have both sides of the argument. I feel as though I am the only one who exists here. You aren't really here. I don't think you care any more.'

Nick looked up, an arrested expression holding him for a moment. 'Isn't that funny. I don't feel YOU care any more,' he said slowly.

Stalemate. Angel wondered if every marriage reached this point, and what made some turn the corner together and others walk off in separate directions. Angel always thought the fact that she and Nick had made something lovely together, a home and a family, was glue enough for a lifetime. That feeling of solidarity was real, but as individuals each of them needed more and the other one didn't notice. It was ironic that they were both so busy making life perfect that they didn't notice their hearts had failed.

And there was a lot of momentum between them for a while; Angel and Nick had toasted one another and made love on the kitchen table on the fourth anniversary of his sobriety. The memory of laughing with him that night was vivid. Angel had one hand over his mouth so the children didn't hear and come downstairs, she was lying back among a chaos of toys, a half-read newspaper and some sprinkled flour with the person she knew best in the world holding her, kissing her, fucking her. It didn't get much better than that, Angel had thought at the time. Someone told her, when she and Nick got married, that if they put one bead in a jar every time they had sex before they got married and took one out every time they had it afterwards, they would never empty the jar. Angel could not believe it at the time, and Nick laughed when she told him. But now she thought that in that imaginary jar lay the secret glue of marriage.

The throbbing between Angel's eyes becomes a hammering as Foss joins Ruby on the bed and they begin to bounce and chant together, *'Take off all your clothes it's getting hot in here.'* Pinned into the bed by the weight of both of them on the duvet, Angel thrashes to the side trying to get out but their solid mass forces her down.

'Ha! Look at Mum, she's our captive.' Ruby elbows Foss, pulling at his pyjamas to steady herself on the bed.

'Where's Daddy, anyway?' Ruby blows a bubble with some gum she has been hiding on the roof of her mouth.

Angel groans. Foss squats down and sits on the lump in the bed that is his mother. He is astonishingly heavy. Angel imagines his bones and flesh carved from alabaster, like a Michelangelo sculpture. Foss pats her bottom with his stone-weight hand.

'I don't know where he is, but he should be in bed too, next to Mummy like proper people.' Nick is not even in the house. He is in the Travel Lodge on the roundabout by the main road ten miles away. That is where he said he was going when he left last night. Angel wants to kick herself now; it is so obvious that he should have slept in the spare room, but it never crossed either of their minds last night.

'Oh, get OFF you two,' Angel screams, claustrophobia catching in her throat as she shoves the children away. Ruby falls on top of Foss and both of them scream then begin to cry, more in shock that Angel is angry than because they are hurt.

'I just wish you could treat me with even the smallest degree of respect. Do you know what the word even means? I doubt it, I very much doubt it.'

Angel storms around her room, yanking open drawers and riffling manically through them. Ruby recovers and begins giggling as her mother attempts to put on a pair of knickers while marching towards the window to pull back the curtains and wobbles for a moment on one leg.

'She can't be properly angry till she's dressed,' Ruby whispers to Foss. 'Whoever heard of a naked tantrum? Not me.'

'No,' agrees Foss, 'but I do know about naked sunbathing because they do it along the beach from where we go. It's called naturing – Jem showed me but there was only one lady there when we went and she was throwing a stick for her dog.'

He slides off the bed and heads to the door. Looking back to stare at his mother he adds, 'She had bigger boobs than Mum and they sagged more – Jem said they looked like raw eggs in tights.' Angel, still only wearing underwear, glares at the children, then collapses herself, giggling on the bed.

'Oh I love you. Do you have any idea how – Oww! Stop it! You're too big!'

Both of them launch themselves back on top of her triumphantly. A physical pummelling from two children is a far more appealing option than an emotional post mortem. Ruby gets up, her bottom lip protruding. She tucks her hair behind both ears and folds her arms. Uneasily Angel sits up, biting her own bottom lip: knowing Ruby, something unpleasant is coming. Like storm clouds gathering on the horizon, a cross patch of frown appears on Ruby's freckled forehead.

'Mummy, I know you say you love me but I don't feel it,' Ruby says dolefully, and spouting tears she jumps off the bed and runs out of the room, slamming the door behind her. Angel gazes after her, panic and astonishment freezing her heartbeat for an infinite moment before the pulse begins racing at double speed through her body and the familiar sense of being hopelessly overwhelmed and under-equipped for life kicks in.

Escaping from this feeling, or trying to, is the impetus Angel needs to drive her to this point where she looks at her life and can say loud and clear, 'This is not what I want.'

Everything is about running, moving, getting on. Getting somewhere. But not out. No matter how fast she runs, Angel cannot get out. Maybe it is shock, or post-traumatic stress, but here in her bedroom on this summer morning, Angel suddenly has the sense of the plug being pulled out. No more impetus to stay on the treadmill.

She lies back down on the bed and examines this new sense of just being.

'Mum, what are you doing lying there like the other kind of Mummy? Where's Dad? He doesn't seem to be here and we're supposed to be playing tennis this morning.'

Jem is in the room too, now, his face extra shiny, hair wet and shaggy from the shower. He twirls his tennis racquet on one finger and drops two balls out of his T-shirt. 'Those were my boobs. Ruby did them for me. She's really stressed – or she was, that's why I had to pretend to have bloody tits. What's going on today? Why is everyone so weird? And where is bloody Dad?'

Jem whacks the bedspread aside and bends to look under the bed. 'Not hiding under there.' He shakes his head sorrowfully to make Foss laugh.

'I'm going out,' announces Foss, scampering gleefully out and down the stairs, making the droning aeroplane noise that for him signifies great pleasure. Jem is still in the room, chatting about a film he has seen, then he coughs and says, 'Right, I think I'll leave you, Mother,' in a joke-stupid voice and he wanders out, whistling.

How incomprehensible that the silent, grunting teen person Jem should have chosen this awful moment to say more, and be more cheerful than he has been all summer. It is as if every conversation he has not had before has been absorbed into him until he has over-flowed and now it is all spiralling out of him in a rippling stream of questions, observations and good cheer, on and on for ever without end, like the music on a self-playing piano.

'Right, I'm off, Mum,' says Jem. 'When are you going to get up?'

'In a minute,' Angel replies to his back view and the door as he leaves.

Angel clambers off the bed again, and on this second attempt opens the curtains. Sunshine bounces in lighting dust in laser beams, whitening the shadows on Nick's side of the bed and ironing them out so the linen expanse glows with supernatural emptiness.

He is not here. Angel looks out at the garden. Spires of foxglove skeletons and giant fennel heads like bronze clouds rocket through the roses, butterflies dance along the catmint at the front in small scoops, fluttering a lacy pattern like a scalloped edge; and even from a floor above, Angel can hear the drone of bees threading clumsily in and out of the lavender. The rioting, happy sunlit garden is absurd.

There is nothing outside to reflect the ethereal oddness Angel feels. She ought to go for a run, to connect with the world, to get healthier and to feel the sense of achievement that this small activity brings her, but she can't today. She moves closer to the window, wanting to dissolve into the glass, to become transparent and to be neither in nor out, invisible and unyielding, there and yet not there. A breeze sighs across the lawn and the morning settles with a sense of heady laziness and the stillness that is summer at its most luxurious. Tears prick in Angel's eyes because it is too late and she can only see the stillness, she does not feel it within her. The summer loveliness is separate and cannot heal her.

Downstairs, the back door judders and Foss and Ruby dart into view, Foss's mad frizz of hair a chrome yellow mop in the sunlight, Ruby still singing breathless teen lyrics, fortunately indecipherable to the normal human ear. The children vanish behind the hedge towards the trampoline and the whispering depth of foliage engulfs the sound of them.

Angel loves the garden. She realises that the gathering sadness of her and Nick breaking up has got in the way of her knowing this. But it is true, and today the lilies in the border beneath her window and a sweep of nasturtiums are vibrant reminders. The vigour and the sumptuous determination of plants, and indeed weeds, is inspiring. Angel decides that she will weed the paths.

The moment she steps outside, dragging a wheelbarrow with no air in the tyre, Angel feels the relief of doing something practical lift her spirits. When she and Nick moved to this house there was no hedge, no deep beds of swooning summer flowers, no Mr McGregor vegetable garden. Angel had very little idea about gardening, beyond the names of a few overblown roses and a vague desire not to be able to see the whole area in one glance, when she began to love her garden. And its success is both a mockery of her marriage and one of its triumphs. She pulls a clump of thistle stems from the back doorstep and chucks them into the wheelbarrow.

Nick's interest in outside is determinedly limited to rectangles of grass for sport. This has its uses, and the lawn is impressively green, flat and flawless. Nick's dedication to it is relentless. And molehills are his speciality. He has frequently sat out all night with a gun, waiting to exterminate the small furry terrorists whose assault on the grass is to Nick an outrage to sense and sensibility. Nick sitting on a kitchen chair in the starlight, the barrel of his gun glinting like a cartoon baddie . . . the memory makes Angel smile. They both played their part, she could see that, and all of the life they made together was worth doing. And Angel had always been grateful that getting him to cut the grass was never a problem – stopping him was another matter. Nick would rather mow the lawn than work, eat, fuck, or talk. Pretty well anything except watching sport and going to AA meetings was put to one side for lawn care. The rules for anyone playing on the lawn often became unfeasible: socks only, no shoes was the first one, then a ball made of sponge.

'I feel such a dork,' said Jem. Nick announced the rules at the beginning of each summer, setting an example for his whole family when he left his trainers on the gravel and skipped on to the grass in his yellow socks. 'There's something about socks that is so pensioner – next Dad will have us all in those grey shoes they wear for bowls. I am not getting my friends to do this and that's final.'

'Don't even think the thought,' hissed Coral. 'He was talking about bowls the other day but I managed to persuade him that it is only for sad tossers.'

Nick's lawn passed from lumpy mess to immaculate untouchable sward without ever stopping at the in-between phase where children could play on it.

The frequent and inconsistent exception to this regime was when Nick himself wanted to play a decent game of football with the children. Then, suddenly it was fine to be on the lawn in trainers, skidding towards the goal and ploughing the surface.

It is smooth now, and Foss and Ruby have dragged a paddling pool out on to the middle and Jem is filling it with a hose while they squeal and run into the cold spray.

'Jem, try and squirt me,' taunts Foss. 'I am out of reach.'

'Oh no you aren't.' Jem runs after him, Ruby trips him up and they lie in a heap laughing.

'Mum, come and save me,' Jem shouts, and Angel leaves the wheelbarrow and joins them, grabbing Foss and twirling him in the air. She is sure for a moment that things will change. Something will happen and life will move forward. It always does.

Nick

Ely Cathedral looms out of the flat green surface of the Fens, improbably large in shades of grey, sailing like a ghost galleon towards Nick as the train jerks into Ely station on his way to London for a meeting. The train judders past the tin roofs of allotment sheds. Solid against the sky, the octagon tower has a cobweb of scaffolding obscuring its elaborate caryatids, and the spires around it remind Nick of the thorns around Sleeping Beauty's castle in the fairy tale. And frankly, as with her thorns, they just don't look worth trying to penetrate. What princess has ever been worth a spike through the arse? And what princess is ever glad you have bothered, or even notices the effort you have gone to for her? None he has known for sure.

Behind the pinnacles and spires and the monumental tower, the sky is watery blue, and the bank of thick clouds clumped on the horizon is the only movement in the scene out of the window. In the opposite direction yellow fields of oilseed rape patchwork the endless flatness, criss-crossed with dykes and dissected by the railway. The open doors of the train send a sudden gust of air into the carriage, and on it the delicate scent of blossom drenched with recent rain. The sun suddenly rolls out from behind the clouds and the Fenland looks full of promise, and flowers and possibility.

Like Angel when he met her. He didn't even notice the thorns around her, they were hidden beneath so much budding optimism. Nick is surprised to find the thought of her all those years ago suddenly in his head. He sees her clearly in his mind now, and what he sees is the moment they met. Here on the train, at Ely where she got on. Twenty years ago, maybe a little more, maybe a little less – and anyway who is counting – Angel walked down the carriage, her hands touching each seat back as she passed. She sat down right opposite him, unaware that she had just invaded his life and was going to occupy it for the foreseeable future. She smelled of roses kicked with musk, the whiff of patchouli oil, and her scent coiled round him, intoxicating his senses while he gazed at everything he had ever wanted. He didn't know that was what she was, actually he didn't know much really because he was smashed – but he was always smashed then. And smashed didn't mean falling over drunk, or not at that point on that particular spring afternoon in May, it just meant a little bit high. It was funny, he would not have thought of Angel as his type. Her strawberry-blonde hair and smudge-grey eyes were too English for him, and her glowing skin and soft supple body were way too healthy. She was out of his league as far as health went. She has no addictions – or none that were visible then. But she peeled off her coat and a purple T-shirt was tight across her breasts and her arms had freckles and fine, pale golden hairs, the sight of which made him shiver. Her throat disappeared into the faded scoop of the T-shirt and there was a dark brown mole on her collarbone, and he was consumed with an urge to lean over and kiss her neck just there. It was the beginning of a hot summer, years before air-conditioning was installed on Anglia Rail and before smoking was sidelined to a single carriage at the end of the train. Angel's bare legs gleamed when she crossed them, absently pulling at the hem of her denim skirt, vainly attempting to get it somewhere near her knees. She hadn't noticed him looking at her yet. All she was carrying was a book, and as soon as she sat down she started to read it. The book was called *Hangover Square*. Nick rarely spent a day without a hangover. The book was clearly a sign flagging the way. Eagerly Nick succumbed to his favourite compulsion, desire. Just now he wanted everything – a drink, a shag, a cigarette, a connection, a conquest. He wanted it all, and yet he would have traded everything for love – his need for love raged through him, unmet and untamed, opening every wound so he could have screamed with pain. But instead of screaming he did what he always did to pick up a girl. He became consumed. He threw himself into falling, rushing desire; a charge so great he could never believe it was not a magnetic force.

So Nick leaned towards this beautiful freckled magnet, his eyes running over her like he wanted his hands to, his elbows on his knees. He was utterly sincere when he said, 'You are incredible. I want to buy you a drink and pay you a lot of attention.' It didn't always work, but he'd had two vodkas already on the train, some subtle opiates at home before he left, and nothing to eat since God knows when. This girl looked good enough to eat and the adrenalin required to be so up front was a fix like any drug. And what the hell; to be turned down was nothing like as bad as not having any drugs. The look he got back from Angel smouldered for a moment then ignited in a smile that was surely all about sex.

'OK,' she said. And at that point neither of them was able to see that the chemistry between them was as toxic as the chemicals coursing through Nick's veins.

Had things been different, perhaps their affair would have run its short course. But Angel was pregnant. She would have left him otherwise, at some point over that summer. She was not in love with him, she was still in love with Ranim; she did not pretend otherwise, though she did not say so either. Nick felt that on some level he had known this. But he wanted her. And everything he was doing at that point of his life was bad for him, so what would have made him pick a girlfriend who was good for him? Angel looked so perfect, she looked like the answer. She was unfinished business. In fact, she was unfinishable business, but Nick wanted to try. When Coral was born, they became a family. Angel tried to find Ranim, but every letter was returned. Nick remained constant. Angel gave up. Nick believed he had won her. Everyone else thought he had rescued her. And at some level he thought it too.

Jem

Sometimes I just feel so real. It is a weird feeling and it makes me realise how not real most of my life is, and how I hang around without really living or seeing or hearing except though a filter of my headphones and my mobile phone. But something about today got to me when I woke up. Maybe it was the fact that the sun had warmed the patch on the pillow right next to my head but the rays had not hit me in the face, so when I moved my head I was suddenly in this warm patch, clean-smelling like the airing cupboard. I was already smiling when I became aware I was awake. Then the cornflakes were super crunchy and the milk tasted just right, and I was standing by the fridge eating the third bowlful and I must have been making a noise because Coral came in and said, 'Are you on drugs, man? – that's just cereal, you know.' And I nodded with my mouth full, thinking, Yeah, she's right, but it's delicious.

I would have definitely eaten the whole packet if Ruby hadn't come in prancing and singing some boy band noise pollution.

'Hey, Roobs, what about the song I taught you about you?'

She does this hip thing, wiggling as if she is twenty-five and performing in a lap dancing club, and it's like punctuation to show she's finished one song. Then she starts on the Rolling Stones. I brainwashed her with: 'Goodbye, Ruby Tuesday', but she breaks off before I can check that she knows the whole verse.

'I want you to grow bosoms now to trick Mummy and Daddy,' she commands, proffering a pair of tennis balls and tugging at my T-shirt. God, small children are insane, but then, why not? Obediently, I stuff the tennis balls inside my T-shirt. Going into Mum's room did puncture the ultra reality a bit, because I started to imagine I was in a time warp and I was seven again like Ruby. Sometimes I can remember things so immediately it feels like they are happening now. This time it was smelling Mum's perfume which she always wears and she has always worn, so it is as much her as the way she laughs, maybe even more so because the perfume isn't separate at all in the way laughter can come into a room with the person not there yet. But the scent is in every room with Mum always, and usually it's hardly noticeable, it's just there, but sometimes, like this morning, it comes and wraps around me like a hug from her.

I don't know why Dad isn't here. I don't notice him by his own personal absence, or by his smell, thank God, but by the presence of things he should be in. His trainers are at the bottom of the bed on the side that he should be sleeping in right now if he wasn't up and ready for our game of tennis and wearing the trainers. Normally though, he is not ready, and is pretending to be asleep with his pillow over his head while Foss and Ruby spring about the place. There is nothing very unusual about him not being here; he's been away on and off for ages, but with the way I feel today it is weird. When I say to Mum, 'So where is Dad, then?' she look at me as though I am talking to her through mists and layers of time and in a language that she has to translate to understand. Basically her eyes are darting about me and she is trying to avoid answering me. She doesn't want to say where he is. And I get it. This is the moment that I know she doesn't love him any more, even though I am not aware that I know it yet. And I don't know if she knows it either. What I am aware of at this moment is my insides have swooped, doubled up like I have been hit in the stomach and on through to my spine and ribs. They are crumbling and if I knew what to panic about, I would be panicking.

Ruby still thinks I am playing the boobs-are-tennis-balls game with her again. I mean we had that one yesterday, why would I want to do it again? The trouble with little kids is they never give up and they never forget that you said you would do something, no matter how throwaway you were feeling when you said it. But I can't. Everything that was real and felt good before I spoke to Mum is flat and heavy now. And Coral isn't here so I can't even talk to her about it.

Nick

Nick wakes up with a bad taste in his mouth and it isn't alcohol, that's for sure. The light sneaks through thick brown darkness in the room, and all of his senses battle to make sense of what he can see is not a familiar place. It smells of old cigarettes, so it is definitely not his bedroom at home. There, Angel's scent and the fresh-air breath of clean laundry mingle in the air with sunshine and sleep. The room is always warm, and always soft, and in his mind he can see it. The odd thing is there is nothing of him or his in it. The pale pink walls with gold-feathered wallpaper, the raspberry richness of the velvet bed-spread, the rack of shoes and boots in the fireplace – all of them are Angel's. Somehow Nick has got into the habit of trailing a small suitcase around with his book, his trainers, a toothbrush and a couple of shirts, and this is the only bit of him he can see in his mind's-eye view of the marital bedroom.

Sighing, he looks around the Travel Lodge room. Everything is nicotine-brown, even the telephone next to the bed flashing an intermittent yellow light. There is a maddening broken buzzing sound; sitting up, Nick rubs his head and allows desolation to seep into him. If any conspicuous way to make things worse were to emerge at this moment, Nick would use it. He experiments with fantasy, daring himself along a familiar tightrope; if the brownness of the room was to yield a bag of brown powder, for example, he could take it. If a gun glinted on the window sill, he could use it. What else? Ah yes, if the mini-bar was stocked with alcohol, he could drink it. Oh yes, hallelujah – there is the key. He unlocks it with ease, and the click of the key in the plastic-fronted fridge door awakens a thousand toxic memories and sets his senses on alert. Inside, there is a row of beer cans and the jewel-bright glint of tiny glass bottles of gin, vodka and whisky. With self-destruction on his mind and not much else, Nick grabs a can of beer and pulls the key from it. He raises it to his lips. He is about to gulp it down, thus annihilating for today at least the good that seven years of being clean has done him, when something in him tugs at his willpower. It is, he recognises, his Higher Power, zapping in to save him in the nick of time.

'It works if you work it,' he mutters to himself, feeling ironic, post-ironic and also hugely relieved. Today he is not meant to relapse.

'What the fuck –' Nick holds the can away from himself as if it is a viper, and leaps out of bed, staggering sideways into the bathroom, not taking his eyes off the lager can in his hand. Sweating and panting he lifts the lavatory seat and pours the brown liquid away from a height, gazing into the loo pan. It would be a good moment to cry, but instead he pees, thinking the release of any body liquid must be good. It is somewhat worrying to be looking into a lavatory pan and see it frothing with pungent brown. Nick gazes on, unable to move away from this depressing position, and gathering in his mind a thousand ways to feel sorry for himself. They all seem to stem from being surrounded by brown. The obvious thing to do to improve things would be to open the curtains, get dressed and get out of the Travel Lodge. But where shall he go? There is something intrinsically foolish about the position Nick finds himself in. Although he has always tried to cultivate an air of mystery and inaccessibility, by never saying where he is going to be, normally he is going somewhere and he is meant to be somewhere. So wherever he is has a purpose, even the negative one of not being where he is meant to be. Dragging his eyes away from the lavatory pan, he returns to the bedroom and lies down to dissect his options.

Maybe he should go home. A bubble floats into his head with his house, the Mill Stone, picture-book perfect with the sunlight falling across the red brick, warming it, and some children tumbling pleasingly and in no way damagingly, across his immaculate lawn. The curtains are all shut in his mind, and the only animation is the somersaulting of the children. Then, like the beginning first act of a play, the curtains are swept back and Angel, her arms stretched the full span of the window, is hovering like her namesake, a twisted smile playing on her lips in the drawing room. Nick flinches involuntarily on his brown bed. God, how unbearable. No, he cannot go home. It is out of the question. He could go to the office, of course. Another bubble pops up in his mind, this one full of desks and noticeboards in an open-plan room with ten-foot-tall barn windows. In the corner, partitions separate a smaller room – and in his mind's eye, Nick enters to find Angel and Nat Rosstein sitting at the large desk, on either side, facing each other, both of them looking as if they are about to rear up and fight. When Nick enters, they glance round but do not move. Nick sighs and continues. No, he cannot go to the office, it is also out of the question.

In a welter of panic, Nick jumps off the bed and walks around the room, pausing in front of the blank screen of the television. He gazes at it for a while then turns it on. The caring expression of a true-life interviewer appears. The discussion underway is fathers' rights.

Oh God. Oh God. Fathers' rights. Nick has never thought that much about his marriage, or his family, until recently. It all happened to him and Angel, it never felt as though either of them was driving it, it just happened. It was fate. They met. She was fleeing, though she did not realise it at the time. He was looking for something to fill his emptiness. They fell in with one another. Did they fall in love with one another? It is hard to remember, and impossible to know what real feelings he had then as Nick was off his head or drunk most of the time. Not rampagingly drunk, but the habit that formed in California of a beer or two at the restaurant he worked in while preparing lunches, became a beer or two for breakfast that was much improved by a vodka shot and a line or two of cocaine. Purely for flagging energy, not because he needed it. In fact, as a chef, there was no escaping drugs or alcohol, you needed them just to get your exhausted body through the long days and nights in hell's kitchen. And the heroin he took was the only way to come down and forget. The only way to take time off.

Being with Angel was such a soft ticket after that. Working for her family business was so relaxing. Nick spent many hours lying on the sofa in the office watching cricket on television, drinking and smoking a bit of heroin – purely recreationally as he told himself. He was waiting for someone to notice, he was waiting for someone to tell him what to do. No one did.

The soft option turned out to be handcuffs, albeit made of elastic and profitably produced by Fourply. Nick didn't mind, why would he? They were so comfortable and so seductive. His mother was in Switzerland on a religious retreat, and had no plans to come back. Nick sent her a postcard when he got married, and she sent one back a while later saying she had prayed for him and his bride. Everyone else seemed to think him so lucky it would have been absurd to rail against his new circumstances.

So the scars from his chef's knives healed and vanished from his fingers and Nick took up golf as a way of communicating with Angel's dad Lionel in his last few years of activity. Aged twenty-eight he could easily have chopped off his arms and legs and not felt a thing, so removed from his heart had he become.

Jem was born and Nick found that he loved him. It was the first sign he had had for some years that he could love. He thought of what Coral's father had lost in leaving Angel. He did not want to lose that too. He stopped taking drugs and believed he had become a functioning human being, though he still drank vodka with his breakfast. Fathers' rights. What rights might they be? Who has any rights over any other human being? The notion is absurd. Running his hands through his hair, Nick picks up his keys and walks out of the door of the Travel Lodge room. He has no idea what he is going to do next. He is utterly alone. Reacting without thinking, he punches Jeannie Gildoff's number into his phone and presses the green button.

Angel

There is nowhere for Angel to hide. She feels hunted and fragmented, she really wants a cigarette even though she doesn't smoke and she is unable to sit down or be still for a moment. If she does sit down, she ought to have a good reason, so she has a telephone like a relay baton in her hands at all times. When it rings she looks surprised, and immediately jumps up and begins marching to and fro again.

'Hello? Who is this? Oh yes – I mean no – Nick isn't here right now. I'm not sure when he'll be back –'

She clicks the off button with an air of finality. Nick will not be back soon. He has gone. The house is full of people. In the kitchen Gosha is sulkily washing up, her back radiating discontent and dysfunction.

'She's got an eating disorder,' says Jem, this morning, having watched Gosha eat six pieces of toast and three bowls of Ricicles with cream and sugar on them.

'She eats that amount every two hours or so every single day and she drinks about three cartons of apple juice a day and the only way she changes is the amount of spots she gets on her face.'

'That is so mean.' Angel stamps past him, sighing heavily. She wanted to stop and sit down in the kitchen, to drink coffee and read the paper by herself, but it simply isn't worth it with all those people in there.

She is dressed – not very attractively – in the electric-blue towelling tracksuit she put on at six-thirty in the morning when she got up, intending to go for a run after giving the children breakfast. This outfit is demoralising, partly because it is a loud blue reminder that she had not gone for a run, and it is now midday and much too hot, and partly because it is supremely unflattering, whether she has been for a run or not.

Three days have passed since Nick left and the unreality is becoming thicker. So what was a mist soon became a fog, and now a wall of opaque density between Angel and the world. It feels impenetrable. Unimaginable that she could go down to the village shop, buy some milk and announce to all present, 'Nick and I are getting divorced.'

The children all know – well, they know something is either happening or not happening and each of them is responding in a uniquely demanding fashion. Foss has found a tin of blackboard paint and has painted the door of the car with it. Now he is watching Jem as he writes 'FOSS STONE TAXI 7p a ride' in yellow paint on the newly black door of the silver car. The more Angel laughs, the more furious Ruby becomes.

'Mummy, why do you find that kind of thing funny because it isn't and it looks really stupid having a car like a taxi which isn't a taxi and how would you like it if you had to go to school in that and have all your friends give you seven p and I would make it forty-six because then you might get enough to buy an ice lolly and –'

'MUM! If you don't stop Ruby going on like that I will strangle her and shoot her and I will have a criminal record and never be able to go to America and it will all be YOUR FAULT!' bellows Jem. He has only ever been angry about three times in his whole life as far as Angel can remember. He is communicating through a loudhailer left over from the fête Angel and Nick hosted in the garden last year, and his booming amplified voice is the only effective competition to his music, turned up to full volume since the morning Nick left.

Coral has vanished. Like a cat, her sixth sense for crisis took her into hiding two days ago. She isn't answering her phone, but she has told Jem she is in Cambridge staying with Matt. Angel is too pole-axed to do anything. Indeed, she feels grateful that one of them is away; the remaining three still outnumber and overwhelm her.

The only way to live through the next nanosecond is for Angel to put down the phone and walk out of the back door and keep walking. Once on the path, she begins to run down the drive, and although the words 'It's all your fault' pound unhelpfully around her in time with her feet, she is away out of the garden gate and up the hill towards the church before any of the children notice.

Going running creates Angel's safety net, and within the parameters of running she can exist and know she will not unravel, no matter how far-flung her reality becomes. She is hot now, the tracksuit like a damp towel draped around her legs, heavy, slowing her so her rhythm falters and she gasps for breath. When keeping going gets hard Angel could slow down and walk for a while and then run again, or she could breathe and count. In. Out. One, two, three, four. In. Out. One, two, three, four. And she will get through the struggle and reach the next level. Rather like the children's PlayStation, she thinks inconsequentially.

Slowing down and walking, then trying to run again, has never appealed to Angel. To her it seems harder, and is imbued with failure, to stop and start rather than to keep going through and get out on the other side. Just keep going. Just keep going. She has been running for ten minutes, the tightness in her chest is burning to bursting point, expanding out of her lungs and vanishing into her veins in a throb of adrenalin. And at the point where it is impossible to go another step, it changes, she changes, and her warmed muscles stretch and flex, her lungs inflate and sink into a rhythm as she breaks through effort into ease, her body working with her mind so she can float for three miles, probably more. Breathing evenly, Angel inhales warm sunshine suffused with birdsong and the dusty-bronze hot smell of harvested corn. Her legs have taken her automatically on her favourite circuit, and she breathes deeply to start the steep incline to the church on the top of the hill, the different vital muscles on the back plane of her body flaring and contracting to change gear. The flooding serotonin delivers an emerging sense of well-being and hope and the possibility of competence. Angel finds these feelings both comforting and seductive. Being fit is not the main reason for Angel's running; she runs for the fix, the high, the mood-altering endorphins pumping through her and making her a smoother, more energetic, clear-minded version of herself.

There was a time when Nick came with her, although he never ran, insisting that he was not built for it, and all the years of smoking would drag him down to the ground and beneath it into oblivion. Whistling and riding with no hands he would accompany her on a bicycle, herding the dog, dragging his feet, pedalling up from behind her and wolf-whistling. There was one autumn evening when she ran round a corner and into a team of ramblers. Nick zoomed past as she was nego-tiating them and called out, 'Nice tits and arse you've got there, pussy cat.' Angel started laughing, running faster to push him off the bike, but though he dawdled for her to almost catch him, he had no intention of actually letting her.

'Come on, chase me more,' he begged, teasing her. Nick used to make her laugh and blush like she did when she was sixteen at school in Ely and was a magnet of attention for the motorbike boys by the bus stop.

The path ahead narrows, a grassy slope takes Angel down to a shady ride between two swollen cornfields, swaying and whispering in anticipation of harvest. Her awareness shifts to the front of her body now and she breathes and pulls back a little to change the pace for going downhill. Beneath her feet, old tractor tyre ruts mould hard furrows into the dusty earth and although it would be exhilarating to let momentum take her faster and faster, she steadies the tempo and runs on at the same speed, focusing all her balance and energy on not stumbling or falling. The path changes again, becoming smooth and narrow, dark grey and cool, like damp unworked clay, and Angel turns in beneath a canopy of twisted crab apple and willow trees snaking back towards the village. Her breathing is even and strong but her calf muscles ache, her lower back thuds with each pace, and sweat sits like a dead skin waiting to be shed, all over her body. It is hot; Angel is thirsty. Ahead of her the dappled shade is cool and inviting. At the end of the path the road becomes visible. The school caretaker's cat is lying in a pool of sunshine outside his gate, writhing to massage its back in the warm sand scattered on the road. Angel picks up speed when her feet hit the tarmac, and she runs the final five minutes home faster and faster, her breath pumping out of her and her feet flying. Getting home is a prize, and she stops short the moment she passes the garden gate, bent double, panting, reeling with exhilaration and breathlessness. If nothing else works again today, this alone is a success.

She opens the door into the kitchen and finds Foss and a tin of black paint occupying the sink together. Gosha is waving the barbecue tongs and saying, 'Take off the clothes for the bin.'

'No. I like them.' Foss squats on the draining board, his feet in the sink, and hammers the lid back on to the paint pot. He waves at Angel.

'Mum, can you put this paint back in the garage? I'll need it again soon. Gosha is really annoying me.' He glares at the au pair, swatting away the tongs she has near his T-shirt.

'GET OFF!' he roars. Angel takes the paint tin and puts it outside the back door. She smiles at Gosha. 'Don't worry, I'll get the clothes off him,' she says, still smiling automatically.

'Come on, Foss, you can come in the shower with me.'

'And my clothes?' Foss looks defiant.

Angel looks at him; it means a lot to him. What does it matter to her? 'Yes. And your clothes.'

Jem

There is something wrong with my parents. There is something going on. It doesn't feel as though anyone is in charge any more. Mum wanders around on the phone all the time. Her hair is bigger than her face by miles. I reckon she has got really thin and she should watch out or she'll end up like one of those scrawny old bags who are too brown and wear loads of jewels and bracelets in *Hello!* magazine. I think they are usually celebrity mothers – that sort of thing – and they all live in Miami. Anyway. What is good, though, is that going nuts has made Mum very generous. This morning she gave me forty quid to go and buy some food for a picnic and she said I could keep the change. So I am on the way back from the shop now. I had to walk because my bike has two punctures, and actually I wanted it to take longer because I can't stand being in the house with the little ones all the time. Mum doesn't even ask me if it's all right for me to look after them, she just treats me like another babysitter. I think she forgets that Gosha is here and works for her. Gosha just goes and sits in front of the TV all day. Yesterday she ate two buckets of raspberry ripple ice cream. I really mean buckets as well. They are on offer in the Spar and the ice cream must be made of pig slurry or something, because they only cost one ninety-nine for the most enormous bucket, big enough to turn upside down and make into chairs. Ruby's got one for her dolls to sit on outside the kitchen door this morning, and four dolls fit on it, no trouble. Anyway, whatever. Gosha managed to eat two whole bucketfuls yesterday. God knows where she was sick, or even if she was sick, but I reckon she must have been. Actually, I reckon she's bulimic because nobody could eat what she does and stay a reasonable size and she is quite small.

So where does it all go? I don't know why I am asking that question because I really don't want to know.

Matt, Coral's boyfriend, does this flick of his hand and I have learned it now. If you relax all your fingers and turn them slightly inwards then flick your wrist hard away and back, your fingers slap together with a whiplash crack, which I find I can use instead of quite a variety of words.

I can use it instead of 'Sod off' when some random person in the street jostles me. I can use it instead of 'Excellent' when I'm watching sport and someone scores or takes a wicket. I can use it instead of 'Oh bollocks' when things go wrong in sport. I can use it when Mum or Dad does something wicked like tells me we are going on holiday or gives me some money – mind you, the holiday thing hasn't actually happened since I learned how to do this and that was a year ago, but when it does, I will be able to express that I am pleased.

It makes Mum laugh when I do it, and I always like her a lot when I make her laugh like that. I think she may not be the greatest mother – although I don't know what is the greatest mother – but I do like her as a fellow human being at those moments.

I can also adapt the finger flick to be a menacing message if people on the bus start taking the piss or something, or if some creep at school gives me a hard time or a teacher goes nuts about homework. Right now, though, it expresses that I am grossed out by everyone – by Gosha and her ice cream eating, by Ruby and Foss, by Mum. And I have cracked my fingers together so much today that the knuckles hurt. I want to talk to Dad, or even see him and watch the cricket with him. He hasn't answered his phone once today. I haven't seen him for over a week and it's crap. Last time we spoke he said, 'I want to spend some time with you, Jem, let's fix something up.' I wish he hadn't said it if worrying about it is what's keeping him away.

I bought two loaves of bread, some soft cheese and a packet of my favourite ham and I still had thirty-five quid. I felt a bit guilty keeping so much money, so I bought three packets of chocolate chip cookies, some sausage rolls and a bunch of bananas, but I still couldn't spend more than seven pounds and I couldn't think of anything else to have for the picnic except cigarettes. So I bought a packet of those too. The picnic is for the little ones and me. I think I'll keep the cigarettes, though. I might see if Foss wants to try one, but that would be evil and corrupting as he is only four. Mind you, because he is only four there is a good chance that he will have a go. No one did that to me when I was his age, but then I only had Coral. And Mum. Mum used to smoke then. She and Dad both did, and I hated the smell like I hate the smell of petrol. For me the very worst of all is still a car with someone sitting in it smoking cigarettes at a petrol station. Bad smell and possible explosion, it's a pretty crap combination. It's funny how it makes me want to puke and yet I can smoke as many cigarettes as anyone else if I'm in the mood. But mostly I don't think about them except as a way to get chatting to people, and as something to do at school. It's so stupid because everyone I know started smoking at school just to have something to do. When I'm on my own I sometimes remember that I could climb out on the roof and have a cigarette but there isn't much point. Dad and Mum know I smoke and they don't mind. Actually, it's more random than that. Mum caught me smoking with Matt watching MTV the other night and she looked at the cigarette in my hand and the smoke, which I couldn't stop creeping out of the corner of my mouth even though I tried to until I could feel my tongue curling up with the poison of nicotine, and the walls of my mouth probably yellowing and all the taste buds dying because I so did not want to exhale smoke in her face. But she stood there grinning and then she burst out laughing. How humiliating is that? Your mum laughing at the sight of you smoking. I think it has damaged me. Most people think I am really lucky that my parents don't give me a hard time, but I want them to give me a hard time about something. There must be something they care about? I flick my fingers together again and try not to think what I feel, which is that they only care about themselves. I am not important enough.

I don't know where Coral is – actually, I do, she's at Matt's house, and even though she is a bossy cow at times I wish she was here now.

But she just said, 'I can't handle Mum and Nick and this atmosphere, I've got to get out of here.' I haven't seen her since. And whenever I call her, she's got her phone turned off. I am pretty pissed off with her in fact, and with Dad, because guess who gets left holding the babies – well, let's just say it isn't Mum, that's for sure.

How have I got myself into being the one left at home? Why don't I have anywhere to go or anyone to go with? I could see my friends, but at the moment, whenever I think of calling them, I think of calling Dad at the same nanosecond and I always call his number first and when he doesn't answer his phone I get this sick-pit-of-my-stomach churning feeling and I can't call my friends, I just go and sit with the Polish eating disorder in front of the TV until the feeling evaporates.

I don't know what the feeling is, but it's getting in the way of my life.

Dad not being here is in the way of my life. Mum and the kids are totally in the way of my life. Literally. Mum appears in the TV room and somehow she is carrying both of them. She staggers across the room and her eyes are manic. Ruby's arms are round Mum's neck and her hands are lost in Mum's thick hair; she is clinging to Mum and Mum is clinging to Foss, holding him out in front of her. His legs are curled up and he is howling.

'Christ, I can't stand this any more,' shrieks Mum. 'You take them, Jem, please, now and go anywhere – somewhere – but I need some space or I will explode and kill all of us with the machete.'

'I want the machete!' roars Foss, squirming in her grasp.

'Well, you can't bloody have it,' Mum pants. 'You are much too young and you should never have got it down. Never. If I catch you chopping up anything – lamps, salami, cushions or people with that machete again I will remove all your privileges.'

'I haven't got any privileges,' Foss snarls back. 'You took them away. They're in the jar on the dresser and you think I don't know they're there but I do and I hate you.'

I wonder what he thinks privileges are.

'What's in the jar on the dresser?' I hiss to Ruby. She is of course being super-angelic and sitting with her hands in her lap, watching Foss. This is a show I know well:

one of them is always good when the other is bad. It's sick, but it makes sense.

'Souvenirs, of course,' Ruby whispers back. 'She took his badges and stuff from the war museum when she found him with the bullets last week.'

An Oscar winner could not have better executed her expression of pious regret, and I would definitely believe she cared about Foss if I had not been witness to an ugly scene last week. Admittedly, on that occasion Foss had a gun and some bullets and they were not toys, and he had tied Ruby to a tree in the garden with the intention of shooting her, but the bullets didn't fit the gun. They were cartridges for a shotgun and no one can remember what happened to the shotgun so they were pretty safe as Foss's weapon was a starting pistol. Ruby was hideous and I would have shot her if I were Foss. She was taunting him, calling him a dork and sticking her tongue out.

When Coral and I were small it was different. Though come to think of it, Dad wasn't around much then either, but that was because he was either pissed or stoned. He was not much good for a game of cricket until I was about eight, but then neither was I, I could hardly throw a ball. I did have tantrums, though. Coral never joined in with my arsy behaviour, and even all those years ago, when I didn't know what I was thinking at all, I vaguely had the feeling that Coral was more grown up than Mum.

There was a day when Mum and I were in the car waiting for Coral outside her school. I was probably six and Coral was eight. It was summer and Mum was wearing a red T-shirt. We were both eating ice creams and playing a game of zooming them past each other and having a lick. Mum zoomed her ice cream past me and it dropped in a huge dollop right on her tits. Actually it was a scoopful, not a dollop, so it just looked like another boob had landed. I can remember how much I laughed. Mum couldn't stop laughing either and she picked up the ice cream dollop and threw it out of the car just as Coral emerged round the corner from her school gate.

'Mummeeee,' she hissed. 'What are you doing? Look at the state of you.' Mum's hair had fallen out of the pony-tail she wore it in, she had streaks of mascara on the back of her hand because she had laughed so much she cried then wiped her eyes. She probably looked about fourteen, and I reckon she felt about fourteen until Coral came along. Mum sighed and twisted her hair back neatly. Coral rolled her eyes and threw her satchel in the open back window so it landed next to me.

'It doesn't matter, you know,' said Mum. 'We were just having fun.' And she leant sideways, reaching her arm across to kiss Coral as she got into the car. Coral bobbed away and her black plaits shone bluebottle green in the sunshine and I looked at her straight parting and the slender brown nape of her neck, and Coral turned her face to look out away from Mum and her eyes shone with tears and disappointment. And I looked at Mum's neck, pinker and with wisps of blonde hair, turning the other way as she started the car and looked down the road and I sensed that Mum was scared of Coral. It did not make me feel great about Mum. And I can remember that feeling exactly, even though it was years ago. Right now, Mum is pink again and she has shoved Foss and Ruby in front of me.

'Can you go now, please. I'll drive you somewhere and you can have a picnic while I get on and I'll come and pick you up later.'

This is always happening. It is crap.

'No, Mum, you come too, you're our mum and I don't want to look after your kids, I am one of your kids. I am not taking them to the fucking beach again for you.'

Mum's eyes widen and she looks mortified. It is a bit like a face lift – there are no wrinkles visible on her face at this moment and what she is thinking passes almost visibly under the top layer of skin – a red flush of anger and then blood pulsing blue through the veins on her forehead and she goes pale with shock.

'OK, I'll come.'

Big fucking deal, Mum.

Angel

Bumping down the track to the creek, the sun shines yellow and metallic and the glare bouncing off the sea invades behind Angel's eyes like strobe lighting in the dark. The tide is out, beached boats are scattered lopsided and drunk on the mud banks. Gorse scratches the doors of the car and the wheels flatten the coarse brown grass as the car inches towards the furthest possible point Angel dares to drive. The grass springs up again behind the car, feathering against the children's bare feet as they sit in the boot, the tailgate open, facing backwards.

'Ouch, it's spiky, Mummy,' squeals Ruby. Angel glances in the rear-view mirror. The ritual of this journey is unchanging; as soon as the car leaves the road and hits the grass track, the children pile into the dog zone in the boot, where normally they would be sick rather than spend five minutes. But a small amount of peril alters it, and Foss and Ruby jostle to sit with their legs dangling out over the bumper and their bare feet catching the grasses. When Angel is in a good mood, 'which is only when we've got other people with us,' remarks Jem as they turn off the road today, she often becomes very relaxed, some might say careless, allowing the children to climb on to the top and hold on to the roof-rack bars to lurch along the bumpy track like monkeys harassing a carful of tourists in a safari park.

A pair of birdwatchers, nylon jackets bunched round their waists, squeeze themselves against the gorse, flattening their whole bodies as the car passes. Angel smiles at them and waves thanks. They stare back, their faces blank with disapproval. This is how Angel interprets their expressions. Actually, they may just as easily be registering blank uninterest. She is aware of her own hypocrisy; if she saw any other cars down here, she would be indignant, even as she drives her own down the almost impenetrable track. But if they walk it will take hours, and Foss and Ruby will moan. Jem will have to carry one of them and she will have to carry the other, and then what about carrying the picnic? And the person missing is Nick, who would be carrying everything if he were here.

Today Angel feels both crushed and heavy. Defeated and convinced everything is her own fault. As if clinging to a rock in a fast-flowing water, she holds on to the belief that breaking up is the right thing to do. She will not look at the possibility of compromise. She can't. Therein lies too much confusion. And her mind is fragmented by shock and she has no conviction that what is happening is right. It just is. So what is the point in debating? Just now she has no instinct, no nothing, beyond scratching, stabbing anger, flaring and demanding like eczema. 'Oh for heaven's sake,' she hisses as the car dips into a gaping pothole and Foss starts to cry.

'He banged his head, Mummy,' shouts Ruby, her voice full of reproof.

'Poor him,' replies Angel, and Ruby's glare in the rear mirror reflects her own insincerity. Some deep exhalations, focusing on the horizon . . .

'MUM! STOP! STOP!' Jem yells furiously. Angel slams the brakes on and turns round.

'What is it? Can't you lot just be quiet for a minute?' But none of them is there. Foss has fallen out and is lying in a pothole some distance behind, bawling. The other two have jumped out and are running back to get him. Angel only feels irritation. And disgust at herself, but now is not the time to foster a whole new culture of dislike.

'I'm coming!' She gets out and runs back. Jem and Ruby have got Foss up, and brushed the sand off him. The three of them are walking along the path with Jem holding both their hands. Angel is not needed. Good. Her phone chirrups in her pocket and turning to the sea she answers it. It is Nick.

'Look, I'm coming back. In fact I am back. I'm at home. We need to talk. There is stuff we have to sort out.'

He sounds far away and separate. Angel feels no desire to bridge the gap, no connection to him. Nothing.

'Yes, there is, but what will you tell the children?' Is that all she can think of to say? Is that how things move forward? Angel, numb with worn-out anxiety, is still amazed at her own capacity for nothingness. And Nick's.

'I don't know,' he replies after a silence. 'I think we need to talk first.'

Angel walks off the path at a right angle to the three children. They are watching her. Foss needs her to pick him up and hug him, but she ignores him to talk to Nick. She feels ragged and distanced from everything.

'How long are you coming back for?'

There is another silence, then Nick says again, 'I don't know. I haven't got any answers to anything at the moment. Look, we'll talk when you get home.'

'OK, see you later.'

Angel puts her phone back into the pocket of her skirt and turns back to the children, rubbing her face in the hope that she can expel the numbness and become carefree.

Ruby grabs her hand. 'Come on, Mummy, let's skip.' Skipping is a monumental effort of coordination between limbs as wooden as a puppet's, and a brain battered by confusion.

Focusing with deliberate concentration, Angel manages a version of skipping, and Ruby smiles and grips her hand more tightly.

Back at the car Foss is assembling three crab lines with

hooks and bits of bacon. His tears are forgotten, and he is businesslike.

'We'll get the crabs and then I want to get some lug worms for fishing in the pond at home,' he tells Jem.

'Yeah, worms are great, but what about a bucket of fish, too?'

Foss considers for a moment then nods. 'Yes, I think so, and then I can put them in the pond and fish them out again.'

'Cool,' grins Jem. Angel catches his eye in the car mirror and they both smile for a fleeting second. Angel's heart springs, loving this tiny exchange, loving Jem.

Driving on to the rutted broad space beside the track, Angel fixes her eyes on the horizon, chooses the largest of three pairs of sunglasses in the glove compartment, and parks the car. So much of her mothering has been carried out by remote control, often in the past because she was trying to work, that it is an effort to remember how to do simple things like going to the beach with the picnic stuff and the children. Nick is back. He could stay. Maybe they can live in the house together and he can just sleep in a different room? Maybe it would be better to have him there like that than to have no one?

'Mum, are you listening at all?' The cheerful companionship among the children has vanished into a storm of crosspatch arguing and car-door slamming. Jem sounds completely pissed off. Foss is bellowing again – what is the matter with that child today? Can he not get some grip on himself and exist alongside everyone else?

Ruby snatches the towel she and Foss had been tussling over and wedges it into her pink bag. Standing, legs apart, with a crocheted white hat on and a pair of red shorts and an old green T-shirt, Ruby swings her beach bag and stares across the marshes towards the frills of waves and the sea. Angel's eyes sting and tears roll down behind her sunglasses. There is a picture on her mother's mantelpiece of Angel at the beach at the same age. The beach is different; in her picture Angel is about to get on a donkey to ride across Scarborough Sands. Clean and ordered, with no idea of the joy of mud sliding, or the warm silk water of a saltmarsh creek. When she was small, Angel hardly ever got dirty or played in water; there was no one to do it with except her mother, and her mother found the beach too hot. She can see the picture in her mind's eye. Ruby's gaze, with her puzzled brow and an expression in her eyes of confusion, shares with it a yearning for something to make sense, which crosses more than thirty years. Angel doesn't know whether the picture in her memory or the one in front of her is more poignant. Certainly the one in front of her is more urgent.

'I want to swim,' says Ruby crossly.

'Let's get across the creek and sit by the black boat,' says Jem. 'We can get a lift if we're quick – I just saw someone sailing back up the creek. If we miss them we'll have to swim – or the short arses around here will. I think I can walk with the stuff on my head.'

He glares at Foss, sniffing balefully but standing still and patient, as he is loaded with towels and fishing nets.

Jem

Dad just sent me a text. 'Looking forward to tennis tonight at 7.' He must be home. I can't believe I've got to spend all sodding afternoon on the beach with Mum crying and behaving like she is totally unstable and these kids squabbling. Foss has got a slug of snot running down his nose and no one has done anything about it since I last wiped it before we left home. Now there's nothing to use. Oh gross. He has just blown his nose on his T-shirt. He is so Third World.

All Mum did was wave as if to a taxi, at some bloke in a boat and say, 'I think he's getting a cold.' Then there's all the palaver of getting in this guy's boat. Of course he thinks he's won the jackpot because Mum, even crying with dark glasses on, is a lot prettier than his wife who is sitting in the front of his boat with a red handkerchief knotted round her slightly sagging neck and a baggy T-shirt disguising God knows what. Mum, on the other hand, is wearing a yellow dress with very small straps and she is brown, and much too much of her body is visible as her dress is wet.

'Mum, put something on,' I whisper as the guy lifts
Foss on to his boat. The wife looks as though four lepers
shedding fingers and limbs are rubbing up against her. I
can't stand it. We are just trying to get across the bloody
creek. 'You are really pissing that woman off,' I hiss.

Mum lifts up her sunglasses and looks at me in astonishment. 'What are you talking about?' she squeaks.

'You're naked,' I reply, beyond exasperation now.

'What? I'm wearing a dress and a swimming costume,'
Mum hisses back.

'Yeah, whatever, but this could be a good idea.' I pass
her my cricket jersey.

She gives me a sharp look but she puts it on. I wish
Coral was here. She is good at getting Mum to pay proper
attention.

It's not so much that I think Mum needs protecting;
it's more that I think I do. I don't want to be in the middle
of some cheesy row where an old bag is offended by my
mum. My mum is nice, she just doesn't notice. Coral says
I notice too much, and sometimes I think she's right, but
Dad always notices a lot, too. I've seen him looking at
people like this bloke looks at Mum and I just have to
turn away or put my music on. I can't stop him, but I
can cover Mum up so this guy can't remind me of Dad
doing the same thing to Jeannie Gildoff at the barbecue
we went to at their house.

That's when my parents started to go psycho, I reckon.
Jeannie Gildoff looks like she's about ninety but with a

kind of Barbie doll approach to age. So she'll wear a dress, but whereas Mum's dresses are soft and feel really nice, hers all stick out in a big bunch of skirt and stiff material and they always remind me of those films where people are going to the high school prom in the nineteen sixties. Anyway, whatever. For some reason Dad finds her sexy and I was having a slash at the back of their swimming pool to get away from their son Heath who thinks he is so great, and I came back past Dad and Jeannie. They didn't see me. Dad was talking to her in a dark green corner where a huge tree makes a canopy over a table made of squashed-up shells pressed into concrete so they look as though major smashing has been going on. But that's not the point. The point is, Dad was looking down the front of the kind of nurse's uniform thing she was wearing and he said, 'I've been thinking about you and me, Jeannie.' And she was presenting herself – there is no other way of putting it – and her eyes glittered and she had coffee-coloured lip-gloss and it had bled around her mouth.

'Nick, it's dangerous to say that sort of thing –'

I couldn't handle it so I coughed and barged through them and went back to the pool. I had to even talk to Heath to stop myself thinking and hitting out at something. Dad gave me fifty quid, which I didn't think was odd until now, and now I think he was bribing me.

Later that night he came and found me in the TV room and he said, 'You know, there are things about marriage that I find difficult.'

If he had poured a can of iced lager over my head it would have felt the same as the seeping of cold rage. 'Dad, can you shut up, please?' I said and turned up the TV.

So this guy in the boat is super efficient, you can tell from the way he pats the picnic basket as he puts it in, and he tucks it away under the seat even though we are only going to be in his boat for about two and a half minutes while we cross the creek.

'Thank you so much, you are so kind.' Mum has a way of sounding completely pleased with strangers, whoever it is – sometimes it's a person at a petrol station who fills our car up for her, more often it's someone she has asked the way from – but how she sounds makes their day and they smile at her and she smiles back and feel-good is radiated and I often feel sick, to be honest.

Right now I feel sick, but not because of Mum, more because the wife of the guy is glaring so badly. Ruby notices, too, and sticks her chin up in the air and folds her arms. She is so good at looking arsy, like Coral. Then Foss notices and he just sticks out his tongue. I have to make myself cough so Foss and the lady don't realise I am laughing, but luckily we are across the creek.

'Sandy Beauchamp, and that is Margot, my wife. Delighted to meet you, Mrs . . . ?'

The man holds on to Mum's hand after she has scrambled out of the boat and is standing up to her knees in the water, holding up the skirt of her dress in her other hand. He is leaning out over the side of the boat and his face is sunburnt and his expression is alert.

'Yes, thank you. I'm Angel Stone, and these are Foss and Ruby and Jem,' says Mum, looking distracted as Foss hurls himself off the boat.

'GERONIMO,' he shouts, splashing in the shallows.

'Foss, bring that basket here, everything will be soaked – come on, you lot.'

Mum waves to the sailing man and turns away and I look down through the opaque water and see a muddled blur of stripes reflected from his wife's T-shirt as they glide away.

'What's for lunch?' Ruby tugs at Mum's dress as we flounder up through sand deep and dry like brown sugar.

'I don't know. Ask Jem, he bought it,' Mum pants, collapsing on her knees at the highest point where we can see the frilling waves of the sea one way across the marshes and the black houseboat moored in the back-water behind us. This small stretch of sand is like a desert island, and is where we have had picnics every summer I can remember. The houseboat has always been there, and I still hope I will get into it one day. Though I never have yet. I have swum up to it and climbed on the roof so many times and the door remains locked, the curtains closed and I have never known what it is like inside.

'I need to get some cockles.' Foss crouches over his equipment and, selecting a bucket and a rake, he traipses off. Mum calls him back and gives him a sausage roll.

'You'll starve and then the fish will eat you,' she teases him. 'Don't go far, please, you are not old enough to be anywhere on your own.'

'I AM old and I AM going on my own,' says Foss, hysteria rising in his voice.

'You won't get any until the tide goes out, so just stay close by, and then we'll all go,' Mum tells him. Then her phone rings and Foss sidles away.

Even though he is only four, he knows there is a lot of escape time when Mum is on the phone. It's a good opportunity for me to get a sausage roll and remove the cigarettes from the plastic bag and I sidle off, too. I know where I am going – to chill out by the houseboat, out of range of Mum. I stop to look at Ruby's sandcastle. She's already made ramparts and stuck a silver plastic windmill on a hill behind it, and for once she doesn't even turn round or expect any input from anyone. She just gets on with it.

Mum's voice is low, mind you, it's always low; Coral's boyfriend Matt says it's full of sex. When he said it, it shocked me so much I couldn't speak for the whole amount of time it took me to smoke a fag on the roof with him. But now she is talking to someone very intensely. Sitting with her legs crossed and her dress all bunched up around her, the bracelets on her wrist glint in the sun as she pushes her hair back, and they clatter and jingle in a way that is as much Mum as her scent. I'm glad she's here, but I wish Dad was too.

A Perfect Life

The houseboat is dense, sooty black; it looks as though it's made of velvet, and it has dark red windows and a red corrugated iron roof. Under my body the sand is warm when I lie down, and a gorse bush shelters me from the breeze coming in from the far away foaming sea. The trickle of sand shifting under my head is so comforting. My eyes close and I let the cigarettes fall out of my floppy hand. I am not old enough to deal with my parents cracking up. They used to be in charge of all of us and I don't think they are now.

Last year when we came here, we brought St Granny – that's what we call Dad's mum. It was really hot and we lit a fire in a pit Dad dug with me and Coral and we had sausages and walked out for miles at low tide. St Granny went to sleep by the fire and Mum and Ruby and Foss collected a basket of cockles. I helped them. I like digging my hands in the mud to find them, and even more I like mud sliding afterwards. Dad and Coral and I had a massive mud fight and we had to walk miles to swim to get it off before we went home. There are photos some-where – I'll find them to show Mum when I get home. It was a lot better than today.

Angel

Cold like a blade rasping down the right side of her body wakes Angel. A sharp breeze from the sea snaking in with the tide, flipping flower heads, twisting stems of wiry sea lavender in its path, coils around Angel's bare arms to lick her flesh, raising goose pimples and an involuntary shiver. She is not sure how long she had been asleep, and the sun is behind a cloud giving the afternoon a flat sullenness. Blinking, stretching, shivering and remembering are simultaneous actions. Angel stands up and reaches for a towel, and looks around for the children.

'Hello-o. Can any of you hear me?' The sun suddenly spills out from behind a bed of cloud and the balmy splendour of late afternoon light unfolds like silk to settle on the marsh, diaphanous and lovely. Angel narrows her gaze to try and absorb the glancing sparkle of water in the creek and brightness stings her retinas, creating an imprint on her vision of tungsten blue and neon green patterns. Closing her eyes, the dark velvet of the lids dances with orange blobs as if she has been staring at the sun itself. Opening them again, it is as soothing as ointment to look at silver-green grasses bent and yielding in the cool sugary sand. Angel puts on Jem's cricket jumper and walks towards the sea. She has a warm feeling of pulled together-ness, she is calm and looking forward to getting everyone home. And seeing Nick. Dealing with it will be good, and however difficult it is, it won't last for ever. Nick will want to get away, he will go and cut the grass or settle into the sofa to watch cricket on television with Jem. He is unlikely to say he is coming back for good; there is no sign that Angel can see that he would want to. He has been away so much Angel feels he has already let go of their life at the Mill House. She feels his detachment, his desire never to be pinned down, is one part of their break-up. It has always been easy for him to say he wants to be around, but in reality, he never is.

There are spare ribs for supper, or as Foss calls them, square ribs, and she could make some kind of pudding – Ruby would know what, and she could get Foss to deco-rate it with the filthy synthetic cream in an aerosol can she noticed Jem had bought this morning. She will get through this. Angel breathes in deep the heady ozone, and smiles, passing Ruby's castle, a sensual series of undul-ations and humps, low-rise but large, very small-town American in its nonchalant sprawl, and highly decorated with sea lavender and razor clam shells.

'Where are you?' she shouts into the breeze. The sun

moves behind a small cloud and light drains out of the afternoon, the smell of salt and mud on the air stronger when the glare has faded; the silence suddenly too long. Angel's heart begins to race, unreasonably fluttery. Where are the children? All she can hear is the sigh of the waves and mournful piping of marsh birds. The drone of a plane cuts through, heavy, rolling across the sky like a lid. Angel takes a breath to shout and nothing comes out. The effort of breathing in again is huge now, as panic shortcircuits her body and she begins to close down, legs jelly, arms lead, voice evaporated. She is rooted in one spot, closing down. Her breath is fast and shallow like a dog panting. Suddenly, into her paralysed hysteria, the low mumble of Jem's voice dollops like cream, pouring delicious cool relief on to Angel's consciousness. And there is Ruby laughing back to him, both voices seeping comfort into Angel's ears. In an instant she dismisses her fears without a backward glance or a moment's acknowledgement. It is time to walk up to the bridge to get back and that will take at least half an hour. And then there is the evening to get through, and the square ribs to cook. Time to get on now.

The kids appear round the end of the dune, and Angel falls in step with them, ruffling Ruby's hair with her hand.

'Hi, you two, where's Foss? We need to get going.'

Jem and Ruby are carrying a bucket of water between them. They both look at her, blank surprise on their faces.

'We thought he was with you. We haven't seen him,' says Jem. 'Ruby came to get me to fill up this bucket and we've been right along the creek, but we left Foss with you.'

Adrenalin and fear surge back, filling Angel from her feet, pushing her breath out of her, hard, like a punch in the guts. She doesn't know how long she has been asleep, how long Foss has been alone, but the timbre of the day insistently repeats, 'He's lost, he is not here.'

Ruby's eyes, Jem's eyes, but not Foss's eyes, stare at her, waiting for her to sort it out. Waiting for her to fix the fault line in the afternoon. If only she could. Angel wants to scream and thump her fists against someone's chest. Her fingernails dig into her palms and she wants the pain because it is real, an effect of something she is doing. Foss not being here cannot be real.

The children are still looking at her, expecting something of her. What can she give them? She hasn't got Foss. Into her mind comes an image of a top hat, and herself pulling him out of it by the ears like a white rabbit.

'Oh. With me? No, he's not with me — I haven't seen him, I fell asleep — I don't know when I — FOSS . . . FOSS!' Fear cannot be contained for a moment more, it is rushing and physical, a torrent bearing Angel away. She can't keep still, she needs to move, pitching herself somewhere in futile defence.

She runs past the children towards the creek, scanning the horizon wildly. 'I should never have fallen asleep. How did I do that? Why did I do that? What have I done? He must be nearby, he must be nearby.'

Running, stopping, running again, the panic inescapable. Red panic, burning in her eyes and ears, releasing a racing torrent of blood through all her veins, starting, jolting immediately to a halt, stopping, piling up, jamming, arresting every thought, anger growling low like an engine, action snarled up and slowed to nothing, over-heating, not moving. Feeling sick with the relentless unending 'stoppedness'. If Angel could scream she would. Her mouth open, a creaking whisper emerges.

'Foss! Where are you?'

The marshes stretch in every direction, empty but filling up with water as the tide creeps in. The mud expanse in front of Angel is wet now, pitted with greasy dark puddles, and as in a nightmare, the day becomes threatening, the light flat and the mud oozing, silent and unyielding. She is afraid to shout again, afraid not to receive a reply.

'Let's ask St Anthony,' suggests Ruby, a mobile phone in her hand.

'Are you going to call him?'

Ruby raises her eyebrows and gives her mother a look reserved for idiots. 'Oh yeah, Mum, like you can actually ring saints up. How would I know his number? I am not God.'

Playground tears spring to Angel's eyes. Ruby is working something out.

'Mummy, how much will you give St Anthony for finding Foss?' Ruby doesn't notice Angel crying; her head is bent over the phone. 'I'm doing it on the phone calculator because I will give him two pounds thirty-seven which is all my money and Jem says he will give a fiver,' she says. 'So how much will you give, Mum, then we can pray?'

'Um, fifty.' Christ, was that the best she could do?

'OK, that's five. And two pounds thirty-seven, and fifty – Mummy, is that fifty pounds or fifty pence?' Ruby, frowning, is at Angel's side. She tugs her mother's sweater, and does not let go. Angel closes her own hand over Ruby's and squeezes the warm fist curled in her palm.

The next hour exists beyond time. Injected with determination Angel runs, her feet echoing on the slapping mud, sound ringing around the marsh as if it is encased in tin. Her breath is rough and painful, and a musty taste of foreboding sits at the base of her throat. She pushes it down and runs, her footprints marking her jagged progress to and fro across the marsh like a damaged heartbeat on a screen. Her mud-caked feet ache as she hits into razor shells and pebbles and her muscles tremble uncontrollably when she pauses, panting. Jem catches up with her. He flips open his phone, squinting at the screen.

'Shit, Dad hasn't called back,' he mumbles, throwing himself down on the bouncy sea lavender, his palms on his face blanking out the sky. Taking his hands away he sits up and looks at Angel.

'Mum, this is pointless, we should call someone. Get them to send a helicopter or the police. I can't get Dad, I've left so many messages on his mobile, and I think

Gosha must be on the Internet, because the home phone goes straight to answerphone. We have to let someone know.'

Angel shakes her head, crouching next to him.

'No, he must be here. We'll find him in a minute. Children muck around like this all the time. Think how many times I've lost any of you.'

'But Mum, we've been looking for an hour and we don't know how long he was gone before that.'

Ruby is a curve of dejection sitting on a plastic box by the creek. 'I prayed to St Anthony so hard. I even told him Dad would do a credit card thing when we get home. Mummy, I'm hungry, and I want to go home. I want Foss and I want to go home. Please.'

She begins to sob huge heart-wrenched gulps. Angel put her arms around her and Ruby is spindly and fragile like a bird.

'I think you're right, Jem, we had better call some help.' Almost gagging, Angel holds tighter on to Ruby. This cannot be happening, it just can't. But it is.

'OK.' All emotion leaves Jem's face, and he lights a cigarette as he waits for his call to be answered. Watching him, with the flashing sunlight behind him making her squint, Angel notices that he is different. The square of his shoulder hunched as he smokes and talks, is an echo of Nick long ago.

Nick

When does an encounter become a fling, a fling an affair, an affair a relationship? When Nick called Jeannie Gildoff this morning and asked her to meet him for lunch here at the motel, were his motives the same as they are now? Over the years they have had the occasional shag. Usually in London, when Jeannie is shopping or getting her hair done and Nick is on his way somewhere. They meet to fuck, and both of them have known that is as far as it goes. Or it always has been. This, though, could be different. For a start they are not in London, they are in the bedroom Nick is living in while his marriage shifts and cracks, perhaps irrevocably. And all the occasional shags add up in the end to something more. Or they don't. Jeannie is neat when she walks into his room; a mint-green handbag swings on her arm, she is wearing a red dress, her hair is flicked up at the ends. She smiles nervously, Nick takes in narrow ankles, black soft leather moccasin shoes and a cardigan swinging on her shoulders. Today she reminds him of someone, and as he kisses her cheek he remembers who it is.

'You look like Olivia Newton John in *Grease*,' he volunteers. 'Before she was corrupted.' Instead of stepping away from her, he moves closer, holds her waist and kisses her mouth. She tastes of coffee and biscuits.

'Seems pretty appropriate,' she replies when they stop kissing, and moves back, sliding her cardigan off. Her bare arms are brown and slim. No one has been in this room with Nick before; her presence is exciting, her whole posture, straight and supple, indicates strength and he always finds her cool exterior erotic.

'OK, Nick, what's going on? Did you get Peter's message about tennis this afternoon?'

'Yeah, I asked Coral to be my partner. I'd like to play you, Jeannie.' Nick slouches against the wall, looking at her, giving nothing away because he doesn't know what he is thinking himself.

'What do you actually want from me?' A sweep of black liner on Jeannie's eyelids contributes to Nick's sense that she is from another age. He wonders if she is wearing one of those satin all-in-one underthings called a kitten or a teddy or some such small cuddly name. He is not certain he wants her enough to go through with this today. The potential for complication is huge. And today of all days, when he has said he is going home to discuss whether or not he is really splitting up with Angel. He is unable to deal with reality right now; he knows that is why he called Jeannie. What he wants from her is oblivion.

Jeannie walks over to the window, tapping her fingers against her still-folded arms. She has freckles on her throat and the curve of her lower back flows into her rounded high arse. Oh, what the hell. He moves behind her, splaying his hands on her hips, sliding them round over her dress on to the flat of her stomach. She sighs, he whispers into her neck, 'Sex would be nice,' as she arches her head back and pulls in her stomach. He moves his hand further down, pulls up her skirt along her thigh and reaches between her legs. She has no knickers on.

'Sex would be fine,' she whispers back as his fingers slide up inside her. He is still behind her, his erection pressing against her. He unzips his trousers and groans; the fabric of her dress is cool and sensuous against his skin. She tries to turn round in his arms, but he wants her from behind.

'Stay there, I'm going to make you come,' he breathes, biting her shoulder, one hand still moving, rubbing her between her legs, the other on her breast, stroking her through the thin fabric of the dress. No bra either. This is fantastic, just fantastic. Jeannie is trembling; he runs his tongue along her jaw, she bites her lip and groans, rears her arse towards him. He pushes her forward so her arms rest on the window sill and light falls in stripes through the blinds. Nick lifts the skirt of her dress up, closes his eyes and pulls her on to him, both hands on her waist, as he slams his cock deep inside her and holds her on him as she comes. She wriggles, gasping, and he

219

fucks her, his rhythm fast, the sensation of her climax pulsing against him exciting, bringing him to sudden, intense orgasm.

Six missed calls from Jem's phone to his make Nick feel hunted and guilty when he picks up the messages after a game of tennis with Coral. Since this morning, when he had to listen to a message recording an argument between Foss and Ruby over a pair of swimming goggles, he has dodged family calls. They are at the beach with Angel, he will see them later, and he will deal with them then. Not now. Jeannie and Peter cancelled in the end. Jeannie, brisk and to the point, called an hour after she left the motel and said, 'I don't want to play tennis with you today, so I told Peter we'd take a rain check. See you around, Nick.' Nick was intensely relieved. He likes risk, but a game of tennis with a woman whose smell is still on him and her husband, is to Nick's mind more or less perverted. Anyway, he doesn't know what his next move is with Jeannie, though she is a great lay. In the end, he plays singles with Coral. He thrashes her. He is feeling great, pumped full of testosterone, sex and success as they walk home from the village court.

He will talk to Angel; maybe there is a chance that they will iron out the problems and he will have his life back. Extra-marital sex? Well, maybe he will stop that. It might be enough to take Angel to a few new places and seduce her. The motel room would be a good place to start. Lost in thought, he is surprised to be home already when they walk in through the gate. Coral turns to face him, a challenge glinting in her eye.

'Nick, I've decided I'm telling Jem and the others that you're not my dad. It's not up to you and Mum, it's up to me, and I'm going to tell them today.'

Nick's instant thought is, Bloody typical of Coral to muscle in and take over as the big story of the day, and his next thought, hard on the heels of that one, is, Good, that will take the limelight off me and Angel.

'If that's what you want to do, you have every right to do it,' he says to her. 'But just out of interest, why now?'

Coral blinks, and waits, shifting uncertainly, twirling her tennis racquet. She looks at him, measuring him up for a moment.

'I have had enough of the lies in this family,' she says, flouncing up the drive, making it clear the conversation is over.

Nick finally listens to the last of Jem's messages, the first to beep into his phone, at about five in the evening. Foss has been missing for two hours, but Nick is unaware of this and unable to detect the level of anxiety in Jem's brief words.

'Dad, we've lost Foss. We need you to come now.'

Another bloody mini-drama like Coral's. Not that Coral doesn't have a point, but why now? There have been eighteen years available for this. Dismissing her from his thoughts for the time being, and Jem for that matter, Nick decides to have a shower. He does not listen to the previous five messages.

As it turns out, it is the best thing he could possibly do. By the time he has shaved and changed, and is just walking out of the house to his car, Angel and the children are back. They look terrible. Foss and Ruby are crying, Jem is white and silent, Angel gets out of the car without even turning the engine off and lifts Foss out of the back.

'What on earth has happened?' Nick doesn't know who he is asking; his heart is thudding, all of them are here, no one is bleeding, but a lot is wrong.

'What happened to Foss?'

Angel looks at him and says shortly, 'Can we take him in first?'

Foss is black from head to toe, though tears have cleaned small white paths on his face. Nick slowly begins to realise that the drama was real. He feels equal measures of sympathy for Angel and inadequacy in himself. He should have known. Poor Angel. Christ, if only he had known.

'I'm going to give him a bath and put him to bed.' Angel's voice is tired and soft. To Nick, it burns like a brand on his conscience and the pain makes him angry. He tries to open the doors into the house for her, but she has done it already, kicking hard with her bare foot, and she starts up the stairs, murmuring to Foss, kissing his mud-caked hair.

Nick goes back out to the car, unease creeping closer, making his skin crawl.

'What's happening?' he says again. He can hear Coral upstairs with Angel; her voice floats out of the bedroom window.

'Oh my God,' she says. 'Oh Mum.'

Ruby doesn't run to Nick like she usually does when he has been away; she remains in her car seat, uncharacteristically wearing her seat belt, with tears coursing down her face. Jem gets out and slams his door, raising pink-rimmed eyes to meet Nick's for a second. Nick tries to win a smile.

'Whatever has happened to you lot? You look like you've been to war. I'm not even getting a look in!'

Jem glares, but his voice does not match the anger in his eyes; it is flat and wiped out like Angel's.

'We lost Foss. We looked everywhere and we didn't know he had fallen in the sinking mud. A man digging bait found him. We thought he was dead when they got him out. He had to have the kiss of life, but the ambulance says he's fine now. I had to cancel the coastguards.'

He stops and walks past Nick, then turns back to him. 'Why didn't you call me, Dad?' The break in Jem's voice freezes Nick.

Cooking pasta, not the spare ribs Angel had prepared, Nick strains his ears to hear where everyone is. In fact, he knows. They are all in the bedroom with Angel. Actually, they are all in the bed, and Foss, like some

Renaissance cherub, is propped in the middle, swathed in pashmina shawls and being stroked by his siblings. Nick knows this because he has been in attendance with a tray. It was Coral's idea to make hot milk and honey, and Ruby's addition was blackberries.

'It's like in *Peter Rabbit* after he was in Mr McGregor's garden. They are good for shock,' she explained, running upstairs with a bowlful. Nick feels that blackberries being ripe already as it is still only bloody August, is pretty shocking in itself, but no one is in a mood for jokes, and he isn't really either, though he has always enjoyed guillotine humour. Or is it gallows? Maybe both were used. He must look it up some time.

So this is it. Funnily enough, Foss's drama has changed everything in an unexpected direction. When he got home today, Nick thought that he wanted to plead with Angel, he wanted to create a chance to try and make it all work again. He was under some sort of illusion that they were still good together. But now, alone in the kitchen with Angel and all the children upstairs, he is defeated, lonely, and to be brutally honest, not especially interested. Why should he be? Angel has made it very apparent that she doesn't need him any more. Time to be realistic here. And it doesn't much matter now when it is that they talk about it; the details are unimportant.

With this thought he pours the pasta from the colander into a bowl containing cream and grated cheese and yells up the stairs, 'Come and get the Last Supper!'

A Perfect Life

They are all too far gone on shock to notice that Nick was not up to the challenge of spare ribs and he still cannot resist gallows humour.

Jem

I can't believe it. After all the drama of today, not to mention letting me down for about a week and behaving like a total jerk, Dad has now been to play tennis with Coral so he's not playing with me tonight. I am sick of being the most invisible member of this family – no, actually I am sick of being a member of this family, full stop.

Mum and the little ones are having a baby bunny nesting party in Mum's bed, and I hung out with them for a while, but there is only so much of the *Mary Poppins* film I can bear. Coral is being all whispery and twitchy and Dad's having a born-again house-husband moment in the kitchen.

I wish I could get out of here. I can't even get out of my head, because I've lost the bit of dope Coral got me and she is way too grumpy for me to ask for more. I would probably be back in Mum's room watching *Mary Poppins* if I hadn't remembered the spray paint.

Shit. If I had known what was going to happen there is

no fucking way I would have sprayed even one letter of graffiti on my bedroom wall. But I didn't know. I was like one of those lambs to the slaughter they have in the Bible or *Aesop's Fables* when Coral came into my bedroom. I was about to listen to 'All along the Watch Tower', so as well as everything else, one of my favourite songs has been ruined for ever now.

'Jem, I've got something I want to tell you – oh my God, what are you doing? Mum will kill you!' She is all angles in my room, and she is looking angry.

'Why? It's my room, I can do what I want.' I don't like Coral criticising me, and the graffiti looks good. I've only written 'Dub' and 'vole' as a kind of practice, and then I was going to do some lyrics. She sits on the bed, and Mum comes in too, holding Ruby's hand. Ruby is all clean now, pink and soft in her pyjamas with clean hair.

'Supper's ready.' Dad appears too, finishing off the audience, and my room is suddenly small and cramped. It stinks of paint.

Jimi Hendrix begins singing, 'There must be some kind of way out of here.'

If only.

Coral says, 'Good, now everyone's here. Jem, you need to know something. Nick is not my dad.' And she folds shut her mouth and clenches her fists as if she is about to be tortured.

'I am sorry, darling, we should have told you a long time

ago.' Mum hugs me, and her soft arms flop against the stone pillar I have become.

'He IS my dad,' says Ruby, never one to be left out. And she scuttles over to Dad. He has his hunted expression on. I never thought he would look like that over something to do with me.

For some reason I ask what is in my head. 'Are you *my* dad?' and Mum bursts into tears, as does Coral.

Dad nods. 'I think you should all come downstairs and we can have supper and talk,' he says. This is when I feel like a slaughtered lamb. We all follow Dad down to the kitchen and sit round the table.

'Where's Foss?' is my next ludicrous utterance. I have no idea what is going to pop out of my mouth, and my whole body feels as though it is moving through cotton wool. No, make that mud. Like the mud Foss was stuck in today.

'He's fast asleep,' says Mum in her soothing voice – and her tone is about as inappropriate as a sledge-hammer at a fairy tea party of Ruby's.

'Shall I explain to Jem and Ruby?' Coral is calm now. Mum and Dad are cowering at the table, but they don't look at one another once. Ruby seems to have taken the news in her stride and is twirling spaghetti on her fork.

Mum just nods, and pushes her pasta away. Dad sighs, and shovels his into his mouth.

Coral reaches out and puts her hand on mine. 'When Mum and Nick met, Mum was pregnant from her old boyfriend Ranim. He lives in India and though Mum really

229

loved him, she couldn't find him to tell him about me existing. Nick came along and rescued Mum from being a single mother.'

So Coral is some sort of fairy-tale heroine. Neither Mum nor Dad says a word. None of it is great, but the worst thing is that they all kept this secret from me. Rage, like a red mist heating my brain, begins to swell. I get up from the table and slam out of the door. On the other side I kick it and yell, 'Why didn't you tell me? What else is there that I have not been told?'

I kick the door again and Dad scrapes his chair back, shouting, 'Cut it out, Jem. You are way out of order.'

'Fuck you, Dad.' Even through my anger I am quite shocked to hear myself say that, but I can't help it. They should have told me.

Angel

It is his back view. Nick in the grocery shop in town.
Angel saw his car when she was parking, so she knew
he was there, but buying groceries was never an occu-
pation she would have imagined Nick engaged in, especially now he has been living at the Travel Lodge for
three weeks. He is at the checkout, and even though it
is only twenty odd days since she last saw him, he looks
different. His hair is lank, and his shoulders rounded.
He is wearing a grey patterned jumper, a middle-aged
man's golfing sweater, the sort of thing her father used
to wear. Angel taps him on the back, having fixed a smile
ready on her face. Nick turns and the sweater is tight
on the swell of his tummy, a swell new to him like a
pregnancy and echoed like a pregnancy in his jowls and
on his cheeks. An extra layer of Nick. There was definitely enough of him already, Angel thinks spitefully. She
gasps, realising she is shocked, groping for a proper reaction to unexpectedly bumping into her husband when
she has broken up with him. Nothing adequate springs

into her mind, just a sliver of meanness, a small shaft of anger that he has stepped into her consciousness when she was not expecting him.

'Hi, Angel.' Nick blinks, stepping back to look her up and down. Aware of this familiar routine, Angel shrinks inside; she had seen him do this so many times and now she is another woman for him to look at.

'You look well,' he says, his demeanour rueful.

'Thanks.' The silence needs to be filled, and Angel is smarting from the pain this encounter is bringing. Determined not to allow anger to erupt, and wanting to protect herself, Angel retreats behind a wall of breezy civility, treating him as though he is a passing acquaintance. She smiles brightly, and says, 'It's very nice to see you, but I've got to go and buy some mousetraps.' She hears herself and has to shut her eyes for a second to regain sense; it may be self-protection, but this is going nowhere and she wants to laugh to break the tension. Nick looks nonplussed, as well he might, Angel thinks. He turns back to the waiting cashier. The shop is about to close, so will the hardware shop across the road. It is true that Angel does not want to miss the mousetraps. And she is flailing for things to say to Nick; ironic and yet it sort of makes sense that with the whole of their life together behind them, it is hard to pick a topic to start with. Impossible, in fact. Angel feels unequal to the challenge.

Nick is still paying, his back turned towards her.

Muttering, 'See you soon, Nick,' she walks away through the frozen food section towards the exit. It would be better if she had bought something, but she can't remember why she came into this shop, and she feels she might burst if she hangs around any longer. Beside the ice cream counter she almost steps on a woman's toe. Recoiling, she recognises Jeannie Gildoff. Jeannie smiles. Angel sees alarm in her eyes change quickly to guarded friendliness as she rakes her fingers through her red hair. Why is she here? This is not her local town. Oh God. Like a curtain dropping, Angel watches Jeannie's red hair swing across her face. She remembers the boys on the street in London. Telling her what she already must have known. Nick was kissing a redhead.

Automatically Jeannie and Angel reach forward and kiss one another on the cheek, Angel half aware of how absurd it is to be embracing in a fucking grocery store and to be kissing her husband's mistress. It is the missing piece, the part of Nick he had not told her existed. Jeannie is the one. And now she knows. Angel thinks all of this, and her instinct of self-preservation pulls her back from saying anything.

Jeannie fills the silence. 'Nick's over there.'

'Yes, I saw him.' Angel wants to run. And she wants to go and buy mousetraps. But she stands quite still, asking Jeannie about her children, her mind shifting, fragmenting like a kaleidoscope.

She says, 'Has Heath finished his exams yet?'

And she is thinking, *Oh God. How can I get out of here as fast as possible? Jeannie is the redhead they saw him kissing. How long has it been going on? What is going on? Is this what Nick's been doing?*

Nick is no longer in the shop, or so Angel assumes. He would certainly want to escape this scene. If he had seen them meet, he would have been quick to get out.

'Yes, he's working for Peter now.'

'Good,' says Angel. As if she gives a flying fuck.

How on earth can she get out? How will this conversation that is about nothing ever end? The two women look at one another and questions tick and ricochet through their minds, while they make polite conversation.

'The forecast is good for the weekend,' says Jeannie.

Is her stomach flat?

Did he love her?

'Oh good. I'm actually here buying mousetraps. We're overrun,' says Angel.

Did they have sex last night?

Does she still love him?

'Oh, they are such a nuisance, aren't they? But at least when you have mice they say you don't get rats,' says Jeannie.

What does she look like naked?

What does she look like naked?

'Really? I wonder why that is?' ponders Angel.

Does she make him happy?

Did she make him happy?

234

'I don't know. I think they each like their own king-doms,' replies Jeannie.

Will they stay together?

Why did she leave him?

'Oh look at the time, I must dash,' says Angel, waving her watch in front of her own face.

Was this what was wrong with our marriage all the time?

I've got him.

I've got no one.

'Yes, so must I. Very nice to see you, Angel.' Jeannie leans forwards and kisses her. Again.

I wonder who she's sleeping with? Peter always found her very attractive.

I miss sex. Even though we never had it, at least I had someone I could have had it with.

'Bye, Jeannie. See you soon.'

Does he love her?

'Bye, Angel, take care.'

Back in her car on the street, Angel hurls the mousetraps on to the passenger seat and sighs, trying to collect a million fragmented thoughts. And Nick appears again, walking along the pavement – well, shuffling really. He passes right next to the car; he must recognise it, but he is looking at his telephone, and he appears not to see Angel or their family car. Angel sits quite still, watching him pass by and walk away. In her rear-view mirror she sees him turn the corner into the car park. And that moment is sad and complete. The end of their time together. How strange that the real end should turn out to be so small.

Angel wishes she were addicted to something as her compulsion to be destructive to herself is a flaming heat as she drives home. Unable to think of anything she can do, she turns up the music as loud as it will go and accelerates. Seeing Nick with someone else has broken the final link between the two of them. They are both free to spiral into nothing or to make new lives. It is sometimes difficult not to succumb to madness. When she gets home, Angel realises she has not bought any food. And she has a thousand other things to do now, but she can't remember what any of them are. The garage on the main road will still be open. Angel sits in the kitchen making a list. On it she writes:

> *Loo paper, coffee, milk*
> *Pick broad beans*
> *Water fucking sweet peas*
> *Tell children re divorce*
> *Call Mum*
> *Book dentist*

What is the worst thing about this list? Well, obviously that she has so little grasp of reality that she could put a time bomb in the middle of a shopping list. Staring at it, part of Angel wants to collapse in self-pity. But why? What good will it do to anyone? The will to survive and adapt kicks in, and Angel feels calm. This has happened, she is still alive and ultimately, so what? Life is full of lessons to learn and things to deal with. Angel has the list she has written to get through, and that is enough for now. She decides to start with the dentist and goes through to her study. The room has been shut too long and is bursting with heat. When Angel opens the door to the garden, fresh air wafts in, stirring the stuffy, hot atmosphere and changing it, like piano music pouring into silence. Angel turns on the computer and listens to the messages on her phone.

'Hi, Angel, this is Jake Driver. I thought I'd let you know how things are going here. It would be nice to speak to you.'

Angel hardly takes the message in at first, she is still staring at the list, but Jake's voice filters into her head finally, and she hears, 'I hope you're having a good time this summer and you are not homesick for work. I think work might be missing you. Take care, and give me a call back sometime. Bye.'

How nice of Jake. Angel smiles to herself, pleased and relieved to be taken out of her own loop by his call. She presses his number on her phone. Jake answers immediately.

'Hello, Angel. How are you? I was just thinking about you. How have you been?' His voice is cheerful and clean and uncomplicated. Angel has never been to his flat, but in her mind it is in a wharf or a warehouse and is full of tawny wood and hard clean steel. Sexy and empty. No clutter.

'Hi, Jake, thanks for calling me. Are you still at the office or are you home?'

Jake laughs. 'I'm not that keen, you know – it's nearly seven o'clock. I am at home, I'm just getting myself together to go out.'

A jolt of desire courses through Angel. She swallows.

'Oh, I'm so sorry to disturb you. In the kids' holidays I get out of sync on what office hours are. I'll talk to you at work sometime. I'll let you go now.'

But Jake is quick to pull her back into the conversation. 'No, it's fine. Like I said, I was thinking about you.'

Another jolt – recognition that he wants her too.

'Were you?'

Loneliness, a longing to be wanted, a craving for physical connection – oh God, a thousand feelings keep Angel on the phone while sense is shouting in a microphone in her ear that she has enough to deal with right now without starting some idiotic affair with someone from the office.

Nick has only been gone a couple of weeks, and here she is, a semi-married woman with four children, flirting on the telephone, coiling her legs around the chair leg, twisting her hair and making her voice a purr to say, 'What were you thinking about me?'

And Jake doesn't answer immediately but Angel knows

he is grinning and she is not surprised when he says, 'I don't think I can tell you that.' She is not surprised, she is delighted.

'Oh good,' she says, after another pause.

Jem

I was waiting for Mum to tell us. I realised that as soon as she did tell us, because it felt like a relief as well as like a fucking enormous kick in the guts. I don't know why she told us all together at once, because that part of it was a nightmare. But I guess it was a nightmare anyway. I didn't want to hear any of her crap so I came outside and lay on the lawn. I wonder how much I care, but it's too difficult to work out. The window is open right behind me, so I got the rest of it like some really lame radio play, wafting out of the window through all the roses and contaminating the summer sky with everyone freaking out. Well, Coral isn't exactly freaking out, she is angry.

'Coral, please stop pacing around like that and talk to me.' Mum's pleading voice sounds desperate – she shouldn't let everyone know how much things matter to her.

'Mum, I am almost nineteen. You cannot tell me what to do.'

I don't know what's the matter with her anyway – he

isn't even her dad – she's got another one. Somewhere. I suddenly think of the whole of the world being full of Mum's discarded husbands – though I don't think she was married to Coral's dad – and them all being morose and alone without any of us, and Mum crying and it is all unspeakably sad for a minute.

'Mummmeeee!!!! Tell me what to do. I don't know what to do. Where is Daddy going to live? When am I going to see him? I love Daddy, why can't you just love him too? I am very upset, Mummy.' Ruby is half crying but she is loud and clear.

Mum says, 'Are you all right, Foss?' and this very small mumble only just makes it out of the window and he says, 'Are you getting divorced because of when I got stuck in the mud and you lost me?'

Bingo. The whole lot of them start crying and talking at once and in the end I have to get up and walk right down to the tree house and climb up it and put one of the cushions Ruby left there over my head so I cannot hear the sound of them. I have never got around to thinking whether or not I believed in God before, and I'm not thinking about it now, but I suddenly found I am praying with all my heart that someone will arrive to help us deal with this. From the shrieks curling like smoke out of the house I can tell that Mum is not handling it. It feels like an old comedy movie, because from where I am in the tree I see the house on three sides and three doors slam. Ruby comes out of one, running towards the gate

– I don't know where she is going. Out of another comes Foss, running as well, and he heads straight to the pond and sits down on the edge. Then the back door opens and Coral shoots out and she throws herself on the lawn like I did a few minutes ago. That leaves Mum, the black widow spider alone in her web, back in the house. Poor Mum. No – fuck that. Poor me. What the hell is going to happen to us now? Where is Dad, anyway? I don't know what I feel about him right now. But I bet Mum decided it – I can't believe Dad would do that. Maybe it's because of Jeannie Gildoff. Jesus, what a waste. Oh my God, that means she'll be our stepmother. I didn't think I could cry but I am crying now and it's all an angry fist in my chest to punch Jeannie stupid Gildoff with.

Nick

The call could not have come at a more opportune moment, which just goes to show that all the flannelling and polishing of acceptance of a Higher Power in the AA has a purpose. It's time to get to a meeting.

'Nick, hi there. This is Jake Driver.'

'Oh. Hello. Um.' Nick pauses in the street outside the office and leans against the glass wall of the building, confused for a moment as he is standing outside the office and Jake must be calling him from inside.

'Hi, Jake. I'm actually just on my way in. Do you want to come and find me in my office?'

'It's not a work-related issue, Nick.'

Oh, how dreary. Nick wishes he had the will-power not to answer his phone when he doesn't recognise the number calling him. Jake Driver is nice but dull. Angel fancies him, Nick can't see the point of him. Though he is good at his job. And friendly. There is no need to be unhelpful, after all.

'Oh, OK, Jake, what can I do for you?'

'Well, I was hoping you might be available to play cricket for the office team on Saturday. And Jem, if you and Angel are happy for him to play against adults.' How nice. Nick is glad he took the call now; it pays not to be a dickhead sometimes.

'Yes, I think Jem will do it too.' Nick wonders what Angel will say. Actually, she won't say anything. There is nothing challenging in this, it's just cricket.

'Yes, Jake, thanks, that would be nice. See you then.'

Nothing special there, but the ordinariness of it is as welcome as a six-figure bonus right now. Where is his cricket kit? Will Jem play? Does Jake know he and Angel have split up? Does it matter? Will Angel let him back in the house to do some nets with the children? Will she come and help make the cricket tea? No, that is pushing it, even as a fantasy.

The cricket pitch lies like an oval pool surrounded by oak trees in the midst of poppy-stained cornfields. A small pavilion painted pale green and cream stands to the side of the pitch, facing the church. Pads on, shades clamped to his nose, Nick squints through the sunlight watching Jem in bat. Jem had been very reluctant to play.

'I hate fucking cricket and I hate playing with a bunch of old wrecks,' was his unsatisfactory response to the invitation. Angel was no sodding help either; she just crossed her arms and said coldly it was up to Jem who he played cricket with. Anyway, here he is, and frankly

Nick feels a bit aggrieved that after all his begging to get his reluctant son to come and play, Jem is above him in the batting – in fact, Jem is number three. And he, Nick, is in at seven. Matt, Coral's boyfriend, is playing too, and he is batting at four. There's no accounting for it, but it stings, Nick has to admit that. Not that Jem seems to notice – he just grunted when Nick told him the batting order.

Angel arrives, driving up to the pavilion with unnecessary flamboyance and one of her God-awful country and western CDs blaring misery. You would think that cowboys had written the book on the agony of the human condition from their endless moaning. Nick is a rock and roll man through and through. For him there is nothing Jimi Hendrix can't say that is worth saying in terms of music.

Anyway, Alan Wilson from accounts is padded up next to him and adjusting his helmet now to walk on to the pitch as Matt, only in for an over, hits a fulsome catch right into the hands of the bowler.

'Good luck!' urges Nick, a pulse drumming in his neck. The game suddenly matters so much to him that he wants to cry. Jem has found a patch of excellent form, and Nick's focus on him is intense. His son hits two fours in quick succession.

'He's a good player. Look at how fluid he is.' Jake squats next to Nick, chewing a blade of grass, his cap pushed back giving him a boyish appearance. Against his better judgement, Nick finds he likes him. Jem is facing again.

Angel comes out of the pavilion, and smiles sympathetically at Matt as he walks in.

'You did well,' she says.

'Thanks.' Matt grins. 'I'm not in Jem's league though, sadly.' And he puts his arm around Coral and walks over towards his car with her. Janet, Nick's secretary, joins Angel on the veranda.

'Wow!' she says involuntarily as the opposition bowls a blisteringly fast ball and smashes Alan's stumps.

Jake groans. 'You're in, Nick. I hope you do better than him – he's out for a duck. At this rate the game will be over by teatime.'

Jake moves over to Angel. Janet has begun talking to someone else, and her voice floats across to Nick as he walks out to the wicket: 'Oh God, Nick's in. And Jake Driver is next. Well, this could be fun, don't you think?'

Angel, laughing at something Jake has just whispered to her, doesn't hear, or pretends she doesn't. Nick wedges his helmet on and twirls his bat. Every fibre in his body creaks with the strain of wanting not to be out for a golden duck. And more than that, but more difficult to acknowledge, he wants to stay in longer than Jem.

He tries to unclench his jaw, but it is set as if in stone. This is probably what having dentures feels like, he finds himself thinking.

The afternoon sun filters the light, yellow and nostalgic. David Bowie's 'Heroes' suddenly fills Nick's head, the denture sensation slides away down his throat and he has a moment of rare joy. He hardly ever admits, even to himself, that there are things he enjoys. Life is to be endured, sensations and emotions are strictly mood-altering, and enjoyment is something he doesn't even know he is missing. A huge grin spreads across his face, partly hidden by the helmet, because right now he really loves cricket, and he is happy.

In a very peaceful surrounding, the absence of white noise allows the tiniest of sounds to amplify, and around Nick the trees rustle, a blackbird flutes some sort of natural love song and he hears Jem whisper, 'OK, Dad.' The bowler's feet thud down the turf towards him and yes – the best sound possible, the thwack of willow on leather as his bat makes contact with the ball and he and Jem run, or, in his case, waddle to the other end. Christ, running in pads is hard work, is Nick's first thought on reaching the opposite wicket, closely followed by, Thank God I am not facing the bowler this time, and At least I'm not out for a golden duck.

Jem hits another four – his fourth of the match, and a small spattering of applause wafts across from the pavilion. Nick's heart cracks, and fatherly love flows through him. Jem, who seems to have grown about six inches since coming on the cricket field, has also acquired a noncha-lant confidence and grace. Or maybe he always had them, and it is just Nick's perception that has shifted. This is certainly the first time he has ever been aware that when he looks into Jem's eyes they are level with his own.

Another ball, another run and now he is facing the bowler again. This ball is fast and he does nothing but stop it dead. As the impact reverberates through his arms and down his spine, Nick's concentration surges and focuses on the game, his restless mind soothed by the gentle unfolding of order, the inevitability of runs notching up, and the clear visibility of what each team is trying to achieve, that is the structure of cricket. Minutes pass, and Nick and Jem bat and run, pause and watch, and implicit trust forms between them. The straggle of spectators is a crescent of colour along the curve of the pitch on the pavilion side, fading to nothing but the odd figure walking a dog at the woodland end and a muddle of cars parked along beneath the wall to the graveyard at the farthest part of the ground. Nick is on seventeen, Jem heading for fifty, and a symbiosis has developed between them which Nick loves. Even more, he loves not noticing it because he is concentrating on play. Fully present in his game.

Jem hits a six off the last ball of the over, and passes fifty. He takes his helmet off and rubs his hands through hot damp hair, looking over at his father.

'How're you doing, Dad?' He grins. Nick wants to cry. He never had a moment like this with his father. He never had a moment at all with his father that belonged to the two of them. You couldn't count the last moment, when he kissed Silas's yellow, puffed cheek in the hospital ward and walked away, holding his mother's hand, not daring to look across at her in case she was crying. His father died of liver failure aged forty-seven, the age Nick is now. Nick was sixteen, the same age as Jem.

A bull-necked farmer comes in to bowl. Nick swipes and it is all over. Like a kick in the balls from the girl of your dreams. And you are set up for it from the moment you first step on to the pitch. His stomach disappears from inside himself as he unscrambles his thoughts, reminding himself bitterly, *This is what life is really about. Disappointment. And the walk in is the longest two minutes of your life since the last time it happened.*

'Oh Dad.' Jem leans on his bat, hunched and sorry.

Nick manages to smile. 'I'm glad it was me, not you,' he says, and is surprised to find that he means it.

Angel

September has a way of inhabiting the early morning air, imbuing it with crisp purpose, a brisk energy that is different from the excitement of spring when everything is new, or the lush presence of summer, but is mature, redolent and strong. Angel feeds the hens and her footprints are a path of soft darkness on the silvered dew. Today she will take Foss and Ruby to school and deliver a letter to their headmaster telling him she and Nick have split up and are getting divorced. The letter is already on the kitchen table and the thought of it keeps her outside, wandering around the house, mentally dead-heading the buddleia but not touching it, pulling browned rose petals off the fat hips as the sun gathers strength.

Jem went back to school yesterday, into the sixth form. Angel took him and his suspiciously small amount of stuff to Ely yesterday evening. Dragging the bags into his room, the smell of polish and the squeak of fire doors swinging took her back to being seventeen at school herself, and how awful, yet also what a relief it was to get away from home at the end of the holidays.

'So, here we are,' she said, sitting down on the edge of the bed. Jem threw himself flat behind her and pulled his cap down over his face. Jem's room overlooked the walls of the cathedral. Angel stared out at the massive wall of stone and the sun going down behind it, softening the towers and the atmosphere.

'I hope this term is fun.'

Jem grunted. There was no chance she would say the right thing.

'I got expelled from here.' This was almost certainly the wrong thing to say, but she was running out of time and to leave with stilted silence was wrong – it was what her parents used to do. Jem pulled off his cap and smiled.

'I know you did,' he said.

'But do you know why?' This was not a confessional; it was just a chance to get a conversation going.

'Wasn't it for running around naked?' Jem put the cap back over his eyes.

'Yes, basically that was it.' Angel wished she had been expelled for something less mortifying for a teenage son. 'I was wearing this trench coat to go into town and for some reason I decided to take it off at the end of the High Street and run back to school with no clothes on.'

'That is so stupid,' said Jem.

Angel laughed. 'Yes. Completely stupid. And I have done lots of other stupid things too.'

'Yes, you have,' said Jem. Angel looked at him. He was still hidden by the hat, but he pulled it off again and looked back at her.

'Mum, I've got to unpack and get my stuff to meet my new tutor after supper.'

Jem stood up. Angel's stomach flipped because she didn't want to leave him. She got up too. Jem started taking his speakers out of the box on the floor. His phone rang.

'Yeah? OK, I'll meet you in a minute.' He smiled at Angel, friendly but busy. It was time for Angel to go. She was not going to cry.

'Bye, darling, have a good time.' There was nothing adequate to say. She hugged him, and Jem was taller. He had grown in the holidays and Angel reached up to kiss him.

'I'll see you next weekend,' she said and walked out of the door as Jem's phone rang again.

'Yeah? OK. I'm coming.'

Leaving Ely in the dusk she was glad he could just get on with his own teenage life. And she hoped he would not get expelled.

Pausing on the door step, the cool dark kitchen and the contemplative ticking of the clock offer a different mood from the busy, gold morning outside with the sound of cars accelerating along the road, a dog barking somewhere and leaves whispering around the house. It is time to get the children up. In fact, it is well past time to get the children up. Racing up the stairs three at a time, Angel erupts into Foss's room to find him sitting on the edge of the bed, fully dressed.

'How did you do that?' she gasps. It is almost sinister: the school shirt and v-neck, the grey shorts and knee socks give a ghostly frisson – a 1930s version of Foss. Even his wild hair, cut yesterday at Hair to Impress, a salon with salt-caked windows on the sea front, is tamed this morning.

'Gosha did it. She's helping Ruby now.'

Feeling grateful, Angel lifts Foss off the bed and kisses him. 'That is so wonderful of her. Now you come downstairs and we'll have porridge.'

'I would rather have cheese strings,' says Foss hopefully, alive to his mother's good mood. 'Or pork pie.'

It was a good idea to wear dark glasses. They are a shield once the children are safely in their new classrooms. Ruby clings to her, wrapping her arms around Angel's waist, lifting her feet off the ground and wrapping her legs around her mother too. Angel's skirt begins to fall down. Mrs Little clasps her hands and keens towards Ruby.

'Come on now, we don't want Mum in here all day, do we? We've got to get started with our work. We're doing the family tree and I know you will have lots to contribute, Ruby.'

'I don't want to.' Ruby has her eyes fixed on the floor,

her face buried in Angel's stomach, tears where her eyelashes brush against Angel's skin under her shirt, like a paintbrush sweeping watercolour over paper. The letter to the headmaster is dismally inadequate. Angel glances around, hoping a small confessional box might suddenly appear so she and Mrs Little could have a quiet moment, during which she can stick a blood-letting instrument into a vein and expel some of the guilt.

The classroom is full of healthy freckle-faced, sun-tanned children, hair neat and cut, clothes slightly big and creased from shop packaging, clamouring for their desks, their pencil cases, waiting their turn to show Mrs Little their lunch money purse, or their newborn baby sister, or their reading book. And beside each small child stands a smiling mother, focused, gentle and interested, each one uniquely engaged with her own child but united in their willingness to make everything easy for their darling offspring returning to school after the long summer.

Angel wants to belong. Ruby is yanking her, like a sandbag pulling her down. It is time to go. Undoing Ruby's grip from around her waist is unseemly, but luckily her concentration lapses as the bell goes, and Angel makes her escape. She is almost out of the playground, when Alice West catches her.

'Oh, Angel, I am glad I got you, how was the summer?' Her hand on Angel's arm is cool, there is a small clatter of gold bangles.

'The summer? Oh you know, full of life.'

Does she know? Is Angel being cowardly not to bring it up? What is the protocol? With no idea, Angel realises she just has to smile and be friendly and see what happens. This is a bad idea.

'We're having a meeting to kick-start the Parents' Association autumn programme and I wanted to make sure we had it on a day that was good for you.'

Oh hell. Oh fuck. It is her own fault. Angel distinctly remembers last summer at the school camp-out, drinking a tooth mug full of whisky and approaching Alice to say, with guileless insincerity, 'If only I knew when your meetings were I would so love to play a more active part in the committee. This sort of thing is what life is all about.' Such crap. Even if she wasn't getting divorced, joining the Parents' Association is on a par with becoming a traffic warden or learning to play bridge on Angel's list of things never to do.

Alice flicks back her hair. Angel opens and closes her mouth, stress or distress gathering like fog. A coffin floats into her mind, inspired by the confession box, no doubt. It is open, and cosily lined with white cashmere, inviting and gentle.

'I must be going mad. I always wondered what it felt like.' Unintentionally, Angel speaks her thoughts; Alice has taken a step back.

'Pardon?' she says, blinking, her face wiped clean of the cool smile.

'Oh, I mean – I'm so sorry, Alice, I've got a lot on this

week. Let me call you from home when I've got a diary in front of me. I'm sure we can work something out.'

'Well, I could give you a few possibilities. If—'

'Thanks, I'll call you from home.'

Angel smiles and flips her sunglasses down with determined finality. It is fine to leave. Alice can't block her path, and now she will walk out, just like that. She takes a breath and the school gate clangs behind her. No footsteps follow, no voice calls out. Angel runs.

At home there is a lot to do and the house is strange with no children in it. Angel drifts through the rooms, keeping away from the kitchen where clattering plates tell her Gosha is clearing breakfast. The shutters in the sitting room are closed, and light spills in through the gaps in bright bars, falling like rails on the carpet. Angel lies down on the sofa and, finding a phone on the floor beside her trailing hand, she calls Jake's number, pressing the buttons fast, not allowing herself a moment to think or regret.

'Jake?'

'Hello, Angel.' He doesn't sound surprised, he sounds pleased, successful, and sexy. The springing adrenalin in Angel steadies to a fast pulse.

'Hello. Jake?' She must have called him before in the morning, but today something is different. Maybe just her awareness, which seems to have taken on panoramic acuteness so every word is open to illicit interpretation.

There is a smile in his voice. 'Yes, I'm Jake. I'm just walking along the Backs on the way to work. Where are you?'

He sounds like he wants to know. Angel presses the phone closer to her ear and hears his breath.

'I'm on the sofa.' Angel's nerves scream, 'Stop!' She is heading into dangerous territory, it is right ahead of her. She does nothing. Holding her nerve takes every pulsing of adrenalin, and her heart thuds in the silence.

Jake takes a while to answer. 'Are you?'

Angel wriggles down and lies flat, pulling a cushion on to her stomach, biting her top lip and smiling at the ceiling. He is good at this game. He has clearly had a lot of practice.

'Yes. And it's dark in here, I haven't opened the shutters yet.' She is not bad either, for a beginner. Crunching footsteps on the gravel outside are followed by the clang of the doorbell.

'Sounds like you've got visitors,' says Jake, and that's it. Gone. The intense flirtation is not there any more. Jake sounds brisk and businesslike, and Angel answers him lightly, following his lead back from intimacy.

'So I have. Let's talk later,' she says, then wonders what they are supposed to be talking about.

'I'd like that,' says Jake. 'I'll call you later.'

What has she done? What is she trying to do? What is she going to say?

Opening the door, Angel is still smiling. A red-faced man stands in front of her; he is holding a red leather collar.

'I caught the dog but it slipped out. It's gone off with

those sheep chasing down towards the school. You should get your animals fenced properly. They could cause an accident.' He waves the collar at Angel; suddenly she recognises it.

'Oh, thank you. It belongs to Vespa. My dog, I mean. What sheep?' Sometimes the effort to focus on the here and now is too much. Inside the house the telephone begins to ring. And she remembers that she does have sheep. Two sheep at the last count. Oh God. Jem was looking after them in the holidays and Angel has not thought about them for weeks. No wonder they escaped, they probably want to be fed. When had Jem last fed them? Yesterday, with any luck. The man turns away, shaking his head, smiting his brow in exasperation.

'People like you shouldn't have animals,' he mutters. 'They said they were your sheep. Small ones. They were standing in the middle of the road, but as I said, they've gone down towards the school.'

The scene sounds absurd and familiar. Angel is trying not to laugh.

'Yes, they are my sheep. How funny that they chose to go that way – towards school, I mean, rather than anywhere else. You know – "Mary had a little lamb, its fleece was white as snow" . . . mind you, these ones are brown, but the next line is, "It followed her to school one day which was against the rules".'

The man gazes at her. 'I am glad you find it so amusing,' he says witheringly.

'Sorry,' snorts Angel. The phone rings again. 'Please excuse me.'

She shuts the door then opens it again to shout to him, 'I'll come and get them. Just give me a moment, please.'

The man marches off down the drive, and Angel slams herself in the study. Animals, divorce, children, Nick, work, Jake. Oh God.

Gosha taps on the door.

Angel is ready for action. 'Oh good, Gosha, please could you come with me, we've got to get the sheep and –' Angel tails off as she takes in Gosha's slippery mauve lipstick, thick spiders of mascara and pale green high heels. 'Oh!' she says.

'Excuse me, do you have the pocket money for me? This is the day to go to college.'

Of course. College. Angel had forgotten this is part of the au pair deal in term time. Feeling guilty for not putting Gosha's needs on her list of priorities, she scrabbles in her handbag for her wallet.

'Oh, I'm so sorry, you must have your money. I'm sure I've got some of it. Oh, ten pounds isn't good. Shall I draw you a map? I'll just see if I can find some more money somewhere.'

Angel dashes out of the room and up to Ruby's bedroom, ignoring the telephone as it rings yet again. Ruby always has money. A small pink wallet covered by a notebook on Ruby's dressing table bulges with cash.

'Twenty-four pounds, thirty-seven!!!!' she reads on the

last page of the book. Feeling sinful and like a baby snatcher, she takes the twenty pounds and writes on the next page, 'Mummy owes you twenty pounds plus interest!!!!'

Nick

Getting through immigration at JFK always feels to Nick like a prize in itself, so to him every trip to New York begins with a bonus. He hadn't really meant to go this month, but the children going back to school coincided with a conference on global manufacturing, and Nick suddenly couldn't bear to be staying in the Travel Lodge, knowing his small son and daughter were going back to school as the products of a strife-torn family. Sliding into the comforting squashiness of a cab and sinking back so all he can really see is the roof, and the coil of greasy black hair his Sikh driver has pinned up under what Nick always thinks looks like a small, crocheted beer mat, he shudders, part exhaustion, part recollection of the night before. There he was, in the Travel Lodge, lying on the neatly made brown bed, channel-hopping and drinking cup after cup of bitter, nausea-inducing coffee from the endlessly dripping filter machine. The football highlights were over, and reality TV had hit all channels like a virus. Even Nick, whose capacity for avoidance was bottomless, could not watch another simpering girl with pumped-up lips and a soppy mind expressing her entirely unoriginal feelings on spending three days tucked up in a house full of strangers. Ten minutes of feverish texting was the next attempt to get away from pain. Before he had even told himself he was going to get a plane to New York the next morning, he was asking Jem if he wanted any music brought back, and composing a balletic dance, avoiding truth, to tell Foss and Ruby he was going away on Angel's phone. There was no reason Angel shouldn't know he was going to New York; he just didn't feel like telling her himself.

Having sent these messages, Nick had the double sense of achievement of having created a new reality for himself and having something to do tomorrow. Content to go to bed once there was no gaping void ahead of him, Nick took two of the sleeping pills he had stashed from Angel's supply and lay down. He did not sleep.

So today he is in transit and fucked up, two of his most familiar states of being, positions from which he feels numb and therefore to some degree comfortable. There is so much to do, and the time lag means that he is safe now to do much of it without anyone from home calling him. His favourite thing about being in America is that he can lead so much of his life while everyone he is important to is asleep and so in some way, in Nick's mind, does not know and therefore cannot be harmed by his antics.

He is here to buy the apartment. The cab stops in a

snarl of traffic stretching from Queens right the way to the tunnel. He closes his eyes, remembering something from the end of *War and Peace*, when Tolstoy makes an argument for momentum deciding outcome, not generals, or battles, even. This applies to Nick and his new roots. Momentum is buying this apartment. And a mortgage with the Bank of America.

Booking his hotel room from the cab on the way into Manhattan, he feels spontaneous and free, and looking at his watch he realises he can make a seven-thirty NA meeting a few blocks away on the Lower East Side. Going to a meeting is the best way Nick knows of feeling he has arrived somewhere.

'Grounding', as his last sponsor was keen on saying.

The community hall door is slightly ajar and the scraping of chairs leads Nick into the right room. He has been to this meeting before, and last time it was packed, but tonight there are not more than twelve people in the room. He sits down on a sofa next to a girl. She is sucking her thumb. It is difficult to look at her, because he is right up against her, but out of the corner of his eye Nick sees enough to make him uneasy. Her legs are folded in the lotus position, pale blue jeans so tight that they look like skin. Even though she is sitting very straight, her head does not come above the back of the sofa. She is minia-ture. Nick is sure she is a child. He glances around to locate her mother; it is unusual to bring kids of her age to meetings, though he has from time to time seen toddlers, hooked around their mothers' legs. Mothers with babies at meetings always cry when sharing. It's a universal truth.

A woman opposite Nick sways from side to side, her arms clasped tight around a purple fluffy hot-water bottle in the shape of a hippopotamus, her legs black sticks, made thinner by the contrast at her ankle, where flesh disappears and her feet are engulfed in pastel-blue slippers decorated to look like racing cars. Nick wishes the meeting would start. A construction worker, still in work overalls, his dark skin pressed with plaster dust, sits down next to Nick, his hands restlessly turning a battered cigarette packet. Beyond him, the polished toe of a pair of handmade brogues taps the air, and the crossed legs of a Wall Street banker make a cage around his soft brown briefcase.

'He was about as inconspicuous as a tarantula on a slice of angel cake.' Nick's favourite Raymond Chandler line is always worth bringing out and trying in a new situation. It works well here. More or less everyone in the room is black and poor. The air smells of cinnamon coffee and hot bodies. The meeting is opened by a pumped-up black dude, gold chains heavy on his wrists, his fingers constantly pinching his nose as he sniffs, clears his throat and talks. Nick is prepared to bet the whole of Fourply on the fact that he is a former cocaine addict, and sure enough, the story comes out.

Nick sighs, listens, and relaxes for the first time in

weeks. He had forgotten the great American godliness, never more pronounced than in a meeting, and there is something utterly inclusive and soothing in the ritual mutterings of 'Amen' and 'Hallelujah' that accompany the familiar structure of the fellowship. Nick has a warm sense of being included and when he introduces himself he finds himself saying, 'Hi, I'm Nick, and I am a former alcoholic and drug addict. Today I understood that my marriage is over, and I feel lonely and frightened. I am very grateful to be here tonight.'

'Thanks, Nick,' choruses the group, and Nick feels his guard drop like a cloak with the sense that no one here hates him and everything might just be all right. He has a tentative feeling of hope, and glances at the faces of all these strangers who wish him well, just for being himself and being here. He realises he has been bracing himself against judgement for months, maybe even years. He rolls his shoulders, stretches and sits back, sighing a long breath of relief. How is it that he has stopped going to meetings? What got him here this evening? He decides to share. A woman finishes sharing her most recent relapse. 'Thanks, Barbara,' says the chorus.

'Hi, I'm Nick and I'm an alcoholic and drug addict,' he repeats, comforted by the familiar repetitive words of re-introducing himself.

'Hi, Nick.'

Nick finds it is always the same when he shares in

meetings. He resists, almost plunges, resists, and then as soon as he jumps in, he is swimming and the muddle that he thought was in his head becomes something he wants to say.

'I just arrived here from London tonight and I am tired, but I'm glad to be here,' he begins. 'And being somewhere new, and in the familiar structure of this fellowship, is helping me see where to go. The changes in my life may look like personal catastrophe from the outside, and I have wondered if relocating to New York as I plan to do is just another escape, like drink was, like drugs were, like sex is, but it is more than that.' He looks around the room. No one seems disgusted; he catches the eyes of the woman with slippers, she looks back at him kindly, steadily.

He goes on, 'It is never too late to get the point of your own life. I'm not confident that I have grasped it yet, but at least I can see it. And that's a start.'

He finishes before his time is up.

'Thanks, Nick,' chimes the group and the collective voice is supportive.

The construction worker follows. 'Thanks, Nick. Hi, I'm Mo and I'm a recovering drug addict and alcoholic.'

'Hi, Mo,' say Nick and the rest of the meeting. Nick feels safe and grateful and accepted. He falls asleep. No one minds.

Six the next morning and Nick is in the gym, rather to his own surprise. CNN news scatters images of war-ravaged Middle Eastern cities and weather-torn tropical islands and Nick pedals obediently up and down imaginary hills, exhaustion forming small crystals in his muscles. He will move to New York after Christmas. Life will begin again. Like it always does.

Lying on his back pushing absurdly heavy dumb-bells up into the air a few moments later, he changes his mind. Foss and Ruby. Foss and Ruby. Jem. Jem, Foss and Ruby. His children. Angel. His wife. Well, ex-wife now, but not someone he can just forget. Indeed, he has experienced several moments of hope that now they are splitting up they might communicate better. It could happen. Nothing is so bad it can't be made a little better.

The girl with the thumb in her mouth shared at the meeting last night after Mo, and Nick cried for her innocence and prayed she could find it again. She was a child. She was eighteen. She had the most startling rasping voice and her face behind the curtain of hair was blank and stunned. There was nothing Nick had not heard a thousand times before in her story of trashed mother, absent father, abuse from stepfather and then on the streets with a pimp and a heavy crack addiction. But this time he heard her and he thought of his own children, and he thought of the choices he had made in life to have come to this point with his children fast asleep in their house in rural England and himself sitting next to another terrified child, hearing her choosing to face the world with nothing rather than continue on the grim path her life has been.

His children, like all children, deserved better. He had no idea of how to give it to them, but he wanted to try.

Jem

The only reason I am going home this weekend is that Coral is having a party before she goes to university and I want to go to it. She called me instead of just texting me at school because she was so surprised that Mum let her.

'Hey, Jem, what are you up to?'

'Nothing, of course, it's so boring here.'

'Mum says I can have a party. She reckons I have had a hard time too and I deserve it.'

'Great.' Mum is really bugging me and I wish she wasn't going to be there. But Melons will be, so it's worth putting up with Mum asking too many questions. She can't help it, I know she's worried, but she set this thing up and she can't expect everyone to just carry on like life is normal. Thinking about going home is weird. Dad doesn't live there any more. He doesn't seem to live anywhere. When I asked him where he was living he said, 'Good question,' which is not much of an answer. So he's gone. I don't really live there now because I am in a cell at school most nights, though I can come back at weekends, and Coral is about to not live there because she will be in Sheffield at university. That leaves Mum and the midgets. They hardly count as life forms, and I bet Mum decides to get rid of Sky TV. If she's got rid of Dad that will definitely be the next thing to go. She hates it and she hates all the cartoons Foss and Ruby watch. Mum keeps sending me stupid texts. The worst so far is: 'I am in the woods, thinking about you playing rugby. Just caught a gold leaf, so am sending it to you with a kiss.'

I mean, what is that all about? How am I supposed to reply to that? Coral says she's doing too much meditation and that sort of hippy shit.

'I think she wants to find herself,' Coral says, giggling, when we speak a couple of days before I come home for the party.

'She's a bit old, isn't she?' I am in my study talking, and there is condensation on the window panes so the nights must be getting colder.

Coral puts on a stupid voice. 'Oh no. You're never too old. D'you want to speak to Mel? She's found herself already.'

There is a lot of giggling. I reckon they have been at the vodka or whatever Coral has bought for the party.

'Hi, Mel.'

'Hey. Looking forward to seeing you at the weekend.' The funny thing about Mel is she has a tiny voice. Big tits though.

'Yeah, me too.'

Mum is at the station to meet me when I get off the train. Jake has brought her in his red TVR. And of course the top is down and he is listening to Genesis. Great. How can Mum have such a geek friend? I can't even go into whether he might be her boyfriend, it is beyond rank. So I am supposed to sit in the back of a spivvy sports car while Mum yaks away about what an exciting weekend we are going to have. I don't see why she should get away with it.

'Where's Dad?'

She more or less deflates in front of my eyes; if it wasn't so shocking, it would be funny.

'He's staying at one of Jenny and Steve's holiday cottages. He says it is like living in an aquarium because it is in that courtyard village thing they built, but he can stay there for the winter and it's quite cosy. I'm sure he'll want to show you it.'

'I might go and stay with him this weekend.'

That knocks the final air out of her. 'Oh, OK,' she says.

Jake has been on his mobile phone all the time since I got in the car. Now he turns round to greet me.

'Hi, Jem, how's it going?' Mum had always said we mustn't make judgements about people because of their clothes, but how can anyone wear a custard-yellow polo shirt with long sleeves? If he is Mum's boyfriend all I can say is she is making a big mistake. And how embarrassing is it for us? He is nearer my age than hers by miles.

We are driving up the hill and away from the sea, and turning down the winding lanes that lead home from the station. I suddenly desperately want Dad to be at home when we get there and for it all to be normal. I wouldn't even mind Jake hanging around if Mum and Dad could just live together and be like they have always been. It isn't easy lighting a cigarette in the back of a TVR with Phil Collins breathing away and wailing about 'something in the air', but it is worth it. Inhaling is a big fix of defiance and my gaze holds Mum's in the mirror. She doesn't say anything. I can't believe it when I see Jake is singing along. It isn't that anything is wrong at home, it's just different in an empty way. Even the fact that Gosha the au pair has left is different, though I don't know why, because au pairs always leave.

Jake drops us off and I leave Mum to say goodbye to him. I don't want to see if he kisses her, or rather how he kisses her. In the TV room, Foss and Ruby are sitting on a pile of magazines each and the sofa is upside down.

'We're looking for the keys to the tractor. Daddy wants them and he says he will give me five pounds if I find them. Mum doesn't know where they are either.'

This is Ruby's greeting. Foss waves a bread stick at me.

'This is nice,' he says, dipping it into a pot of yoghurt. Basically, they have gone feral. I am so relieved none of my friends came home with me this weekend.

'Where's Coral?'

'They're having sex,' says Ruby without looking up from the TV.

'What? Did Coral tell you that?'

She giggles. 'No, not Coral, silly, the people on this deserted island who are camping. Look, they're both in the same sleeping bag.'

'Oh yeah.' I watch for a moment. It is some pornographic crap. Finally it sinks in. It really IS some pornographic crap, and I react. 'What the hell are you watching?' I grab the remote control. They have got on to one of the Sky adult channels.

Ruby pouts. 'I've seen it before. One of the babysitters Mummy got for us last week was watching one about a plumber.'

Oh my God. We need a new au pair.

Angel

Agreeing to Coral having a party was the easy bit. In fact, Angel wished she had offered it first.

'You deserve to have a good time,' she says when Coral comes in waving the invitations which are in the shape of pouting red lips.

'Do you think so?' Coral looks disbelieving and, pinning one of the invitations on to the kitchen noticeboard, she leaves the room. Angel's hopes that the party might mend broken lines of communication with her daughter dwindle again. Coral is unreachable, distant. She is either on the phone, or waving a hand as she disappears out of the door and into Matt's car, arriving home at the heart of a group of girlfriends, all jangling identical earrings and smiling secret smiles. Matt goes back to university a couple of weeks earlier than the others to do a course, and Coral finds a whole lot of new interchangeable friends. Angel is not sure where they have come from.

Talking to Jenny, whose daughter Ally is the same age, is a relief.

'The girls look twice the age of the boys, and the boys look like they could have half-fares on the train. I can't believe they are old enough to drive,' says Jenny, and Angel laughs.

'The ones Coral brings home are either like that or they look about thirty. I don't know which is worse.'

Angel and Jenny are walking through the village to collect Foss and Ruby from school. Angel goes on, 'None of Coral's friends seem to have anything to do. Having a job doesn't feature, and when I suggested to Coral that she might go to the village pub and earn some cash waitressing, she glared at me and said, "That is not what I worked my butt off for at school, Mum. I am having a break, just a few months, not even a gap year like lots of people, and I start university in October. Is that OK with you?" I was pole-axed. So I didn't even react.'

Angel laughs it off now with Jenny, who has a similar story about her own daughter, but at the time, she was confounded by Coral's fury. Coral's hands were on her hips, her jaw was thrust forward, and Angel retreated, shaking, not sure how she could have done it differently, but quite certain that there were ways to handle children so much better.

Coral had been at boarding school for the past five years, so Angel was quite unused to the daily presence of a grown-up member of her family in the house. Her privacy was gone at the moment she was convinced she needed it most. And as Jenny suggested, Coral probably knew it and resented her mother for needing space.

Right now, though, is lunchtime on Saturday, the party is tonight, and Angel has had enough privacy this morning to send her into a decline. Jem is still asleep, Ruby and Foss are waiting, with a packed rucksack between them, at the bottom of the drive for Alice West to pick them up and take them to a play date.

'We would rather wait down there,' says Ruby, 'because then you won't waste time talking to her like mums always do, and she can't have coffee.'

Waving them off, Angel ponders their unpredictability. Until now, through all the years when Angel was working and unavailable, Ruby swung on her arm every time a friend came to play, pronouncing orders she wanted carried out from the moment of the friend's arrival.

'What you have to do, Mummy, is say to Mrs Killross, "Would you like to come in for coffee?" And you have to make sure you have some cake on a tray and get one of those white pots for coffee which has cups and saucers.'

'Oh yes, and then what?' Angel is always fascinated by Ruby's visualisations, or indeed hallucinations.

'Then you talk to her, like she's your friend.'

This also clearly has an agenda, and Angel wants to know more. 'What might we talk about?'

Ruby considers for a moment. 'Well, probably it would be things like your daughter's ballet exams and things like that,' she says. Ruby's vision is so solemn, consuming and important to her; Angel is uncomfortably aware that she has never had a conversation about a ballet exam with any other mother, nor has it occurred to her to do so. All this must change.

Today, though, there is not a moment to practise ballet conversations as the need to get all the sleeping teenagers to get up and do something presents itself. They clearly had a practice run for the party, after the pub last night, if the stack of bottles and cigarette packets in the fireplace in the sitting room is anything to go by.

Throwing them into a bin bag, Angel wonders if she has got this wrong too. Is it a mistake to let your teenage children drink and smoke in your house? Oh probably, but who is making the rules anyway?

Wandering into the hall, Angel shouts hopefully up the stairs, 'Is anyone getting up?' Returning to the kitchen she begins to pace between the fridge and the table, thinking of all the things that need to be done for Coral's party.

Clear the barn, find a lot of candles, set up the trestle tables, get the music out there, and then someone has to go and buy some more drink. And it would look so nice if they put lanterns along the top of the wall. Writing a list in bigger and bigger writing, as if the size of it will make things happen, Angel quickly becomes carried away.

A quick coat of lime wash over the barn would give it a real lift and the whole thing could look like the Buddha Bar if they got that sea grass matting up from the cellar and put it down with a few beanbags and candles floating in a bowl or something. The familiar reflex of managing and perfecting kicks is like a buzz of adrenaline. Angel is hooked immediately; all that needs to be done is for someone to make a start, and who better than she? Coral and her friends can take over when they get up.

Angel makes her way out into the yard. It is a softly beautiful day; the damson tree droops with purple fruit, their dusty lustre like cabochon garnets, Angel's favourite stone. She pauses to look across the fields and the smell of autumn in the air fills her with a sense of aching loss. Blue smoke drifts from a bonfire, and otherwise everything is still, basking in gentle autumn sunlight. Reaching to unbolt the barn door Angel forces herself to remain focused on her plan. Doing something always makes her feel better. She just needs to get on with it. So it is surprising to hear a clear voice inside her shout 'STOP!'

'Why?' Angel wonders, ready to dismiss the voice. Being busy, and making things perfect, is so reassuring, so familiar, so soothing. It's like staying in a bath that is no longer hot enough – if she keeps all of herself submerged and tries not to create any movement on the surface, it is fine, but any unusual action which might bring her into contact with the world above the water will be uncomfortable and dreadfully cold. This is how she feels about being organised. Suddenly she is just too tired. None of it matters. Coral can do what she likes for her party, or she can do nothing, it is all the same to Angel. The thought of spending the afternoon scrubbing a barn for a bunch of teenagers is absurd, a mind-blowingly unnecessary and unrewarding project. But what can she do instead? How about nothing? There are a thousand things that need doing. Angel finds herself walking past them all, past the kitchen where Coral, Mel and another tangle-haired girl are coughing and shuffling food from the fridge to the table, their faces pasty with mascara rubbed beneath their eyes. Angel glances in, but backs out again. Her sympathy is roused by the skimpy neediness of their bodies in T-shirts and baggy pyjama bottoms, but it is subdued again by her own tiredness. And suddenly she is in bed, with the curtains drawn, sinking in, but so empty she can imagine evaporating and not being there in the bed when she wakes up and looks for herself. An out-of-body experience is how Jem would see it if she told him.

'Hey, Mum, I've got you a cup of tea.' Jem wakes her, a bit like a ministering angel, but only because he is wearing a white gown. It turns out to be a boxer's satin dressing gown Angel has never seen before. Switching the bedside light on creates a well of warmth in the lilac shadows. It is late.

'Are Foss and Ruby back?'

'Yes. Foss is green.'

Angel sips her tea. Jem sits down on the bed. His face has changed since the end of the summer, and features that were too big then, like his jaw and his ears, are now in proportion again. He is balanced between childhood and being a man. Not realising she is smiling fondly, Angel stares at him over her cup.

'Why is he green?' she asks.

'Oh, he wanted to be an alien or a frog or something at the party they went to. He says he's not going to bed, by the way, and he's gone to help light the bonfire. Coral's friends are all coming in about half an hour. Can you stop looking at me like that, Mum.'

'Sorry, I was just thinking.' Angel rubs her eyes, then jumps. 'Oh my God. What time is it? We haven't done anything! I can't believe you let me sleep so long.'

Angel slops her tea on the bedside table and throws off her duvet. Jem throws it back on.

'Mum, chill out. It's all done. Matt's here. He got back an hour ago, and Mel has brought the drink and they're setting up a tequila bar. Ruby's dressed up as a belly dancer, and I wanted to know if you thought I should wear this?'

Angel looks at him again. He stands up and turns around. She gets out of bed and switches the overhead light on. Jem fills a lot of the space in her room.

She hugs him. 'You look great,' she says.

Jem hugs her back. 'Thanks, Mum,' he says, and digging into his pocket, he takes a cigarette out and flips it from his hand up into his mouth. He grins at her, a measuring expression on his face, and says, 'By the way, your boyfriend Jake called.'

Angel raises her eyebrows. Jem raises his back.

'Yes, Mum?' he says politely.

'He is not my boyfriend,' says Angel, throwing a pillow at him. 'We are friends. That's all.'

'Whatever,' says Jem and, grinning, walks out of the room.

So now she knows what he has been thinking. Angel sits down on the bed again. Jem has presented her with the memory of an encounter she had not thought of for years. It must be the dressing gown, or maybe the heart-breaking hope that is youth. Or maybe it was the mention of Jake and the possibility attached to him. Twenty years ago, when Angel was at art school, about to finish her degree, and she went to an election-night party. It was the only time in the whole of her adult life that Angel had shown an interest in politics, and even then her interest was purely a reaction against her father, who had six months earlier given a large amount of money to the Conservative Party to coincide with his inclusion on the New Year's Honours List. She could not even remember who was standing for Prime Minister. Anyway, it didn't matter. What mattered was the boy. A beautiful boy.

Now, lying back down on her bed and closing her eyes to focus her mind, she cannot remember his name. But he had sexy, sleepy eyes and he was wearing a white dressing gown over his clothes. At the party they leant on a window sill together and looked out at swans floating past on the river beneath the derelict shoe factory next to the art school, and they talked about belief. Angel must have been drunk, because she often was then, but despite this she could remember what happened. She could see him by her side as they walked along the river towards the house she shared, and his dressing gown gleamed in the street like the swans had gleamed in the water half an hour before.

At the door of her bedroom, a chance remark by Angel brought them to the election, and by the time they were inside the door, he was defending the Conservatives and sounding just like her father when he said, 'And there will come a time when you will change.'

But he was beautiful, tall and lean and she wanted him. Inside her room, he asked her what she had voted.

'I didn't get round to it,' she replied, reaching up to take off his dressing gown.

'You didn't? Think of the suffragettes who died so that you could have the vote.' He took off her shirt and pulled down her bra so it fell like a lace belt around her waist and he licked her right across both nipples then picked her up in his arms. She kissed him back, wanting him and pushing him away at once. He put her down close to the bed.

'It's my business and my choice,' she said, but maybe he didn't hear because he was taking off his shirt over his head then folding his strong arms around her. Too tight. Her breasts hurt, pressed hard against him, but it was exciting, too. She struggled, he held her tighter. His eyes mocked her. He bent and kissed her hard, and bit her lip gently.

'Doesn't sound like choice, it sounds like apathy to me.' He kissed her breasts again, and he bit her nipple this time. She gasped, throbbing everywhere, wanting and not wanting pain and pleasure from him. His mouth was on hers, and his hand on her breast massaging softly where he had bitten.

'I don't like you,' she said, and pushed back out of his arms. He laughed and pulled her back towards him. She was curious and afraid. Her body wanted him; his hand moved down between her legs and she squirmed away, avoiding showing him how turned on she was. The conflict was arousing her more; she ran her hands down his stomach and pushed her fingers down inside his jeans. He took them off, and pulled her skirt up like a fan around her. They lay together on the bed; he moved on top of her, pushing her arms flat on the pillow behind her head. She looked at his face, and all his beauty was just bits of flesh bolted together, and his eyes were flint-cold, oily with desire, and they flickered across her like a snake's tongue. And she realised that she was probably looking at him in just the same way. She wanted him. She didn't like him. She had never fucked someone she didn't like before. It turned her on.

It is funny now, twenty years later, but she remembers how powerful she felt when he came. It was her only one-night stand, and it was great sex with a man she never wanted to hear from again. In fact, this is the first time she has so much as thought of him in years.

She gets up and goes downstairs. In the hall it is difficult to navigate the lower stairs as a bank of beanbags and cushions block the way. A small green goblin and a mysterious belly dancer with a purple veil are dragging them out through the kitchen to the barn, where music pulses fast and erotic in the gathering dusk.

Excitement catches in Angel's throat. Even though she is under strict instructions to stay at the other end of the house and not talk to anyone, a party is a party, and Coral has pulled out all the stops.

'Hey, Mum, what do you think?' A cloud of citrus perfume, and the sugared smell of cosmetics mingled with tobacco, envelop Coral and Mel. They are both sparkly-eyed and with their skin gleaming, anticipation in their pouts and their laughter, and even the provocative way they blow a kiss to extinguish the candle guttering by the barn door. They prop themselves in the doorway and light cigarettes, looking out, chattering to one another, their eye make-up flashing kingfisher-blue above smooth cheeks. Anticipation and sex, promise and risk hang in the air, heady and exciting, intoxicating as champagne. Angel folds her arms then unfolds them and enters the barn. Wisps of sleep hang around her, and she feels clumsy and slow. The beams twinkle with fairy lights, the space smells of sea and flowers, and someone has artfully heaped cushions on a velvet bed in one corner.

No words come to mind for Angel, just a sense of relief that she hasn't had to do anything, and a proud welling of recognition that Coral can make things nice herself. She wishes Coral's father could appear – probably, she thinks dryly, on a cloud of mind-altering drugs, but it would be satisfying to share with him the celebration of their daughter becoming an adult. Angel finds it odd to think of Ranim now with no heightened feeling. He would be middle-aged, late middle-aged, and he has missed out on knowing Coral. The sadness Angel feels in this thought is for Coral, not for him.

Having dreaded this rite-of-passage moment ever since Coral embarked on adolescence, Angel now finds herself accepting it easily. Maybe the morphine of tiredness is colouring her reaction, or maybe recognising this change is making her tired, Angel isn't sure which. She sits on the purple velvet bed and looks up at the sparkling stars Coral has hung from the beams. She is not responsible and it's a good new feeling. This is Coral's evening and Angel does not need to do anything to make it happen or to make it a success.

Jem

Waiting outside the headmaster's rooms for another sodding lecture is just so pointless. I don't know why they bother. Mum doesn't care if I smoke, Dad smokes and he used to jack up heroin every day, so what does it matter if I go and smoke a roll-up on the River Fields? It's not illegal. I am sixteen. I'll soon be seventeen. I don't want to be here anyway. It was all right getting back here after the summer. In fact, it was good to be away from everything at home. I didn't have to think about Mum and Dad at all. But now I miss home, even though it's weird there.

School is run by a bunch of losers. I mean, who cares if you walk on the grass or don't do up your shoelaces? And the new kids are so tedious and they've got over that silent and polite bit when they first arrive, and now they are all acting like they are auditioning for *Just William*. Someone told them about speech day and how these guys took a car to bits and took it up the octagon tower of the cathedral and reassembled it there and now they never stop taking things to bits. It is so random.

'Ah, Jem, come in, please.' Mr Manson – named after a serious killer, according to Dad – pokes his head out of his door. I hadn't noticed before how tall he is, but his head appears round the door miles above where I was expecting to see it. In the room he waves me to sit on the sofa, where I know from past experience that if you throw yourself into it, you more or less vanish. It is so deep your feet don't touch the floor, which is a disadvantaged position to be in. This time I just sit down perched on the edge.

'I am sorry to see you again, Jem.'

Jesus. What kind of life is this? I mean, do I need to be called into rooms by people just to be told they don't want to see me?

'I'm sure you are, sir,' I say, as a silence yawns between us. There is no way I am going to look at him, though his small eyes are fixed on me the whole time. I find a carved bunch of grapes on the fire surround and look at that. Mr Manson's swivel chair is to the right of the fireplace. He moves in it and it creaks. From the corner of my eye I notice that the arm rests are engulfed by his massiveness, and the stand with its little wheels looks way too small. It will tip up soon, I hope.

'Your parents have written back to me in response to the last letter I sent about your smoking. I dare say you have spoken to them?'

Have I? Why did they write to him? I don't think anyone mentioned that they were writing to him. Mind you, I hardly ever speak to them anyway any more. Dad's been away for so long that I wonder if he's really in jail, not in America at all, and Mum can't be bothered because she's too busy getting divorced and talking on the phone to her friends. And probably getting together with Jake, though I asked her at Coral's party when I was pissed and she said she was just friends with him and we had nothing to worry about or some crap like that. Anyway, she isn't so busy she hasn't got time to interfere right now. Manson is looking at me just like I imagine his serial-killer relation looked at his victims.

'I shall read it to you,' he says.

'Good,' is all I can think of to say. He gives me a filthy glare – more hostile than murderous – and he reads:

Mr Manson, I was surprised and disappointed to receive your letter concerning Jem and his inability to follow the school rules. I feel Jem has huge integrity and that given the right support, he will do well in the rest of his school career. If you decide to ask him to leave, you will be doing him a great disservice.

I can't believe Mum has done this. For a moment I wonder if Manson made it up, but, weirdly, he is frowning too. I would have thought he would be pleased to get Mum backing him up like this. She has betrayed me. I shouldn't be surprised. I mean, look at the other things she's done without telling me. I feel like all my escape routes have been blocked and I am stuck in childhood with stupid rules for the rest of my life.

My next thought is maybe she is on my side in some coded way, but that, too, has to be banished when Manson folds up the letter and presses his fingers together. It would be too much to say that he looks triumphant, but let's say he certainly does not have the air of someone who has just been warned off by a kid's parents. And that's the other thing. Has Mum told the school that she and Dad are getting divorced? I wonder why I hadn't thought about it before. But if she has, they will all be expecting me to crack up, so I may as well get on with it. God, why does everyone expect so much of me? I just want to get on with my life and my mistakes. I wonder where Dad is?

Nick

Driving is good. Ruby up in front next to him, Foss in the back. Straight to Woolworth's to get one of those DVD players that go in the car, and a stack of films featuring slugs and molluscs. That sorts Foss out; Ruby is different. And the way she is different is that she is like Angel. Guiltily, Nick tunes back in to her monologue; he has not been listening since they left Woolworth's. He has been thinking about Angel's back, her lower back – a part of her body she has never seen. A part of her body he always felt had been created to have his hand placed upon it. This morning she bent to pick up Foss and kiss him goodbye and when she lifted him into the car her T-shirt rose halfway up her back and he wanted to touch her there more than he had wanted to for years. Why is that? Why want her now? She is unavailable. What is the fucking point?

'DADDY! LISTEN. I AM TALKING TO YOU!' Ruby waves her pale blue cap in his face, calling him to attention.

'Daddy?'

'Yes, Ruby?'

'You know Tom, don't you?'

'Uh.'

She has her large grey eyes fixed unblinkingly on his profile. He has no idea who or what she is talking about. There are no references in that sentence, no clues. Maybe Tom is the man who now puts his hand on the small of Angel's back and pulls her towards him –

'Anyway, Tom sits next to Michael and he's got dark hair. It's darker than fairy hair usually is – he had the cat's brain, remember?'

Christ. Doesn't sound Angel's type, unless she's gone very Aleister Crowley, but maybe Ruby's talking about a horror film.

'Cat's brain?'

Ruby nods, distracted. 'Yes, but they're not real. You know Mrs Peel, she's the one you asked about my piano music?'

Nick spots the clue – this is school she is talking about, not a film. 'Oh yes,' he says untruthfully.

'Well.' Ruby crosses her legs, brushing her skirt smooth and the gesture is so familiar to Nick as the way Angel punctuates conversation, that it is hard to believe this is not her beside him in the car. He pulls himself together, making an effort to bring his mind back to Ruby here and now. There is no more Angel in his car. That is finished. Ruby chatters on.

'Mrs Peel is Tom's mother – did you take me to school the day when he had cat's intestines or was it Mummy?'

'Cat's intestines?' What sort of school is it that she and Foss go to? As far as Nick can remember it used to be quite normal, so what's with all the foulness?

'Yes, he had them in the classroom one day. I really like Tom Peel, you know, Daddy. The cat's intestines weren't real.'

'Oh. Good. What were they for, then?'

'Oh science, I suppose. Actually, I think the day you took me he had a huge snail. Do you remember? But it wasn't real.'

It wasn't real. What is real? Nick wonders, and what the fuck is he going to do with Ruby and Foss? It is Saturday morning, ten-thirty. They have already spent a couple of hundred quid in Woolworth's, it's raining, and Angel is not expecting them back until Sunday night. They think he knows what he is doing; worse still, they trust him to know what he is doing, and he has no idea. Indicating out into the traffic on the main road, Nick pauses as a lorry swishes by. He pulls out behind it; the wipers clean an arc like a curtain, pulling back over and over, rhythmic and repetitive.

'Anyway, Tom Peel has got freckles and he had to wear a hair slide and pretend to be a girl in our drama lesson because he was being Achilles when he's on the island of Skyros and he is hidden among the maidens and then he can't resist catching the ball they throw.' Ruby giggles at the thought. Nick glances across at her and can't help laughing too. God, she is cute. He feels he has made a terrible mistake until now. He has not noticed the full extent of Ruby's adorableness. He needs to catch up.

Suddenly he knows what they should do.

'Let's go to the Larkham lighthouse. Maybe we can stay the night there. I'm sure someone told me it's a bed and breakfast.'

Ruby is dubious. 'But it's raining. Do they work when it's raining? I think it's a waste of money to have them on when it's raining. And is it expensive to go to bed and breakfast? Tom Peel went in a taxi to his dad's house in London and it cost one hundred and forty-five pounds and his dad paid it himself, well, I think—'

Foss interrupts with elliptical assurance from the back. 'No, they are meant for rain because storms are when they get wrecked. Ships get wrecked in storms, don't they, Dad?'

'Mmm.' Nick shoots the car into a garage forecourt. 'Go and buy some sweets,' he says, giving Ruby a fiver. 'I'll wait here.'

Ruby is gleeful. 'Five pounds. Yippee! Shall I give you change, Daddy? Or is it two pounds fifty each? I think Foss is a bit young for that many sweets, you know.'

Ruby jumps out of the car and opens the back door for Foss. He climbs out and puts his hand in hers and they walk into the garage. Nick bangs his fist on the steering wheel and grits his teeth, pinching the bridge of his nose. He shuts his eyes and sadness like a blade pierces him. Just now he cannot remember why this has happened. What is he doing on a rainy Saturday with Foss and Ruby and no Angel? He cannot feel any faith in his ability to function, to be with the children, to survive the next twenty-four hours. It's just too lonely. He bangs his fist on the steering wheel again and reaches for his phone. He doesn't have anyone to call, but using it is one of his pain-masking reflexes. He turns it on; it beeps a message.

'Hey there, Nick, it's Carrie from Holder and Casey in New York. It's kind of early here, but I didn't get a chance to call you yesterday, and I thought you would want to know as soon as possible that all the paperwork you signed last week is in place now and the deal is through. Your keys are here. Congratulations.'

Carrie. Honey-blonde hair and red knickers. A lovely afternoon a while back. He hadn't seen her when he was signing, a thin man had dealt with him, but it was nice to hear her voice. Nice but not the answer. None of it is the answer. Nick turns off his phone again and finds he is crying. He puts his head on the steering wheel and does not try to fight it.

Angel

Rain. Closing all the open windows, running around the house to pull them shut, Angel enters empty room after empty room. How strange to be in the house for a whole weekend with no one here. There are so many things to do and now she can get cracking. The first place to tackle is her study, where the filing needs a good two hours, then there is washing up and tons of jam to make. The damsons are building up, creating an arson in fruit bowls around the kitchen, and she has a recipe for pear and ginger pickle that she wants to try out. Angel sits on Foss's bed, and her strength seeps out, down to her feet. The sensation is like wearing Wellington boots full of water. She draws her feet on to the bed, musing about jam jars and wondering if she is the same person as the Angel who used to think nothing of making ten pounds of jam in a morning. She feels as if that part of her had been removed surgically, and replaced with a cavern of black. She shudders, not wanting to investigate any black right now.

The red flannel sheet is soft and cosy; Foss's bed is surprisingly comfortable. Angel pushes aside a festoon of camouflage netting and gets under the duvet. She has never lain in this bed before, or even slept in this room, unless it counted to perch on the bed to read a story to Foss. The eaves create a ceiling like the Egyptian pyramids upside down, and along their sharp sides, clouds and saints float. Foss's neon set of saints, given to him last Christmas by Nick's mother, Naomi.

When Nick told Naomi that he and Angel were getting divorced, she sighed and walked out into the garden and on into the nearest field. Nick said it was ghastly. He felt she was passing on the news to God and getting His spin on it, and when she came back in she just said, 'I pray for you all,' as if the plague was coming their way.

Bloody typical, thought Angel. She and Nick used to laugh about the remorseless nature of her piety. 'She is so full of sack cloth and ashes she's got no room for a heart,' was one of Nick's descriptions of his mother. Angel misses Nick's spiked humour often. She has a lot of it in her head, and sometimes she plays it back. She feels less overwhelmed now, to think of leaning on him in bed, his arm round her, whispering because Naomi was staying with them, sleeping – or probably praying – in the next room. He was talking about his mother's reaction to his father dying,

'But Naomi could never throw her arms open and comfort anyone, she always acted as if pestilence was on its way.' Nick laughed, Angel whispered, 'Shh! She'll hear us.' Nick rolled over beside her, pulled the sheet over both of their heads, and said in a voice full of laughter, 'I reckon in another life she probably served the Last Supper. All her human kindness is based on the belief that others are heading for acute suffering. And only she knows it's coming.' It must have been six years ago, but Angel can feel their shared laughter like a real presence now.

Curled up in Foss's bed, Angel has no desire to witness her mother-in-law's pity for her and Nick. Angel wishes that the world would just let her get on with life without showing its kindness. She prefers judgement to kindness at the moment. Yesterday's encounter at the school gate was classic.

Foss and Ruby were on the climbing frame, Angel was loitering, reading some bumph from the Parents' Association about a nature night and feeling guilty as usual when a flurry of energy and a smell of nappies rushed up to her. It was Nicola Hallam, Foss's best friend's mother.

'Angel, Angel, God, I am so sorry. I've been meaning to catch up with you but everything's been so busy. You poor thing, you've got so thin, is it stress? I don't know how you can bear to go through with it.' Nicola pushed back stringy hair and thrust out her ample hip to balance the large toddler more easily on it. Her whole demeanour radiated honesty, goodness and bafflement at Angel's inexplicable behaviour.

'I'm not a bit surprised you're looking haggard, though,

it's just such a nightmare getting divorced, it's so awful for the children. Listen, I've got to go, I'm making chocolate ladybirds for the school nature night, but call me if you want anything, and some evening when Hamish is away you must come and have supper.'

Angel's rage was so intense she had to hold on to the school railings for a moment to stop herself pushing Nicola over or pulling her hair. Thankfully, another mother reversed over someone's bike, so no one noticed and Angel bit her bottom lip and whispered in her head, 'Actually, fuck you, Nicola. And fuck you for meaning well, too. And fuck you again for only wanting me to come to supper when Hamish is away. Are you scared I might try and tempt him away from you? Please don't worry, I wouldn't touch your pompous husband with oven gloves on.'

Listening to the rain beating the end of summer into the countryside and on to the house, Angel hugs a small khaki frog and rolls her eyes. Of course it doesn't matter, and now, with distance, she can smile and be grateful that Nicola had got in her car, blithe and unaware of her death stare. In fact, it is good to feel a bit of clean contempt for Nicola and her narrow-minded view of the hazards of life with divorced women in the area. But yesterday evening the anger had rolled on, grumbling like thunder in the back of Angel's mind as she grated cheese over cauliflower, erupting in a mini-storm when Foss and Ruby said in unison, 'Urgh, it's cauliflower cheese and we hate it.'

'Oh shut up!' Angel threw the wooden spoon across the room. It landed in the dog basket. Foss and Ruby looked at it, looked at one another, and began to laugh.

Angel took a deep breath, counted to ten and walked out of the room. 'I must not take it out on them,' she intoned, marching around her usual cooling-down loop. First out to the hen house, round the washing line, and back into the kitchen again. The anger subsided, rolling like a metal pinball across the floor of her mind while she bathed the children and put them to bed. She hugged them for twice as long as usual, because they were going to Nick to stay away for the first time.

Rage flared again when she listened to her messages later in the evening.

'Look, hi, Angel, Nix here. I've checked the diary and I've got an evening next week when Hamish won't be back until about eleven, so why don't you come for early kitchen supper at about seven-thirty and we can have a baked potato and a chat and I'll be tucked up in bed by the time Hamish gets home.'

'I would rather suck shit through a sock,' said Angel out loud to her answerphone, pleased at last to use the phrase she had relished Jem using when asked to Jeannie Gildoff's son's beach party. Stupid cow. And Angel went to bed, glad she was getting a bit of spirit back, and poised to do battle.

Today, though, she is not so sure. The emptiness of the house is shocking, its silence rising inexorably, filling every room.

Raffaella Barker

The phone rings; Angel can't be bothered to move. It is probably Jake, and she doesn't want to tell him she is on her own. She wants to be on her own. Acknowledging this feels new, exciting and good. Angel stays curled up in Foss's bed, listening to the rain dripping and spattering from the gutter outside. She will get up when she wants to. Or not.

Nick

Sunday morning, another shop. This time the newspaper shop in Larkham. Nick goes in while the children listen to *Just William* in the car. He buys crab lines,
sherbet fountains and the Sunday papers. Nick has a warm
sense of contentment, which reminds him of the TV advertisement he had known in his childhood. The advertisement showed a boy who had eaten Ready Brek cereal going
to school with a red and yellow glow around him.

Staying the night in the lighthouse was a success,
though in the night Foss had woken, wailing dry-throated
and empty, his eyes wide with fear in the dark and calling
for Mummy. Sleep-fogged, Nick didn't think or panic. He
knelt by Foss's bed in the silver black night and put his
arms round him.

He felt his small ribcage shake and he whispered, 'I
am here and you are safe,' over and over while Foss heaved
with sobs. After a while Nick lay down on the bed, curving
around Foss tucked in a ball under the blankets, and fell
asleep. In the early dawn the smudge-blue daylight filtered

in over Nick, and the roar of the heating starting up warmed his body; he was chilly in boxer shorts and a T-shirt on top of Foss's bedspread. It was six in the morning. Nick thought about getting back into his own bed, but when he moved his arms, Foss stirred and wriggled closer to him. Nick smiled and drifted back to sleep.

Breakfast is in the parlour, a round room with curved windows like something out of Beatrix Potter. Knives and forks clattering and the whisper of conversation at the other two tables create a soothing atmosphere inside which echoes the gentle motion of the sea outside. Foss, his bad dream forgotten, sits on the floor next to the table arranging his collection of razor shells from beachcombing the afternoon before. Ruby orders porridge, to the astonishment of the landlady, and is discussing the Spartans.

'Daddy, if we go on holiday, please can we NOT go to Sparta. It's really harsh there with rules for everyone. You know if you are a boy in Sparta you are taken away from your mother aged seven and sent off to try and survive, and if you are a girl you have to do wrestling EVERY DAY.'

She pauses to receive her porridge, and Nick coughs and turns away so she doesn't see him grinning as she tucks her napkin into her T-shirt like Desperate Dan.

She is only silent for a moment: 'We have to say, "For what we are about to receive may the Lord make us truly thankful," at school,' she says. 'Should we say it at a hotel too?'

Nick considers his own beliefs. 'Uh. I'm not sure. I

think God usually knows what you are feeling, but there's nothing wrong with telling Him as well,' he says, surprised to find that is what he thinks.

'OK, hands together, then,' says Ruby, bending to tug Foss's T-shirt. 'Come on, Foss, we're saying Grace.'

'But I've already had breakfast,' objects Foss.

'Oh yes,' Ruby laughs. 'We'll do the other one, then. The one for when you've finished.' She turns back to Nick. 'This one is almost exactly the same so you'll have to listen carefully. "For what we have JUST received may the Lord make us truly thankful".'

Nick puts his hands together, conscious of the elderly birdwatching couple to his left who are smiling indulgently. He suddenly wishes Jem was here too.

'I know another prayer too,' Ruby says after a moment's contemplation. 'It goes, "Hail Mary, mother of Grace, please find us a parking space." It's Catholic, I think. Mummy taught it to Foss and me when we went to London. How many do you need to know to be a qualified nun?'

'How many what?'

'Prayers,' says Ruby, pushing her empty bowl away.

'I'm not sure. Why don't you ask my mother, St Granny, I mean?' says Nick.

'Good idea. I'll write her a postcard on a picture of a church as well,' says Ruby. 'She'll like that.'

'She will,' Nick agreed. Ordering more coffee, he wonders how he has managed never to notice before how easy it is to have a nice time.

Jem

I always thought being seventeen was going to be the best thing ever. I know it sounds stupid, but it was the birthday, apart from twenty-four, which I haven't got anywhere near yet, that I have always looked forward to. I think it comes from living in the middle of nowhere and knowing that the day I am seventeen I can get in a car and go – admittedly with L plates and a co-driver – but I can actually leave home with horsepower. So how it turned out to be so crap is a mystery. It's always in half-term, so when I asked Mum if I could have my first driving lesson on my birthday I was gobsmacked when she said, 'Your birthday is a bit of a problem this year, Jem.'

I was on the phone. I was lying on my bed in the cell that is my room at school, and I was looking at my Led Zeppelin poster. Coral gave it to me at the beginning of term. One of the guys looks a lot like Dad, and the sad thing about that is that the picture was taken in the seventies and Dad still looks like that. I have told him he looks like the guy in Thin Lizzie, which I thought would get

311

him down to the barbers right away, but he seems to be grateful for any personal remark that isn't an outright insult.

Anyway, Mum sounds like she's swallowed some great lump of bread, all snuffling, and then I realise she's crying. SHE'S crying and it's MY birthday they've cocked up. What has she got to cry about? *I* should be crying. Actually, at the time of the phone call I had no idea I should be crying or that there was anything to cry about but I did know that she shouldn't be.

'Mum, why are you crying?' It's so horrible when Mum cries and it's worse on the phone because if I am there at least I can see when she stops.

'I don't know, tired, I suppose,' she sniffs.

'So why is my birthday a problem?'

'Dad is taking his furniture out of the house on that day to put in the cottage he's moved into at Jenny's.'

'Why?'

'No one realised until too late to change it.'

Fucking great. That's my family all over these days.

So in the end, here we are on my birthday having supper in the Chinese restaurant in Cromer. And Mum and Dad are both here, but Dad looks like his eyes are about to pop out of his head he is so unrelaxed, and Mum is trying to be jolly, which of all the ways Mum can be, has to be the worst.

'Now, has everyone got what they want? Foss, stop that, please, it's Jem's birthday.'

Why that is relevant to Foss flicking some small camou-
flaged army man into the special fried rice is a mystery
to me. Coral and Ruby are listening to Coral's iPod. Coral
has not said one word to Dad since he turned up at the
restaurant, even though she talked all the way here about
how great life is in Sheffield and how we are all missing
the point by not being in the North.

'I think I'll stay up there when I finish,' she says, chin
up, looking at Mum with defiance.

'Well, if you like it as much after three years as you do
after three weeks, you would be daft not to,' says Dad. He
orders a Coke and drinks it in one big swallow. Coral looks
as though she is going to punch him for a minute, then
she relents and laughs.

'I guess you're right, Nick, but it is really good fun,' she
says. From her that is like handing out the biggest olive
branch on the tree. Dad looks like Christmas has come, he
is so bloody pleased she is speaking to him. He orders another
Coke. He looks a lot older than usual, I think it's his hair.
Or maybe the popping eyes. Mum looks weird too. She's got
a new posture. I reckon it's to do with yoga, but she always
looks as though she has been arranged at the moment, and
she turns her whole body when she's talking to you, not just
her head. I prefer not to look at either of them, so I gaze at
my favourite thing in this Chinese restaurant, a gold-framed
picture of 3-D swans in front of a waterfall. The swans ripple
across the water past lily pads. It is a combination of kitsch
art and computer-game graphics that I love.

Suddenly I get Mum's attention and a breath of her scent comes over me and my memory kicks in to the whole of my childhood with her kissing me goodnight and hugging me and smelling of that particular perfume, so I am not listening, I am remembering, and I suddenly notice that everyone has stopped eating. It is something Dad is saying.

'As we are all together, and this will not happen very many more times, I think it is the right moment for me to tell you that I am going to be spending a lot more of my time in New York after the divorce. You can all come there, of course. I hope you will like it.'

Ruby starts crying and rice falls out of her mouth. Mum looks like she's been hit, so does Dad.

Mum pulls this smile that looks painful to hold and says, 'Well done, Nick,' like she really means it.

He says, 'Thanks,' and they both start looking more normal than they have all evening.

Coral stands up and shouts. 'Christ, you guys are crap. Can't you keep the carnage of your existence to yourselves?' which I think is a bit over the top. Foss and me are sitting next to one another. I take one of his army men off my plate and put it in his hand.

'Fanks,' he whispers.

The waiter arrives with a plate on which is a round chocolate-orange ice cream sitting on a clear plastic stand like a rugby ball tee. A sparkler is fizzing on top. He comes round to where I am sitting and puts it on the table in front of me.

'This is a bombshell surprise,' he says. 'Many Happy Returns on the house.'

Ruby cracks up first and then I start laughing too. That's all I can do.

Angel

May Day. White cherry blossom blurs the edges of the trees in the wood in front of the house, festooned like lacy curtains around the view. From across the field under the canopy of a wide chestnut tree, Angel and Ruby gaze at the soft haze of the wood carpeted with bluebells. Behind them, among the roots of the tree, Foss squats, breathing heavily over a nest of ants.

'Tell me again what happened in your bluebell wood when you were little.'

Ruby sits in a kink in a low snaking branch of the tree, swaying and swinging her legs. 'Tell us the unicorn story,' she begs.

Angel is slow to answer, lost in a floating peacefulness, absorbed in the gentle warmth of the spring afternoon.

'I'm not sure any more if it really happened or if I imagined it, you know that, don't you?' A ribbon of images, of many spring days, many memories suffused with joy and sorrow, never one without the other, flicker through her mind, spooling through all her life until here and now. This moment when the tree smells green, and sunlight lies in pools on the cows huffing interest at a safe distance and she is here with her two youngest children. Happy. Ruby kicks a foot on the ground and the branch bounces gently.

'I know, and sometimes when you tell me the story I think it's true and sometimes I know you made it up. It just depends what I feel like believing.'

'Mum, I need a jar or a box, can you get one?' Foss appears in front of Angel, his hands cupped around something.

'What have you got?'

'A chrysalis. I need to keep it warm.'

His whole face, his embracing stance, reflects his earnest desire to look after the creature. Angel cannot imagine how so much passion will ever survive. Foss's enthusiasm for small and often rather disgusting creatures is growing with him. It is not shared by anyone in his family, indeed it is largely ignored, but he does not care. Angel is suddenly moved by his solemnity.

'I haven't got a box or a jar. How about a hankie?'

'How about no?' Foss turns away, as if shielding the chrysalis from his mother's crassness.

'Oh.' Slightly taken aback, Angel looks around. 'I don't know what to suggest then.' No shelf of jam jars emerges helpfully from the tree.

'I do.' Ruby swings off her branch, and brushing her skirt smooth, she runs around the trunk and stands on tiptoe, reaching into a small hole on the other side.

'What are you doing?' Angel is fascinated. What could possibly be in the tree trunk?

'I've been here with Jem, smoking – and he always leaves some matches and his cigarettes here for next time.' Angel is little shocked that Ruby has a life and experience that she, Angel, did not know about, even here at home.

'But won't he have taken them back to school?'

Ruby grins triumphantly. 'No,' she giggles, waving a packet. Angel begins to laugh. Foss shuffles over to his sister, his hands still clasped over the black blob of insect.

'Quick, throw those away and put this in,' he commands, and Ruby shakes three cigarettes on to the ground.

'Perfect,' she murmurs. 'Perfect,' echoes Foss. Angel can't stop laughing.

'You two are so adorable,' she says.

Foss and Ruby give her a surprised look.

'Come on, Mummy, let's have the rest of the story now,' says Ruby, tugging her hand as they move away from the tree, the cigarette packet safely stowed in Foss's trouser pocket.

Angel begins. Outside is a new setting for the story she normally tells sitting on the end of a child's bed, often when they are ill and need the extra comfort of something familiar.

'OK. Well, years and years ago, when I was just about your age—'

'Whose age? Mine or Foss's?' Ruby loves detail.

'Probably just a bit older than you,' says Angel after a pause. 'So when I was eight or nine, I used to ride my pony through a medieval wood near where we lived when I was growing up.'

'A long way from here,' says Ruby, her eyes far away in the story.

'Yes, far away, and long ago,' says Angel, smiling, 'and at this time of year I often used to take a picnic with me and I would ride all day, and when I got tired, I would get off and lie in the bluebells.'

'And what happened to the pony? Why didn't it run away?' asks Ruby, wanting to picture every moment.

'I used to tie him to a wild lilac bush and he would eat the leaves and swish his tail to get rid of the flies,' replies Angel.

'What kind of creatures were invented in your day?' asks Foss, trying to take an interest. 'Did you ever have dragons around you?'

Ruby answers, deliberately flattening, not wanting her story to head off in his direction: 'None of your sort of creepy crawlies, just unicorns and butterflies.'

They are nearly at the wood at the bottom of the field now. Holding both their hands, long grass cool on her legs and the whirring presence of swifts darting above the grass for invisible insects, Angel has a sudden moment of joy, sharply focused, fleeting and yet enduring.

She continues, 'And my mother had always told me

that there were unicorns in this ancient wood, and that she had seen one when she was a child, and I never believed her because I had never seen one, though I had looked and looked every time I was there, and I had seen badgers and deer and sometimes a fox.' Angel stops. They are at the edge of the wood now, and the bluebells are as high as Foss's knees. She helps him over the ditch at the edge and follows him and Ruby into the intense blue.

'One year I walked to the woods. My pony had got old and died the winter before, and I still wanted to go to the woods. I don't know why, as it was a long way to walk. Anyway, I was there and I was remembering him and feeling very sad and lonely, and I lay down on the blue-bells.'

Telling it now, Angel remembers every detail as clearly as if it was yesterday, not thirty years ago. 'The smell was just like this now, and I'm glad we are in here so you can describe it yourselves.' She pauses and breathes in the soft scent.

'Mmm. Smells like smoky bacon,' says Foss dreamily.

Ruby shoots him a filthy look. 'No. It does not. It smells delicate, like lace,' she says crossly.

'Anyway,' says Angel, moving on quickly, hoping she is not going to have to break up a squabble, 'the sky went dark, as though it was going to thunder, and the air was purple and still, and all the buds on the trees were such a bright green I had to blink. And I looked down through the glade of bluebells. Where the path turned away at the bottom I saw a horse emerge quite silently from the woods.'

She pauses again and looks down at Foss and Ruby. Both of them gaze unblinking at her face, their argument forgotten; she smiles and squeezes each of their hands.

They both squeeze back and she continues, 'My pony was grey, and at first I thought it was him. Or a ghost of him, and I was a bit scared. But then I realised it couldn't be him. This horse had dappled grey shoulders and hindquarters and its body was dazzling white. It had a long mane and tail and big dark eyes. It was so beautiful and so quiet, I just looked and looked. And it felt as though it was there for ever, and had been and would always be, but it also seemed to be there for just a moment. Then it began to walk away. I felt very sad watching it go. I thought I would cry, but the sun came out and glanced through the trees, and it caught the head of the horse, and for the briefest moment I saw a unicorn's horn. The horse disappeared in among the trees, and even though I ran to where I had seen it, there was nothing but the flattened grass of a path created by an animal's feet.'

Somehow, in the story, the three of them have stopped walking. They climb on to a fallen-down piece of fencing a few metres into the wood, under a veil of cherry blossom. 'It was this kind of bright white,' says Angel, nodding at the flowers above their heads.

'I wish I could see your unicorn.' Ruby hugs Angel tightly, her arms around her neck.

'I wish you could too,' says Angel, kissing her forehead.

'I can see it! It's come!' shouts Foss, standing up on the fence, gripping Angel's coat with one hand, pointing into the wood in front of them.

'Look!'

They look. 'I can't see anything,' Angel says faintly, not sure what Foss is imagining.

Ruby darts forward, threading a path through delicate white garlic flowers and the first pink campion and then up into the smoky blue of the woodland, her whole body crackling with excitement.

'I can see it too, Mummy, look!' It is true, something is moving in the foliage, something separate. Light glints, but through the shadow of afternoon sun on leaves and festooning undergrowth, it is impossible to make sense of what it is. It could be anything. Excitement rushes through Angel, and a sense of wonder, long forgotten yet familiar. And at once Ruby is climbing, slipping in her excitement on long bluebell leaves curled like cats' tongues, the sap from the stems hanging in translucent spools. The soft scent of spring in the air, the damp shadows of the wood and the magical blue light make anything possible. Foss, just in front of Angel, holds out his hand.

'We'll show you, Mum, quick, come and see!' he says, yanking her over a fallen branch. A tree stump with a sweep of wild honeysuckle leaves cascading over it blocks their path, and behind it something is moving. Ruby looks back at her mother and brother, and the smile on her face is so open, so lit with excitement, that tears spring in Angel's eyes. Holding hands, all three of them step around the tree. A silver and white helium balloon bobs among the bluebells.

'It's a butterfly,' says Ruby.

'From a chrysalis,' agrees Foss.

'No, it's a balloon butterfly,' corrects Ruby. 'It's from a party, not a chrysalis.'

'It's got a message on it,' says Angel.

'It doesn't need one,' says Ruby. 'We know why it's here.'

RAFFAELLA BARKER

Green Grass

No matter where you land up, the grass is always greener somewhere else – and Raffaella Barker's captivating new novel will take you there.

Laura Sale has become invisible in her own life. Her domestic existence in North London with thirteen-year-old twins Dolly and Fred, and their father, the fascinating but ridiculously demanding Inigo, seems relentless, while her professional life fostering Inigo's career as Britain's most successful conceptual artist is frustrating and unfulfilling. What does she really like? What makes her laugh? Is a passionate existence passing her by?

A chance encounter with Guy, the man she nearly married twenty years ago, is the catalyst she needs. Change comes in mysterious guises, and Laura finds herself confronting old ghosts, ferrets, a goat and a collapsing relationship, back in the rural Norfolk of her childhood holidays. As she starts to savour the space she has craved, she begins a new stage of her life with its own surprises, demons and delights. Taking control of her destiny, Laura finds it lit with possibility.

0 7472 6747 2

headline
review

Now you can buy any of these other bestselling
books from your bookshop
or *direct from the publisher*.

FREE P&P AND UK DELIVERY
(Overseas and Ireland £3.50 per book)

Come and Tell Me Some Lies	Raffaella Barker	£7.99
Hens Dancing	Raffaella Barker	£7.99
Summertime	Raffaella Barker	£7.99
Green Grass	Raffaella Barker	£7.99
Left Bank	Kate Muir	£6.99
Out of My Depth	Emily Barr	£6.99
The Vanishing Act of Esme Lennox	Maggie O'Farrell	£7.99
My Latest Grievance	Elinor Lipman	£6.99

TO ORDER SIMPLY CALL THIS NUMBER

01235 400 414

or visit our website: www.madaboutbooks.com

Prices and availability subject to change without notice.